Flag by Meganne Rosen O'Neal.
Acrylic and aerosol on board, 4' x 4'. 2013.

MOON CITY REVIEW
2016

Moon City Review is a publication of Moon City Press at Missouri State University and is distributed by the University of Arkansas Press. Exchange subscriptions with literary magazines are encouraged. The editors of *Moon City Review* contract First North American Serial Rights, all rights reverting to the writers upon publication. The views expressed by authors in *Moon City Review* do not necessarily reflect the opinions of its editors, Moon City Press, or Missouri State University.

All other correspondence should be sent to the appropriate editor, using the following information:

Moon City Review
Department of English
Missouri State University
901 South National Avenue
Springfield MO 65897

Submissions are considered at http://mooncitypress.com/mcr/. For more information, please consult www.mooncitypress.com.

moon city press
springfield missouri

STAFF

TABLE OF CONTENTS

Fiction

Poetry

Nonfiction

The Missouri State University Literary Competitions

Contributors' Notes

This issue of *Moon City Review* is dedicated to the memory of Dr. Jane Hoogestraat: poet, teacher, editor, friend.

Michael Ramberg

LAST KING OF THE GORILLA SUITS

1. Lake Harriet

His first time was while watching old shows on the local station. With the setting sun sending rays of gold through greasy windows, he lay stomach down, feet up kicking dust motes. On the TV, Gilligan was scared by something in the jungle. A dark face, black hands, a grunt of menace in the tropical air: a gorilla. Enamored, the beast kidnaps Mrs. Howell, throwing her on his shoulder and waving a hairy fist at the castaways before vanishing into palm fronds that quiver in his wake.

After that first time, gorillas were everywhere. For years Lenny saw gorillas on *The Addams Family*, apes on *The Beverly Hillbillies*, monkeys in squad cars and on trapezes—even a white space ape, a horned ridge on his back, his poison fangs leading to almost certain death for Captain Kirk.

He watched the apes at home, or at his friend Robbie's house. Robbie had a TV twice the size of Lenny's, and his mom—Robbie had a mom—would pour corn chips into a glass bowl she set on the floor. Robbie said, "Dad says it's not a real ape. He says it's a man in a suit."

Of course it was, Lenny answered. He'd known that already. Which made him wonder: What kind of man did that? How was it to see the world from under heavy, coal-black brows? To feel the costume shift on his shoulders as he lurched down the street, to feel the confusion of pedestrians, the shrill shriek of beautiful terror as he frolicked on the rocky backlots of Los Angeles County, chasing bikinied women as the camera recorded his every move? There was only one way to know.

As the credits rolled he stood up but not all the way. He cupped his hands and swung them low till the knuckles brushed Robbie's mom's deep green carpet.

"What are you doing?" Robbie asked.

"Ooh-ooh ah," he said. His first words in ape. Robbie's mom laughed and clapped before pouring more chips.

Back home, he ape-walked around the house. Through the hall, up the stairs. Leaping from sofa to chair, floor to ottoman, arms flailing about.

"Make him stop," his sister said, but his dad did nothing, only stayed in the office with his piles of numbers.

"Ooh-ooh ah-ah," said Lenny.

"You can't be an ape," said Heather.

He stood up, reverting to human form. "I don't want to be an ape, for your information. I want to play a gorilla. On TV."

"You're crazy. You don't even look like an ape."

"So I'll make a suit. Easy. Dad says I can be anything I want."

Dad was an independent accountant, doing books for small businesses in the neighborhood. He spent his days in his basement office, punching numbers into a boxy computer, preparing tax returns for grumpy entrepreneurs. On weekends he took Lenny down to the lake where they fished from the public docks and the conversation wandered to hopes and dreams. Don't let them tell you who to be, he'd say. Chase your dream. But he didn't say it like someone who'd lived that advice. Like someone who'd been whipped into a whole different life from his dream, was how he said it.

He went to the mall with Robbie to look at movie magazines. When they reached B. Dalton's, Robbie waved him to the back. "You're gonna love this," he said. In the automotive section, hidden behind the manuals for Harley Davidson motorcycles and Evinrude outboard motors, men hid adult magazines to look at in relative peace. That's where Robbie pulled out a copy of *Hustler*, already dog-eared and Slurpee-stained. He flipped through it, pink shades of women fluttering one by one under Robbie's hand. Then stopped at a full-page spread. A woman on the back of a boat, her hair spilling like a hurricane from under a white captain's hat, her head tipped and slit-eyed to evaluate whoever was looking at her. She was spread invitingly, her arms thrown across the gunnels, her glossy huge breasts lolling, her legs separated across two deck chairs, white oiled highlights leading up her thighs to that space where her legs joined in a glistening tangle of hair and pink flesh.

Robbie put a finger on the woman's patch of hair and whispered, his voice wet in Lenny's ear: "That's for your thingie, there. It gets big, and it goes in there to get small. It's what my dad said." He nodded solemnly. It did not seem possible that such a thing could happen. Not on a boat or anyplace else.

They stared, turning pages with sweat-soaked hands, until the manager emerged to chase them away and they ran, faces red, to the food court.

The picture haunted him. When he saw station wagons hauling fishing boats, her eyes, tilted and judgmental, leapt from memory to vivid life. He wanted to see her again, to trace her outlines, see again that mystery where the legs met. He went back alone, but this time the automotive section held no pornography. Instead, he found a different magazine hidden in the back: *Fangs and Claws*, its pages holding stills from slasher movies and articles describing how the effects were done. Blood pumps, latex wounds. He paged through it anyway, in his chest a pang of fascination and dread as distinct from what he felt for the naked ladies as it was similarly powerful.

And there, in the back, an article that would change his life. The title was "King of the Gorilla Suits." Its subject was Janos Klawiter, who made his living as an ape man in films and television. There was a picture of Janos, wavy remains of his golden hair flapping in a Southern California breeze, the golden hills of television land behind him. A gorilla head tucked under his arm, brutal even in repose.

You could do it, Lenny realized. Janos had. You could pretend to be an ape for real. And make a living at it. Anything you want to be, Dad had said.

He practiced at home. Dad brought home a VCR, and Lenny rented any movie he could find with an ape suit. When the ape came on he stood up, thrashing more dust into the golden light. He stood as the ape stood, beat his chest, mirroring the movie ape's motions, echoing the staticky ape noises.

He asked his sister if he could carry her across her shoulder. That happened in every movie, and he needed to practice. She peeked up from the *Teen Valley High* book she was reading and made a face like he'd just farted. "C'mon, Heather. It'll be fun," he said. She set down the book.

"You get one try."

She fought as he tried to lift, real fighting, hands pounding his back, and he set her back down.

"You need to help me a little. You can scream a little, and fight a little, but that's it. OK?"

"You're weird," she said. But they tried again. Once she was aloft he discovered it was hard work to carry her and stay stooped, to make his legs stay bowlegged and keep his balance under such a load.

"Eek," said his sister in a lazy monotone. "Eek eek. Can I get back to my book?"

His hand had crept up the back of her thigh to keep her balanced, and was now near the place where her legs met. That's where it goes to get small, Robbie'd said. His own sister, Lenny thought, as a strange motion flipped his lower stomach. He put her down.

"Why are you doing this?" She tugged her shorts legs, straightened out her shirt.

"I'm going to be the next king of the gorilla suits," he answered. "And I'm going to be on TV."

"You're just weird," she said.

In high school, he made a suit. He started with fake fur in the costume shop, and then discovered estate sales often had hidden caches of torn fur coats. He sewed together an oversized shirt, low-hanging pants, and bulked it up with parts of shoulderpads filched from last year's football equipment. He experimented with latex, asking the art teacher for help molding hands, and sculpted a template for his ideal gorilla face.

Finally it was ready. He stepped in and zipped up. The misshapen feet splayed against the carpet, his hands flexed and broke the poorly cured gloves. Too-thin suspender straps bit into his shoulders. Chunks of fur fell from his shoulders and arms. The second model, already begun, would be better.

He lowered the mask, Velcroed himself in. The world through the mask was different, tinted with the smell of banana oil and polyester fur. He bowed his legs and stooped. He brushed the floor with his knuckles. His breath in the mask was an echo of waterfall on palm fronds, sound-fossils of ancient jungle noises resurrected within him the cries of common ancestors fighting to rise from primeval soup. A tentative thump on his chest, then another. A cloud of fur rose into his face as air escaped his lungs with a cry of freedom and birth.

"Jesus," said his sister. She was lurking in his doorway. "What a freak."

Now he needed a camera. He needed a script, actors, a director. Because he needed a demo reel to take to California, to show the world he was ready.

He still hung out with Robbie, who now wanted to be an actor. Robbie had grown into a handsome boy, with a rugged but delicate chin, high cheekbones, and a broad-shouldered sexiness that had, he reported, already yielded to him the cleft of woman promised by that long ago copy of *Hustler*. He related each conquest to Lenny; his tally included cheerleaders, most of the Drama Club girls, even someone's divorced mother. And he'd learned a secret: "It doesn't make you smaller," he said. "Just the opposite."

So together they had the same needs, and together they went to the AV Club, where Ellie Johnson swiveled away from the film splicer to face them. Ellie, they'd heard, knew how to run a camcorder and had access to editing equipment at the cable station's public access studio.

As she listened to them she crossed her legs, putting the smaller one in the air. She had one short leg and a slightly scoliotic spine, a birth defect that lent her walk and attitude an otherworldy charm.

"So you guys, what—you wanna make a monster movie?" she said. Her eyes were slanted, skeptical, the way that made Lenny's heart weak. Lank hair on pink skin, pale as the imperiled maidens of jungle mystery films.

"He's got nice hair, and I have a gorilla suit," said Lenny.

She shrugged, her freckled shoulders rising against white halter straps. She said she had nothing better to do. "I'm in."

His sister put down her teen romance novels long enough to write a script for a five-minute romp she titled *Oops, an Ape!* A gorilla escapes from a traveling zoo at Lake Harriet and terrorizes a young couple on their first date. She wrote a stirring speech for Robbie, stealing the best parts from her favorite book. It was about how he hadn't been sure he loved her till just now, and that he'd do whatever it took to keep her, including going toe-to-toe with that stink-ball ape. Then she wrote in a passionate kiss because she was cast as his date and hoped for long, complicated rehearsals.

They set up on the banks of Lake Harriet. Passersby formed a small circle to gape at Lenny in his gorilla suit and Ellie directing from under a parasol held by her little brother. Ellie stalked the shoot, framing shots with her hands. Stand here, she said, then, when the light was wrong, she said, No. Here. She filmed Robbie and Heather, took a close-up for Robbie's first speech about undying love as Heather melted under his eyes. She filmed Lenny—Come here, Oops, she said—lurking behind a tree. Then it was time for the action. For a minute Lenny thought he couldn't do it. Jumping around in the back yard was one thing, but here, in front of strangers, he had a crisis of faith.

The film depended on him being as ape-like as possible. But, because he was essentially human, he suddenly realized full apehood was impossible. Sure, he knew the craft of it, the actions to make, but still he began to wonder: Who was he, and what was this thing he was trying to become? Was he simply a man playing an ape? Or was he, as suggested by Oops' humanlike qualities—juggling here, a quick soft-shoe there, a wolf whistle at a woman in a bikini—instead a man playing a man who was playing an ape? Or, thirdly, was he a man playing an ape that thought it was a man? That is, how many times removed was Lenny from authentic humanity, and exactly how recursive was the ape-to-man self-awareness?

He thought of Janos, the greatest of the apemen, the immigrant who had built himself into an industry. Janos would tolerate no existential hesitation. Janos was a professional; so, also, would be Lenny. He leapt from behind the tree, arms over his head, and landed on half-collapsed legs. He scraped his knuckles and shuffled forward, beating his chest. His cry echoed over the lake and drew gasps of fear and delight from the crowd. His savage yowl skipped like stones across the rippling water to the ears of the boaters and kayakers. He felt his human self receding, a calm sentience making suggestions, but the ape—Oops—the ape was its own pure source of volition and energy, transcending itself and Lenny, his puny humanity, a receding speck in the rearview mirror. He was Oops the ape, that's what he was.

Ellie filmed it all on her father's Camcorder, the rough footage writing over their Christmas videos—they'd never watch them again anyway, she said. Later, during editing, he discovered how fascinating she was. Firm and in command. And she liked Lenny. She liked the suit, anyway. Once, for fun, he put the suit on and carried her around the school. She was nothing like his sister. Ellie was light and joyous, a woman who knew how to ride a wild ape. Slumped over his shoulder, light as kindling, her waist bouncing against his arm, she squealed "Eek" with gleeful terror, her fists pounding his padded back. Later, after they'd left the principal's office, detention doled out, she pulled him into an alcove between lockers and kissed him hard while grabbing at his crotch through Oops' soft hair. "You have a gift," she said. "For the absurd."

Absurd wasn't what he was going for, though. Not at all. But he did not stop kissing her.

She came to his house to show him the final tape. They watched Oops and Robbie on the flickering screen and spoke of the future. He told her about Hollywood, she read to him from her own screenplay. She told him to put on the suit. Sit here, she said, pointing to the recliner. He did. She reached a soft hand into Oops' lower regions.

"You need to find a way to make this part more accessible," she said. She leaned the chair back and walked up his legs, her one short leg and bent spine bending her into him like a clothespin gripping a bath towel. What she did then—her hand was still in his suit—he could not describe after. What he could remember is her saying his name over and over in rhythm to what she was doing. But not his name, not exactly: Oops, she said. Oops, Oops, Oops and then with her final release: Eeeek ....

2. Los Angeles

Robbie went to LA first, taking his copy of the VHS demo tape of *Oops, an Ape!* Lenny's sister's dialogue must have been good, because it impressed the agents. That and his cheekbones were enough to attract the eye of a man who put him in a commercial, then in a TV show about troubled teenagers, and finally in a movie that broke box office records. In two years, he was a star.

Lenny stayed behind, working at the Blockbuster, putting away enough cash for gas to get him out there, a down payment on an apartment. He put the final touches on Oops Mark 3, whose face was harsher, more antagonistic. This was Argos, Oops' evil twin, in case the studio wanted a more menacing ape. Ellie finished her screenplay, and her visits were less frequent; finally she told him she'd found a new boyfriend. "He's kind of hairy," she said, "but you knew I liked that."

He was leaving anyway, no need to be sentimental. If things worked out, she'd finish her screenplay and join him, or not. He had the suit, he had the moves, he had the demo reel. Ellie had played her part in the birth of Oops; he was ready to head out to Los Angeles for his life's second act.

It felt like a time of opportunity, because the old guard was gone now. He'd seen Janos' obituary a year ago, in the back pages of *Fangs and Claws*: "Hollywood Stuntman Moves On." A picture of Janos holding the white spaceape with the rhino horn tucked under his arm. His face ruddy but noble, his hair waving like spun gold, the ochre stone outcroppings of Paramount's back lot over his shoulder. So there was a need for someone to carry on Janos' work; the island was ready for a new gorilla.

Lenny came in on Highway 15, the light that same yellow from his childhood on the carpet, that moment he saw the first gorilla man tossing coconuts at Gilligan. Argos and Oops rode together in the trunk. He got caught in traffic, paid too much for a basement apartment with a soggy floor. Every time he left, walking up to his car, he was assaulted with light permanently the color of the day he'd first seen the ape on TV: syrupy, unreal, a thing he breathed. He was ready for whatever could happen next, except for what really happened next.

From Robbie he got the name of an agent, a guy who cast stuntmen and animal actors, and first thing Monday Lenny barged into the talent agent's office just like he'd imagined doing. Live your dream, his father always said, and if his dream was filled with awkward forced meetings, he'd do it.

He set the box with the ape suit on the floor and sat down. "I want to do gorilla work," he said.

"You want to do apes."

"Just like Janos Klawiter," he said.

"I don't know Janos."

"I have a suit," he said, lifting the lid of the box. Argos' face, a dark menace, the glint of lower canines, peered from the darkened depths.

"You got a suit." Dumbfounded. He peered into the box, then leaned back, ran a hand over his bald head. He chuckled. "Kid brought a monkey suit. Kid, you seen a movie lately?"

"I can do lowland silverback. I can do chimpanzee, orangutan. I can even spell orangutan, not everyone can. O-R- ...."

"I believe you, kid."

"And a tape." He handed it over. The agent sighed, checked his watch. "Kid brought a fucking tape. You make it work, I'll watch," he said. He pointed to a metal stand where an ancient television stood over a dusty tape player, blocked in by CD cases and takeout boxes radiating a stale funk. During the cleanup cockroach shells thumped to the carpet. One of the shells flipped itself, scuttled away. Lenny plugged the VCR into the wall and waited for the ancient technology to come to life.

Finally the television burned dull orange, and the agent ended his phone call. And there he was, Oops the ape, turning cartwheels on the lawn of Lake Harriet. He climbed the bandshell, juggled coconuts in the rafters. He was a man. He was a man as an ape pretending to be a man. He was all these things knotted up. He paused the tape when Robbie gave his final speech.

"Is that Rob Goodfox?"

"Sure."

"Huh."

He skipped ahead. They watched Oops hand-walk across the floor, jump into the fountain, thrash his arms about, and yowl. Afterwards, Lenny had spent six hours waving a hair dryer at Oops' sodden fur and been threatened with a lawsuit over clogging the fountain's filters with ape hair, but Ellie had nailed the shot. Oops was primal, a force of nature, but there, in the closeup, you could see in his eyes that he was also justified, that Robbie had wronged him, that revenge, should he get it, was his due.

"So you know Rob?"

"Sure," he said. This seemed to tilt something in his favor, that he knew a legitimate actor. The agent nodded and rolled his lower lip with an index finger.

"I'm ready to be the next king of the gorilla suits," Lenny said. He'd printed business cards. It was his destiny.

"Kid, have you even seen a movie in the last five years? When was the last time you saw an apesuit outside a used car lot?"

Lenny sat quietly. He'd seen so many, but the year of the movie or show? Insignificant detail. As far as he was concerned, apes existed in myths beyond the rules of time. The agent said, "Let me show you this." He opened his computer, fumbled with inserting a shiny disk. He turned the monitor to face Lenny. A film clip started. A man and a woman in a car. They stop, dumbfounded: What had they seen? The man sits up, removes sunglasses, stands, the camera rising with him. Then the camera cuts to what he's seeing. Dinosaurs. Dinosaurs walking, standing on hind legs, swarming verdant fields.

"CGI," the agent said. "That's coming out next year. Sure, he did some suitwork, but computers. That's your future. No one's doing guys in suits. Not in any production you want to be in. The nerds with the computers, those guys do the apes these days."

"Those are dinosaurs," said Lenny. "I do apes." It was a thin reed to cling to, but all he had. He thought of Ellie's contact information on his cell phone, how her smile would rise when he told her how the meeting went. His success would lure her out. It would have to! "I got a suit," he said again. "How much nerdier can you get than that?"

"Are apes all you do? I suppose if you're married to the suit, I can get you store openings. Pet shops. Kid's birthday parties. Maybe a wine tasting. Or if you leave the suit at home I can get you extra work. Cause you got moves, I can see that. Or there's mob scenes. You're lead zombie material, maybe. You catch a director's eye, he can get you motion capture, with the balls and a green suit."

Motion capture. Wasn't that what the camera did? Capture motion? What was happening to Hollywood? He'd been here a week and it had disappeared already.

Robbie invited him to a party at a bar that was half swimming pool. Women's tan bodies against blazing white tile as if all for Robbie who stood in a white suit, hair ruffled by a Pacific coast breeze. They chatted like old times, but then Robbie would become distant and opaque, as if his golden-boy good looks had hardened into a bronze shell. Whether there was a real person in there anymore, Lenny didn't know.

He told Robbie that Ellie was done with him, that she wanted to write novels, that she and his sister had started a workshop. Every few days Heather posted to the web another chapter of her story about a virginal girl in love with an asshole movie star. She got thousands of hits a day.

"I know you liked Ellie," Robbie said. Lenny nodded. "Tell me, did she ever come across?"

Of course, he said, but then he thought about it. They'd done plenty of things, but had he ever put his part in there for sure?

Robbie nodded, twisted his mouth into a bro-smirk, bumped Lenny's fist. "You should get plenty of action out here," he said. "I know I do."

"You're a movie star, Robbie. That's to be expected."

Robbie smiled, removed his sunglasses, and rubbed his cheek. For a moment he was in the same pose as the Rob Goodfox on his blockbuster hit's movie poster, that golden alchemical ratio of glib, magnetic, alluring, and insufferable. "I guess that's right," he drawled, a dead ringer of his own tagline. Lenny wondered if Robbie knew what he was doing—whether he was playing at being Rob Goodfox, or Rob Goodfox occasionally reverted to the Robbie Gutenberg Lenny had grown up with. At least Oops could come off when Lenny left the set. At least that much was clear.

In any case, there was enough of the childhood friend left for Robbie to pull some strings. He was famous now, he knew people who were doing a space epic with various aliens, and maybe they could use an apeman type.

"They won't need Oops," Robbie said. "They'll do it all green screen. The apes come last, from computers."

The knowledge that no one needed Oops settled in Lenny like concrete hardening into a sidewalk. He slept on it, this hard cold fact, and in the morning he took the job.

Also, he took the job because his car's check engine light had been glaring red since Denver, and because his rent was due, and because Oops was a dying, bankrupt dream. He spent the first day of orientation signing safety wavers with a dozen other extras. His was a tiny cog of the massive production, cast for B-unit footage of alien life forms in an adaptation of a lesser-known comic that had been popular in the seventies.

His coworkers were Olympic gymnasts, trained dancers, understudies for Cirque du Soleil. They moved with a measured elegance, as if shaping the air with their limbs as they passed through it, and when at rest were completely still, conserving their kinesthetic gifts until they were absolutely necessary. One of them, a woman with orange hair slicked back so tight it appeared painted on, talked to him outside the studio. "I do apes," he said. Her eyes took severe angles to her nose, her cheeks hard as gemstones, a talon of ponytail bobbing. She touched him, fingers flat on his arm. She said, "Is that all you do?"

Maybe she meant well by it, he thought later. Maybe it was flirtatious. Instead, doubt crashed down upon him, and he fled. He began to suspect the entirety of his dream, his continental-seeming ambition, would not be enough.

He kept Oops in the car, in a box, in the hatchback. Oops, his animal guide and protective force. And so he and Oops spent the next morning inching along the freeways to the lot, where he gave his name to security and parked by the studio, a big white box flaking strips of paint. By the door, Lenny paused to push his face closer to the warmth of the sun. That golden unending California light that had powered movies for generations, abandoned now for green walls and little white dots.

Oops was in his box in the car. One last glance showed the corner of his box, a tuft of fur, the glimmer of latex paw. His ghost stood by the door, a man playing the bones and spirit of an ape, other fur and flesh to be added later. The ape playing a man playing an ape. Opening the door and entering the dark.

Ron Riekki

FINDING OUT THE GOOD NEWS

The saddest I've seen people
is after the good news.

The chemicals in your body
crash. They drive off of cliffs

into quicksand marshes,
the rope to save your life

catching on fire, so it burns
like a comedic wick, except

the comedy is that you're going
to die a mud-death. You will eat

mud, and right after all that good
news, where you thought there'd

be no more pain, except pain
waits in the dark, patient

like a lighthouse that's been closed,
haunted, ready to create a new spine

for your schoolboy insides.

Jeannine Hall Gailey

NOTES FROM BEFORE THE APOCALYPSE

There was a halo around a gibbous moon.

The horses all lay down in their fields.

Children died in a school holding hands.

Tornadoes right through the city centers ripped up everything we had built.

The hives of bees were empty. *(Do Not Fly Apart.)*

The bridges collapsed leaving people stranded.

There were knife attacks, guns in malls and theaters, bombings at the races. Flus, pneumonias, resistant bacteria, virulent strains.

Every day in spring the snakes flew through the grass.

We could not escape.

And all we dreamed of was death. A plague. A warning sign. Sporadic shaking. Moons out of orbit. Water in the basements. Earthquakes along state lines. Our bones grew cold while we slept. There was no distraction. Everyone threatening a different weapon. Nature turned on us, furious. We had a bad case of burnout. Then no sleep at all.

☾

We tried to hold together. We prayed. We lit candles. We huddled for warmth. We marshaled resources. We held hands. We looked to the animals. Someone told me to pull it together. I was busy writing down the stories. Even with the barns burning, the last glow on the horizon, I could not stop taking notes.

Jeannine Hall Gailey

AN INTRODUCTION TO SALVATION

Are you ready to be saved? It's best to do it
here, by the water, where the pure white spirit descends upon you
like a dove. Or out in the desert, among the stars and locusts.
In the trenches, too, that's a popular choice.

Are you truly ready, my brother, my sister?
What is the cost now that we are in our darkest hour,
here at the end of civilization, and all that we can hear
is the sad broken slap of water wheel upon water,

the sound of malfunctioning machinery?
We dream of robots, of zombies, of plagues and comets,
of tidal waves that wipe our world clean. We dream of the end
because we long to disappear. We keep building bombs,

lighting fires, pulling dead children from dead women in muddy fields.
Do you claim your hands are clean? But look at the blood
you've spilled just to get here. You'll never be quite free
no matter how you pray. You'll never claw the scales from your eyes.

Marvin Shackelford

ANGELS, EXILED

The angels have taken, lately, to sitting on the front steps of the old monastery, smoking cigarettes and watching the sun crawl over their faces, down their backs to leave them in shadows. Their tiny, crippled wings catch the breeze, flutter enough to show they're useless. They otherwise don't move. Maybe they don't even think—they're shutting down and paying no attention to the world they're part of, the world they are. I've walked by their low perch enough to be sure they're still beautiful, just as wonderful to look at as ever, and filled with the dull but effusive light that, seen from above, is easily mistaken for a halo. But there's nothing more pitiful than catching their gaze, getting the flicker of a smile, and knowing whatever their purpose is they're not fulfilling it. Their parts are aligned but deprived of power.

We didn't notice their withdrawal from the goings-on of town at first. They left their jobs, no notice, and we eventually noticed the holes they left around us. Students at the high school were suddenly without the means of learning Latin. No one waited to cut and arrange bouquets in the flower shop. My buddy Lucius stopped coming into the garage each morning to toil away in grease and oil and sparks. He's a genius beneath the hood, like he'd driven chariots with 408 big blocks and tiny European four-cylinders dropped into them. He hadn't needed automotive and diesel college. I had. I got along fine but missed his input, his little tricks and steady fingers ferreting out knocks and faults. It took days after that, though, for us to realize they all were gone—we were alone together, equally abandoned.

I'd never have thought you could look around and miss an angel, but it's easy enough. You don't expect an enormous monastery at the edge of our town, either, but we had it, two hundred years old and crusted with neo-Gothic trim. Two long dormitories stretched behind the cathedral, once abandoned for longer than it had been in use. This is Jesus country, not papal. It seemed if not natural at least reasonable for a few dozen scarred and fragile men of God to come retake it, restoring its wood and replacing its glass edges, and walk among us as they pleased. We take them for granted, maybe, impressive only to out-of-towners and the youngest of kids, the sick and old who wish they shared their knowledge of what's next, what's outside of us. For most of us they're good luck or guardians but normal, unremarkable in the everyday, at least until they took their leave, waiting at their home while we go on about our business. We're unsure how to handle their sudden withdrawal, what to make of it. The hope is they come back to work, go shopping, make themselves available to us, and all will be well.

I head home after work. It's raining and I walk quickly, cutting past the monastery. Even with the weather they're out front, huddled beneath the eaves to stay dry. Lucius is among them, tucked into the recess of the monastery's twin oak doors. He lifts a cigarette to his lips, stares ahead. I wave to him. He nods solemnly, a small benediction. Sooner or later I'll have to convince him to speak again, if not come to work then at least visit our home. I have a '77 Ford pickup in the yard, still in solid shape and with its yellow factory paint job but unwilling to so much as turn over. I've replaced plugs and parts until I'm out of ideas. I can just see Lucius lay his hands on the frame, wrinkle his brow and dance his fingers a bit, and tell me the magic of my problem. I won't push him, though, so I duck my head and go on, waiting for better weather.

Lil's waiting for me at the front door, apron on and smiling. We stay in an old farmhouse that belongs to her uncle, tall and just a spire away from Victorian, and she looks like a pale tooth lipping from our home's broad gray mouth. She has dinner ready and rushes me in, yanks my slicker off and forces me to the head of the dining room table. She's lit candles and set out flowers and slow-cooked a roast. Lil rubs my shoulders a second, runs to the kitchen for me a beer. She ladles food onto our plates and sits, still flashing me that weird little grin. She asks how my day was and I tell her between bites: three sedans, a pickup, and a little Honda hybrid.

"You wouldn't believe," I say. "Boring little turd, but the way they wire them together."

"You like the little details. You like fiddling."

"I like that it's different."

"Then you'll like this." She drops her fork, pushes back from the table, and stands up in her chair. "Who's got two thumbs and is six weeks knocked up by Glenn J-for-Jeffrey Banks?"

Lil points her thumbs at her face and does a dance, twisting and turning and laughing. I jump up and grab hold of her, lower her to the floor, part because I'm excited and part I'm suddenly scared as hell to see her up so high. I spin her and kiss her face over and over because, yeah, I'm proud to be a daddy and we've been at this a while. We do a small happy-dance, closer to the floor, and I rest my palm on her stomach beneath her belly button. She's still flat and firm.

"Six weeks?"

"Yes, sir."

"I have no idea what you should look like. Or it."

"He's about like this." Lil holds her fingers less than an inch apart. "So not much for me. He's starting his eyes and ears and mouth. Just enough to get himself in trouble."

"Him."

"Or her."

"Shit," I say. I imagine a little he-she pink caterpillar smiling at us, something from another world. "I have to get the truck fixed."

"Priorities, priorities."

"You'll have to drive to the doctor. You'll have to drive the baby everywhere. Come on, now. I'll get Lucius over to help figure it out."

"Lucius," she says. "Right."

"I love you," I say. I kiss her on the lips. "I'm gonna be a daddy."

"Right." Lil's not right there with me. I can see the backtracking rolling in giant steps across her face. "Lucius. Six weeks, Glenn."

"OK?" I say, but I already know what's coming.

"They hole up in their church, and I get pregnant."

"Come on," I say.

"You know how I feel about them."

"Sure," I tell her. "Come on. Forget that. Enjoy this for a minute."

I spin her around, lifting her off her feet. Lil laughs and lets me have control of her small body. I dance us to music only I can hear, high and airy and full of strings and crashing cymbals. After a few turns around the room I throw Lil over my shoulder, her squealing for me to cut it out but not fighting a bit, and I carry her upstairs. God bless her, but she about ruined it for me. Not everyone cares for Lucius and his brethren, thinks they're good markers or even benign, and Lil's one of them. She's from a superstitious lot, still clings to those ideas when it strikes her right, and she's convinced our angels are a bad omen. Or in this case a fine omen, their withdrawal accompanying our new little life. Nothing about them has ever struck me wrong, but I let it go, sure it doesn't matter, and I celebrate with my wife, celebrate for her, and for a while all's as wonderful as can be.

For all I like Lucius, and as much as I'm charmed by all the angels and appreciate that there isn't, probably, a thing wrong with them, I understand Lil's aversion. Their abandonment of everyday life, their sitting on their stoop, waiting for no one knows what—it's funereal, the long hours of a wake. Even I have a hard time, the longer they stay still. For all the physical quirks, their different carriage or habits, they're mostly like us. They laugh and have their interests, they weep and they love. They don't grow old but die the same as a regular person. Their current funk has grown long and unbearable, so total that it looks to become unending, but it's like what we've seen before. It's understandable.

A couple months ago Makar took his leave. He was eldest of the angels, or so they said. It's hard to tell, looking at their smooth features and white hair, who outranks who. Makar taught at the college, ancient history from a standard textbook. Students often asked if he knew more than he was telling, if he'd seen destructions or births, and he only answered with a smile and shake of his head. He left the monastery in the middle of the night, dressed in the ceremonial robes we rarely see them wear, and walked downtown to the courthouse. He must have stood a moment, staring up at the clock tower backdropped by the moon, and smoked a last cigarette or two. He made his way to the tip of plaster and wood above the four cardinal-pointed clocks and took a last look. Then he went, a leap with no flight. The custodians found him in the morning dark, splayed on steps they scrubbed roughly and quickly before business hours.

They came in the forties, thirty-seven angels just after the war. My father was a boy and remembers the astonishment and delight, everyone's theories that they'd materialized with the bomb or defected, a European secret, from the spread of Communism. But in any case they've dwindled, with Makar's flight, to fourteen, and all but one have thrown themselves from the courthouse. They die on their own but with force, without explanation. Those left behind perform their mourning—days of shiftlessness at work, temporarily imposed silences, or sometimes sackcloth and ash. Makar has struck them different, and we know that's why they've withdrawn. The eldest, throwing off eternity in our town and knowing, we think, for what.

It's his brethren's reaction that breeds distrust in the spooky, uneasy sadness in the rest of us. If they've seen the Lord our God, if they descended from Heaven, warped and lost or not, why do they mourn each other so? We've spelled ourselves so long with stories of what comes after death, believing it makes the passing worthwhile, it's difficult to imagine their choosing the passage, time and time again, only to mourn it after. I've never thought to ask Lucius about it, or at least never had the courage. Maybe someone's asked, but there's no answer floating around. We give them space, take casseroles and desserts to the monastery to help ease the burden. Even Lil paid respects, made a potato casserole we carried over the day after Makar was collected from the courthouse steps. None of us wanted to see suffering, and beyond these quick, simple kindnesses, we wait for them to return to themselves, return on their own.

We are the opposite of sadness, Lil and I. We're all the joy there is for a while. Lil teeters around the house leaning backwards, hips set like she's already far along, and I bring home ice cream, fold laundry, work on the pickup. She's ready for bedroom decorations and tentative names. Our coffee table sits in a pile of paint swatches and legal pads covered in names, boy and girl, she's pulled from books and TV and family photo albums. She arranges them over and over and asks if I love her enough to run to the gas station after dark for candy and drinks. I'm happy to oblige, smoking on the way—we've decided to stop for the sake of the baby, but I'm taking to it slower. When she catches me she wags a finger, already parenting.

"What is this world without love," she says. "Can't love without life. Put it out."

I don't perfectly follow. Lil asks for names, but I offer only Junior and Glenda. I act like I can muster nothing better, though I can but know she won't be happy. I keep thinking *Makar* or even *Lucius*, other angel names like *Wilhelm* or *Leonid* or a simple out-of-the-Bible *Michael*. I still feel respect, a love for those outlying men, I can't quite tamp down. They've begun to end their exile, coming back to the flower shop and deli and high school. I'm proud for them, and though Lucius is still holding out I look forward to his being back in the garage, tinkering away. I'm excited for him, for having it all together again and so much good on the horizon.

Our festivity takes a bump when Lil calls work to say she's sent for one of our town's two cabs and I should meet her at the doctor's. I wash as much grease from my hands and arms as I can and get a ride from Steve, my boss. He has three kids the picture of health, says not to worry. These are almost always surprisingly good bits of news. Luck disguised as tragedy. He asks how far we are, and I tell him nine weeks. He drops me at the office complex across the street from the hospital, all smiles. The first one, in the early going, is always a terror, he says. I look up the beige brick of the building a few minutes. I imagine climbing its outside, making it to the top and staring down again, searching for something I don't know I've lost.

The nurses in the office lead me directly to an examination room where Lil sits on the table, stirrups pushed to the side, while the doctor talks in a low but cheerful voice. Dr. Zeng is a tall white woman with blond hair and a deep Southern drawl, her name a careless misdirection. I stand by Lil and put an arm around her shoulders, feel her lean into me. She's paler than usual, rumpled and displeased. I start to ask what's going on but Dr. Zeng speeds ahead of me.

"It's a normal thing," she says. "Or a common thing. It's not good, but we can work with it. A quarter or so of early pregnancies experience this, and most of those are fine."

"What do I do?"

"Take it easy. Just rest. The spotting should pass. And if not we'll go from there."

"Spotting," I say.

"Bleeding," Dr. Zeng says. "There's nothing at this point but to wait and see."

"You're bleeding?" I say, and Lil works her lips. "Is the baby OK? What do we do?"

"Wait and see," Dr. Zeng repeats. She smiles and stands from her rolling stool. "We won't know until we know. Just let me know if there's a change, OK?"

We're dismissed, and the doctor goes on about her business, other patients with other problems but none, I think, as immediate as ours.

I feel certain I arrived too late to fully understand the situation. We gather ourselves without speaking, see the nurse at her glass window who assures us the insurance will be billed, and take the elevator to the lobby to recall the cab. I wait for Lil to tell me whatever it is I need to know. She leads me out the doors to the low wall fronting the building, takes a seat, and asks for a cigarette.

"I didn't tell you because I didn't know," she says. "It's just a little blood. Here and there, last few days."

"Yours or his?"

"Are you serious?"

"I don't know how these things work."

"Right now," she says, "it's a grape. It has a heart."

"Can you not hold it? I mean, will it not hold?"

"We'll see."

I don't see her source of calm, how she seems so easy. I try to think when she noticed, her mood changed, but I can't place it. Lil stands and walks to the curb before I see the cab coming up the street, and I think how dependent we are on everything, how everything depends on us or someone like us. I get her home and she goes upstairs, deprives the predicament of its mystery. She plans to lie in bed, not move, cling to herself. I make her dinner and haul the TV up so she can watch it without coming down. She's ready for the long haul, she says, and I feel all the faith of her roiling up, a tall cloud that marks her spot, marks where she aims to go.

I go to the monastery my next day off and find Lucius still on the steps. It's down to him and Farid, their brethren returned to work and making up time on the weekends. Lucius wears his bluish-gray jumpsuit, covered in suggestive blots of grease and oil stains, and I figure he must be close to returning. I don't feel as bad asking him to break his watch, lend a hand. I nod to Farid and take a seat next to my friend, offer him a cigarette that he takes. We smoke for several minutes without speaking—I'm showing reverence without really thinking about it. The sun crawls over us and I imagine sitting here, days on end, to the last sundown I can imagine. The breeze catches Lucius' wings, their delicate white feathers loose but staying put. I sometimes search them over when his back is turned at work, wonder if he was born or made with smallish, useless wings or if they've atrophied since. Maybe he once soared, maybe he was a sort of Icarus, or maybe he knows no more of Heaven than I do.

Lucius gets through half his cigarette and crushes it beneath the steel toe of his boot. He stretches and clears his throat and holds out a hand to shake. All of the angels are, sooner or later, helplessly, almost insufferably, polite.

"Did you read the paper, Glenn?" he asks. His voice is accented with gravel, between Dracula and Churchill. Frightening in its exhortation but sad enough I'm tempted to pat his shoulder. "An early winter. Patterns given to snow. Are we not somewhat south for snow?"

"Not far enough. That's what they're saying on TV."

"It has been several years. I prefer the warmth. Mild." Lucius produces a cigarette from his sleeve, filterless and marked with foreign letters, and lights it with a match. "You are not here for work."

"Nah, didn't want to bother you."

"So your truck." He nods. "Yellow Ford. Half-ton. Nineteen and seventy-seven."

"Yeah. It won't crank."

"Still. Still won't. Have you not had time to figure this out?"

I don't know what to say, search a moment, but Lucius laughs. He's joking, dry and sympathetic.

"You must take Lilith places. You are tired of walking. I understand. These roads are long."

I don't have to tell Lucius things. He lets me know he knows. He stands, straightens himself, and waves me on. I'm both solemn and grateful as I follow him down the street, to the edge of town and my home. It's easy to feel like a pilgrim with Lucius. He hums and scuffs the pavement with his feet, the song large and full of pomp. It's old and calling to something as great and ancient with its lengthy arrangement. I can believe, witness to his pleasant toiling along, any story of guardians and messengers. It's good to have comfort, good to have help and guidance.

Lucius is quick onto the truck, wasting no time. He peeks under the hood while I list my attempts to make her turn. He nods and steps back, smoking and looking the vehicle over like something will jump out and declare its problem. I wouldn't be shocked if it did for him. Shortly he takes my small toolbox from the tailgate and climbs into the cab. I let him go on his own and glance at the house. It's dully contained by sunlight, refusing to reflect and shine. Lil is unhappy with our visitor, and I know she won't come say hello, even look out the window. We're barely into her self-imposed stillness. She leaves the bed only for the bedroom. I imagine she'll ease off eventually, whether the shakiness of her body passes or not, but for now she's determined. There's still spotting, she tells me, still something loose. I deliver her meals, do what I can.

It takes him only fifteen minutes to dissect the steering column and dash, and Lucius begins testing wires by licking his fingertip, touching the end of each unscrewed strip. This is a magic he carries, something that lets him feel without device or intervention the lack of spark in the tiniest part of the largest frame. It's more than catching a jolt. He searches out the glitch in a dead line, determines the point of disturbance or simply somehow *knows* the problem. And God bless him, he traces a heavy line from key switch to starter and then yanks it loose, replaces it with a slightly heavier gauge. He reassembles the coverings without checking his fix and then turns the key in the ignition. It floods to life in smoke and a roar, and I stand in the fumes. Lucius smiles at me, says it was only a tiny, hidden break somewhere along the way.

"Sometimes things just go," he says. "You fix what you can."

He kills the motor and restarts it several times, succeeding on each attempt. After we take a seat on the porch and light cigarettes. I offer a beer, or just some water, but he turns me down with a small wave, only wanting to rest before the walk home. Through the screen door I hear Lil up and moving, downstairs for the first time in days. I holler if she needs some help, but she only bangs around the kitchen, doing I don't know what. I start to go inside after her but feel afraid, suddenly, what she might say. Lucius and I sit in silence until our smokes are out, and then it occurs to me to ask something I know I probably shouldn't.

"What about people?" I say. "Can you tell about them?"

"Tell what?"

"How they work. What's wrong." I glance over my shoulder, where the house has dropped to silence again. "Lil's had some spotting. Blood. The baby."

"I am sorry," Lucius says. "Your doctor?"

"Says it's not necessarily the end of the world. There's nothing to do but wait and see."

"I am sorry, Glenn."

"What if you just touched her," I say, and I lay my hand on his elbow, feel the heat flowing from his body. "Tell us if there's something wrong or not. Where."

"I am sorry, Glenn." Lucius pats my hand and then levers to his feet and flicks his cigarette into the dirt. "There are mysteries. The body is a mystery. I will pray for Lilith."

"Pray," I say. I'm disappointed but stand with him, shake his hand, and walk him to the street. "Thanks for the help."

"See you at work," he says, and given it all I'm glad I will.

But of course it happens, and of course, I think, of course we're not lucky or blessed or whatever people need to get by unscathed. Lil is all business, and I know by watching her that all is lost. She spends a long time in the bathroom, letting out a single wail. When she exits she takes all the sheets from our bed, her long rest finally ended, and carries them to the burn barrel in the backyard. She lights a fire immediately, careful with matches and a little kerosene. She returns to the bathroom and carries her bucket of cleaning supplies. Stays a while before coming back to tell me what I already know. She is streaked white and red, sweaty with sunken eyes and a mouth that turns neither up nor down in the corners. Plastic and defeated.

"No more," she says. "It's over."

I want to drive her to the hospital, but she only gets on the phone and calls Dr. Zeng's number, leaves a message, and waits for a returned call. They have a quiet conversation in the kitchen. I can feel her twisting the cord around her fingers, asking how close to death she is, and I wait for her to come tell me we need to hurry. But when she does hang up Lil comes out on the porch, takes one of my cigarettes, and says there's nothing to do but watch the bleeding, wait, let herself clear out. She sits in our swing and pushes back and forward, like she wants the air to catch her. We'd made it ten weeks, so close to the safer ground of another trimester.

"I was close to maternity clothes," Lil says. "He was growing fingernails."

"How do you know all this?"

"They've studied it. He had fingers. He could touch."

"Where is—what did you do with it?"

"He's swimming. He's a voyager. Conquistador."

"Jesus," I say, imagining a little dollop spinning at the eye of a hurricane. "Why that?"

"Well. You tell me."

I don't know what to tell her. I want to say sit tight, we'll do better next time, only in many more words. No more setting money aside, less worry, but these aren't reliefs. I don't have magic of any kind, nothing that lets us do-over or reset without loss. I wish I did. She finishes her cigarette and then walks inside, gets on the phone again to let people know she'd let them know too soon. I stay on the porch and watch the sun fail. Lil bustles around the house, calm and quiet now. There isn't much else in the world but a red sky and black little words of love behind it, and there's nothing to try and turn it around. More waiting, endless see-it-once-it's-happened.

The worst at first is phone calls, condolences from people we'd told. Each bit of sympathy drains Lil and makes me cringe. We even get a card, thinking-of-you, from an aunt. She sets them atop the TV, now returned to the living room, like they're Christmas cards, and it's a reveling in disaster I don't understand at all. She cooks every night before I come home, leaves the food on the stovetop and disappears upstairs. I spend the nights on the couch. Steve offers me as much time off work as I need, but I don't want any. I'm scared to be in the house. I pick up overtime where I can, say it's to put extra on some bills. I shut off thinking about anything beyond bolts and filters and the bare motions to get me place to place.

I take to thinking of our dead, or at least unborn, child as a little girl, and she's been lost in the woods. I daydream something like Alice wandering Wonderland, only with more dire a consequence, and I imagine her blond and petite and quite a little specimen of our bloodlines. I give her my forehead low beneath Lil's hair. Long, strong fingernails and feet with second toes longer than the king, something neither of us has. I don't know if it works genetically. But when I think of that tiny girl traipsing through a maze of trees, never finding daylight, something clicks in place better. Makes no sense, doesn't have to make any, but I want to move on from it some. Lil grows a little less morbid and a little more social, and I think about going back to the bedroom at night. The talks we have to have, life to ease back into, are looking closer.

Saturday evening Lucius arrives to pay respects. I'm surprised to see him. I'm on the porch with a beer and watch him up the street, carrying a tinfoil-wrapped dish. He waves from the pavement, pauses a moment before stepping into the yard. I tell him hey and he takes a seat on the porch rail, holds his offering with one hand, and fishes a cigarette from his pocket with the other. We smoke together without saying much and then he stands, shakes himself, and asks if Lil's home. I holler for her. Lucius smiles and shrugs, little embarrassed.

"You will not mind if I speak to your wife, I mean."

"No," I say. "Of course not."

"Hi," Lil says when she comes to the door. She looks at the screen a moment before pushing it open and stepping out with us. She eyes us both warily. "What can I do for you?"

"I want to offer a small comfort in your time of hardship," Lucius says. He hands the casserole to her. "It is in your bowl. I thought this an excellent way to return it to you."

"Two birds with one stone," I say.

"Yes, good. Thank you." She pulls the foil up from the dish, looked and sniffed at it. "It's about suppertime. Why don't you come on in and eat with us?

"No," Lil says, cutting off his protests. "Come on and enjoy it with us. I insist."

"Of course," Lucius says. "As you like."

Both of them surprise me. Her politeness and his willingness to step into our lives a moment. I know they do but don't think I've ever seen an angel eat. They'll come help, like Lucius did with the truck, but they don't visit like friends. I lead him to the dining room while Lil throws some bread in the oven, toasts it up, and pours us glasses of tea. Lucius sits tall and stiff at the table, looking around at our small china cabinet, the couple yellowed family photos and crosses Lil has hanging on the wall. He seems to think no more or less of any one thing than another. I wonder what they have inside their home, if they brought art or sculptures or simply settled in with the plain monastery walls, if they enjoy the plainness.

Once we're settled Lil uncovers Lucius' food and ladles some onto our plates. He bows his head, closes his eyes. If he's praying, though, he does it silently, so we give him his moment before we start eating. Lucius is slow and measured, his manners almost dainty. Lil picks at her food, nibbling on a slice of the bread and hardly touching the casserole. Something's on her mind, and I wonder what. I poke at it a couple times—broccoli and rice, no meat, some kind of soup filling and firming the mixture. I take a bite and it near knocks me down. It's clear Lucius knows his way around a kitchen, especially the spice rack. I have no idea what he's used but it pops, something garlic and something more, something else smoky and tangy, rich. I shovel through my helping and go back for another. I enjoy it and feel better for just sitting and chewing.

Lil excuses herself, asking if we need anything before shuffling to the kitchen. I hear her opening and shutting drawers. Lucius and I finish and sit back in our chairs. He bows his head again, another prayer I guess, and when he looks up I wonder what to say to him. I appreciate his kindness. We share loss, at least in part. We've passed comfort back and forth. For a moment I think about just asking what happens when we die, when angels die, if it's all the same and what exactly it is. He might simply tell me, I think, in a moment caught with his guard down.

"Thanks for dinner," I say instead. "It means a lot."

"It is a small thing," he says.

We light cigarettes. I grab an ashtray from the hutch and push it to the center of the table. Lil returns and I start to ask if she wants a smoke—she still hasn't bought a new pack, just keeps taking from mine—but she stops behind Lucius and raises her hand. She's holding a hammer. It floats, green handle and rust-spotted head, like a twiggy halo what seems like forever. Then Lil brings it down and from across the room I feel its *thud* against Lucius's skull. He falls forward onto the table, twitches and shakes. Lil stands over him, no expression on her face. I jump up and scream at her but am too afraid to come around the table. She doesn't blink. Lil speaks calmly.

"We've all had this coming, Glenn," she says. "Now it's going to be very simple."

She explains what she wants. I listen to all of it, wait for her to finish, and then can't bring myself to move. Lil is patient. I expect Lucius to lift himself up, stand and flee. I hope he will, but he doesn't. When I can feel my legs again I step around the table and do as Lil instructs.

Twenty-three angels have died since they came to town, each has been mourned, and the one who didn't leap from the courthouse, the only to die otherwise, won't leave my mind. I was a kid when it happened, the one named Adil shot three times and wings cut off and left on the side of a dirt road. People went crazy wanting to know what happened, who did it. Names were tossed around, accusations made and houses searched for evidence, but no one was ever arrested. We'd probably still be locked down and half at war with one another except a guy named Peters turned up dead, Adil's wings sealed in a box in the closet of his mobile home. The circumstances were sketchy, but the sheriff ruled it suicide. Everyone moved on, relieved if nothing else.

He just wanted to see if an angel would die, I think. He was curious. I'm not sure what I want from Lucius, now. He lies in the basement, wrists tied by metal wire to exposed water pipes. Lil wanted the wire because she says they can open locks without keys. For two days Lucius doesn't even wake, though, and I wonder what we're supposed to do with him. He sits on the cool floor, head lolled. A dark patch of dried blood crowns his scalp, a flattened bit of skull. I think Lil aims to finish it, sooner or later. Why she's waiting for him to wake first I don't know.

While she goes about her business I go to work and come home to sit in the basement and watch Lucius. I study his wings, find nothing particularly special. They should just be on some other animal. I guess he's white, maybe a little something else, but can't be sure. He's not even all that memorable, his features sandy and dull. He's carried nothing with him, no ID or cash. I think about praying for him, and then praying to him or through him, like a saint. I set up a cot on the opposite wall. I eat and sleep and wait beneath a single unshielded light bulb for something to change. In the end it's Lucius that wakes me, early Tuesday morning. He wails and thrashes against his constraints, shaking near a seizure, but he can't come loose. After a bit of it he stills, rolls his head back, and spots me with his flat eyes. He shrieks again. I run up the stairs, stumble through the dark house and out onto the porch. I fling myself to the ground and lie in the grass, soaked with sweat and all of a sudden lost.

Lil cautions patience. He's awake but not himself. She wants him aware, able to answer for what he's done. Or what she thinks he's done, whatever in our connection to him she feels sure made her lose our baby. She says to watch, wait for the screaming and madness to end, and then she'll make good on it. I try. One day at work Farid drops in, asks if I've seen Lucius. I say he'd delivered the casserole, eaten with us, and gone home. They haven't seen him, of course, and I worry they'll come by the house looking for him, catch a whiff of his wailing, and bring the whole world down on us. Lil isn't as concerned. She goes about our home, cleaning and cooking meals I can't work up an appetite for. She tells me it's all right. We'll be fine.

"I've never been clearer," she says. "We're doing the right thing."

"We need a way out."

"This is it. Think of it like before they had justice, when it was every man's responsibility. The West."

She lights a cigarette and walks away, like she's explained it all. In the basement Lucius quiets when I enter. He's gone from screaming at all time to taking advantage of an audience. But none of it's what I want to hear. I ask him what's on the other side, what I can expect for a dead child. I ask how to fix Lil, put an end to all this and make things right.

"Everyone, secrets," he says. "You want the name of Jehovah."

"I want to figure this out."

"I will tell you where all ends. I have seen the fiery throne. You are not to know."

"Lucius, please."

"It moves as what you think of as a rocket, and it is everywhere," he says. He coughs and I see a glint in his eyes. "Deep in the north. Do you know what it is to be separate?

"Do you understand the lifting of His hand and the day you no longer can see the separation of His fingers? He holds to you a number, and it is all your life. And you cannot set eyes on the glory.

"You want the glory and fire and the name," he says, and he drops his head again. "But you shall not have it."

I beg him for something that makes more sense, but he gives nothing. I go upstairs again and he returns to shrieking. Lil is drinking coffee in the living room. She pats the couch beside her, wants me to sit and hold her. I do like she wants but can't get comfortable. She feels thin and sticky, like she's oozing apart from inside out. She radiates heat and a sweet, sickly scent.

"Just wait," Lil says. "He'll answer for what he's done."

"What's he done?" I ask, afraid I'll make her mad but hoping she'll flounder for an answer and realize how crazy we've become. But I don't faze her.

"Maybe you should sleep in the basement again. He's quiet when you're there."

I don't answer. I know I'll do as she asks, and she knows. Lil has taken charge, and all I know to do, now, is follow along.

"Glenn," he says, waking me. My name in his mouth is soft but firm, and another time I'd expect a message from God, a mission charged. "Glenn. Glenn."

"Lucius," I say, cautious.

"Why am I here?"

I crawl off the cot, ease to him, and lay the back of my hand on his forehead. He's cool and calm, eyes dulled but focused. We've made it through the worst, or to the worst. I sit back and eye him, trying to decide how to proceed. He's patient, now. I notice for the first time he's grown no facial hair, these days in our basement, and it keeps him from looking quite as bad.

"Lil. She aims for you to—I don't know. She blames you."

"Your child. She is one of those," he says. When I don't answer he nods. "You must let me free, Glenn."

"I'd like to do that."

"This is not meant to be."

"How do I fix her?" I ask him. Even with his wits he offers me nothing, repeats he must go. I must let him go.

"I can do this no more. I am not holding it against you. Glenn, please."

I walk upstairs, find Lil in the half-dark kitchen. The sun isn't quite up and she's getting ready to bake a cake. I watch her back, her short, choppy motions with the mixing bowl. I think about telling her it's time to forget all this, that we're not going further. I'm not scared of her, she doesn't hold a power, but something stops me. She might be right. Lucius could have brought this on us; I can't be sure she's wrong, and that keeps me going along. I wait for her to turn and notice me. She smiles and pours her batter into the pan, loads it into the oven. She lights a cigarette and settles against the counter.

"He's awake," I say. "Lucius."

It's all she needs to hear. I follow her back to the basement, wondering what she'll do. Or how she'll do, when she'll do it. She settles cross-legged on the concrete floor, and I wait at the stairs. Lucius straightens as best he can and they stare at each other several minutes, neither speaking. I expect accusations from each, curses, and maybe even begging, but they only watch and wait, for what I don't know. I don't see anger or haste. They're disappointed and patient. Each injured but pressing along. Lil presses her hands together like she's praying, or wants to pray, and Lucius bows his head. I don't know who God would have to answer in this situation, and I don't know why or how they're having a moment together. I start to tell them to cut it out. They finish on their own, though. Lil stands, spins away, and pushes past me to the stairs.

I walk in her wake to the front porch and sit by her when she hurls herself onto our swing. The sun's risen, slicing red over the trees, the edge of town. Lil's starting to crack, face flushed and eyes watering. I hope she's turning the corner, realizing what she's done and coming to grips with what's inside her. I put an arm around her shoulders, offer to let her lean in, but she isn't interested. She shakes and cries and rattles me off of her. She stands and paces a circle, sits again, strikes a thinker's pose. Bobs up and down, almost celebratory in her frustration, I suppose ecstatic. She's elated, if tortured, and my wife scares me.

"So, what?" I ask.

"He dies in the morning," Lil says. "He knows it. Let him think it over today, and then we do what must be done."

"You're sure?"

She leans over, finally, and kisses me roughly on the lips. I feel the stubble of my beard drag over her cheek, smell a sour sort of liquor to her breath. She doesn't answer, except for that. Really, that's all I need. Lil tells me what she's making for dinner, pork roast and all else, and tells me to sleep upstairs tonight, in bed. She wants my body next to hers, wants the comfort of closeness, her husband. We'll wake in the morning and cleanse our house, the whole earth, of that little-winged man, same as she did for our poor dead child.

"And leave him alone. This is his time, and then it's ours," she says and grabs my chin with her stained fingers. She kisses me again. "Just help me through and we'll be fine."

"OK," I promise. I can't tell if she's sincere or only keeping me where I need to be, but I mean it. Lil stands, still holding to my face, and bends to kiss me once more. She heads inside and leaves me alone. I mean what I say, I will help, and I will see us through.

"I have seen sons taken."

"I think she was a girl."

"Even so," Lucius says. "I have seen them taken as well. I imagine no greater sadness than the child, lost."

"I'm not sure what she was," I tell him. "It just broke Lil a little. Broke me a little."

I started off talking about an engine we'd had at work, an original from a '57 Chevy. He likes those old motors, no gimmicks. We're moving on to things we've seen, things we know. Lucius doesn't mind acknowledging factual occurrences. It's late now, or early. I left Lil upstairs, kicking in a fitful sleep just deep enough not to break. I couldn't sleep, whether worrying about her plans or being in the bed with her again after weeks of distance. It seems decent to spend these hours with Lucius, awake. I stick a cigarette between his lips and light it for him, offer some food he declines. Says he's good on water, too. His body's requiring little.

"We've always been all right. Nothing remarkable," I tell him. "We liked screwing around so we got married. A kid just seemed natural. This is normal."

"It is."

"That's why it doesn't make sense, because it does. This is really, plain, boring stuff." I look at him. "Is the kid in Heaven?"

"We are not to answer these questions."

"You were talking about that fiery throne," I say, and he winces. His face carries more pain for a few seconds than he's looked in all the rest of this time, and I feel a pang of guilt. "Listen, it's simple. Is she all right? I don't want a theology or nothing, just a little child is all right."

"She is fine," Lucius says.

"It wasn't anything you did."

"Absolutely. Of course it was not."

"And Lil."

"I cannot possibly know of her."

"No. What do I do with her?"

"She is her own, Glenn. You are her husband. You know this. You can do nothing but love and help her."

"I want to let you go," I say, changing the subject but not.

"I will not tell you what to do. Soon it will not matter."

"It always matters."

"No," he says. "It is my time. Soon, Glenn."

"Even if we don't."

"Even so. This is not as I desire, but I cannot demand different. There is little point."

We sit in silence. I dangle another cigarette from his lips and light it before I go upstairs and back to our bedroom. I look at Lil's dark shape in the bed. She tosses, mumbles. I know she's sweating without touching her. For people so free and drifting and without a solid point in the world, of no interest to anyone, she sure has come to have a fire burning, driving her forward. I think this and then imagine her waking in a while, finishing her supposed business with Lucius. After that she won't simply settle in and carry on, even if she wants to, expects it. I feel it on me, responsibility to take care of it all. I step out and shut the door between us, leave her to darkness.

I find a pair of pliers and take them to the basement. Lucius stays still, watching, and I figure this is where I set my misery in stone. I lean over my friend, reach down his back to the wires wrapping his wrists to pipe. I twist the end until they unravel and he's loose. I expect him to leap up and smite me with something like brimstone, but he doesn't. Lucius pulls his hands into his lap, rubs the scabbed-over ruts where the wire has cut into his flesh. A tremble runs the whole length of him, goes down his arms and seems to have to shake out his fingertips. He gets his legs under him and tries to stand. I take him beneath his shoulders and help him to his feet. He sways, an unsteady tower, but doesn't drop as long as I keep hold of him. I nudge him toward the stairs. We shamble along together, easily enough.

"Your people," Lucius says to me. He lights a cigarette and lolls his head against the cracked-open truck window. "Mankind. Your greatest gift is you see nothing coming. And what do you do? You call upon psychics. You are desperate to know the end. You are fools.

"But blessed fools," he adds. "Here. Turn here."

I drive him, in the truck he'd fixed for me, down a street near the college, and he points to a yellow-painted home. It sits dark and looks empty, no cars in the drive and blank windows. Lucius waves me past when I start to slow, and I turn us back toward downtown.

"I once made love to a woman who lived there," he said. "This is strictly warned against, for me. For us. 'Frowned upon,' the saying is. The frowning face of God, I suppose."

"Why won't you just tell us things, though? If you're hedging on the rules anyway."

"Your people." He snorts. "Fools, but blessedly so."

I think he'll want to go by the monastery, or concede to the hospital, but Lucius doesn't change his mind. We see his former lover's house, he smokes and talks some about what's wrong with all of us, and we close in on the county courthouse where, he says, everything that needs to be made clear will be. I don't believe him. For all he looks like hell, he wears a smile on his face like it's going out of fashion. It's not a look I recognize on him and leaves me a little less than easy. I'm at fault, I've done wrong, and though he says nothing of it, I don't forget.

Along the empty streets I think about Lil. We're a couple hours from daylight. Soon she'll crawl out of bed, stretch, and look around for me. I see her heading downstairs, and instead of starting breakfast or bathing or whatever simple ritual she aimed to perform before murder she'll rush to the basement and see neither me nor Lucius waiting for her. She'll tear something up, shove over a living room chair or toss around small appliances in the kitchen. I've betrayed her. She takes up the knife or hammer or whatever tool she intended for Lucius and she waits with it. Lil settles and waits, and that's all my doing the right thing amounts to. When I walk through that door again I'll have to answer, whether it makes sense or not. Nothing much does, and I don't understand how Lucius can't see why we want to know, why we question.

"I hope this is worth it," I say.

"It is," he agrees, but I'm not sure we mean the same thing.

We pull to the courthouse and kill the lights, and I wait for Lucius to do what he'll do. I wonder if he'll scale the outside or knows some way in. Maybe he levitates, for all I know. He finishes the cigarette he's on and rolls up the window. He looks up the face of the stone building a few moments and asks for the time. Nearly four, I say, and he shakes his head.

"Late." He turns his head to stare at me. "You will help me, yes?"

I can't say no. He knows that. I run around and get him out of the truck, brace around his waist with his arm thrown over the back of my neck. We stumble, a little more quickly than we had coming out of his basement holding cell. I feel his muscles wanting to give, drop him to the concrete. We get to the front doors and stop. Lucius reaches out a hand, points at the knob.

"Kick it in?" I ask.

He shakes his head, leans himself toward the locks. They turn without key, something from his body riveting into the door and opening the way. I lug him in and get the door shut.

"Normally I would lock that back," he says. "But you will need to exit this way."

The courthouse innards are dark, office doors to either side shut tightly and lit only by emergency lights spaced widely down the hall. They have security cameras up, too, but they look dull and sleeping, useless. I start to ask Lucius if they'll see me, watching the tape back, but figure it doesn't change the situation. If helping him at this point is the worst I have to answer for I'll be lucky. At the center of the building, open beneath the upper floor's balcony and the high ceiling, the clock tower, we take the small and damp-smelling elevator up. Lucius looks around, nods to an undersized door off the balcony. Behind it a narrow stairwell turns tightly, hopelessly toward the tower. It's too narrow for us to pass together.

"Come on," I tell him. "We'll get it."

I turn and bend down, and he crawls onto my back, scaring me for a moment that he aims to choke me with his arms around my neck, but I get hold of his knees like this is any old piggyback ride. Lucius is heavy, like he's filled with a small and compressed weight that isn't human. At the first switchback I think my legs will give, but I push on until we end at a platform sealed by a thick door. Lucius slides off me and steps ahead without assistance. He pushes open the door, and I follow him into the square of the clock tower. We stand on a landing, a ladder leading upward into cool, dark air. Above us are the clock faces, one directed to each cardinal point, and the speakers that sound the hourly bells. Lucius searches along the wall and finds a small service door, opening to the building's exterior. He swings it out into space and the nighttime breeze wraps around us. Lucius sighs, turns back, and asks me for one more cigarette. We smoke, and he finally clasps my shoulder.

"I will tell you something," he says, "one thing. You will not care for it."

"Then don't."

"What will happen happens. That is all."

He's right, I don't like it, but that's Lucius' good-bye. He flicks his cigarette out the door and then ducks through, onto a ledge. He stands a moment. His little wings twitch. He takes a step, then, out into air, and my stomach lurches. But he doesn't fall. Lucius hangs, his crippled-looking wings quivering and his body holding in space. As I watch he moves up and outward, higher than the tower's spire and clear of the courthouse's rounded roof. For a moment he floats still as can be, hands folded and feet weakly drooping, unnecessary. Part of him is falling, where I expect, what I know, but Lucius rises, too. He lifts, and as much as I'm witnessing tragedy, I think it's more a beautiful, small pause in gravity, all the world, and then he's gone.

Jeff Coomer

1:OO-2:OO A.M.

The god who rules this hour is the god of flushing toilets, scampering mice, and distant radio tower lights. No longer having any ambition for advancement, he goes about his modest work with a philosophical outlook lacking in the God of Noon. Those feathery clouds that just blurred the full moon, for instance, don't particularly trouble him. He's a specialist in doubt and regret; his favorite music is whatever you listened to alone in high school. "Put on *The White Album*," he says as you settle in to reorganize your collection of unhealed wounds by descending order of date. He watches you work from a corner of the bed, singing the familiar words and occasionally interjecting a helpful observation. You're only half finished when the hall clock chimes, and his voice fades like the whistle of a train you were too late to catch.

Jennifer Met

FALLOUT

... in the white dress which is as cool and
evil as a glass of radioactive milk ...
—Lynn Emanuel, "Like God"

an image upon which people always linger but
growing up in 1950's New Mexico she says it
was commonplace to Geiger-counter your milk
to live with the dark threat of radiation poison
and she didn't give it much thought beyond that
context—I guess—how in the milk a tint of blue
is normal—until you look—and then it seems so
white that it's impossible and you imagine gray
slipping through and what you think you know—
the outside appearance—is wrong and deceiving
like how this excerpt suggests that God is in the
dress or how back in college while I studied DNA
half-lives and other things I hadn't given much
thought as to why hospitals were white but one
theory suggests that albinism is genetically linked
to sterility—and here the roots of the poet's lines—
our mother—warm and life-giving—in reality
sterile and thus not ours and of course the obvious
fear of our own diminished effect or what Freud
would call castration and when my lab partner
accompanied me back to my dorm room and we
found the microwave running—door open—the air
full of unseen waves and he stuck his hand inside
to see if it was really on and it didn't hurt but turned
his finger black for the rest of the semester and then

I never saw him again—I didn't give it much thought
but now I'm starting to worry a German nightmare—
a "doppelgänger" story where your shadow separates
itself and turns against you—cancer—and I watch
others eyeing the dark clouds gathering over Sendai
full of radioactive evaporation from the flooded plant
something that you can't give much thought because
what can they do—they think—what can I do—
and can radiation be called evil when it doesn't feel—
has no malicious intent—really what could God do—
even knowing the split beginning inside the safe body
of these clouds threatening rain and starting to shadow
black—we all just watch—cool as radioactive milk

Nandini Dhar

After Bergman

A thud reverberates over and above the children's voices
      memorizing their lessons: the sound of the fish dying.

My sister whispers, rushes to the window to catch a glimpse
      of how death is trickling in through the collective

pores into our neighborhood: the broken sidewalks, the cracks
      in the petals of the marigold, the worm-eaten coconut tree.

Unmindful, Mother thwacks her on the head, but my sister
      was already whistling to the neighbor-boy—our friend

Babua. Waiting for us underneath the guava tree. Mother knows,
      she cannot keep us locked. Mother knows, between her

two children, there are four eyes. Four eyes that would
      remember what hasn't happened. What is about to happen.

Sister pushes mother's hand away, mouths words that cause
      mother to wonder where she has picked them up from: *son*

of a swine. The heritage of whittling curse words from nothing
   never escapes a generation. I stand up, push the chair back.

A crater size cavity on the schoolroom floor, and the arithmetic
   textbook falls, falls, falls. Underneath, a little girl who grabs it,

caresses its pages. Her name is neither Fanny. Nor Alexander.
   Not even Alice. Our fingers entwined, we leave the threshold

of our home. One cannot witness the crafting of marrow maps
   secondhand.

A. A. Weiss

CHALLENGER

Mom and Dad only used the chandelier to illuminate special occasions and serious conversations about things I'd done wrong, so I was afraid. I held the key to Dad's gun cabinet deep down in my pocket. The metal was warm in my little fist. The nice white plates with blue oriental scribbles were already on the table; *Something special this way comes.* Her voice echoed from the kitchen. I'd been summoned and there wasn't enough time to return the key to Dad's study. She called me *Honey* (instead of Vladimir Ivanovich Thompson!) and my shoulders dropped to where they'd be useless for protecting from body blows. When I answered her my voice hinted at the tenderness of a potential victim. Mom had never hit me. Dad had never hit me. This body crumpling was something instinctive from before. Healed red markings crisscrossed all over my back. She'd entered the dining room with good news but didn't want to continue now that I'd shriveled into a ball. She hugged me and took away the tension from my head with a warm hand on my neck.

"Oh, honey. Everything is fine."

She was wearing makeup, which she did occasionally for things like fund-raisers in Portland or Renoir-themed community picnics.

Dad got home. Mom and I waited at the table until he changed his clothes and then we ate dinner off the nice plates. I was careful not to stab through the meat or scrape the plate with my fork (such forgetfulness once led to a well-lighted talk about behavior). Dad had removed his tie and button-down, but somehow seemed more formal than before. *Why would he tuck in his polo shirt for dinner?* At last, Mom and Dad folded their linen napkins to hide the stains and placed them to the side as though they've never been used.

"So," said Dad, nodding without eye contact, either pleased by the meal or by his thought. "Here's the news, sport." Now he looked at me.

Mom smiled, and while Dad spoke, I focused on a small patch of red lipstick on the tip of her front tooth.

"Oh," I said.

They weren't going to mention the key. They didn't know about the key.

So I was not in trouble. Or not yet.

But the tension inside me didn't go straight to happiness, didn't resolve at all, but rather went sideways to somewhere else without a name (at least not a name I knew in English). I'd probably known it before, this feeling, but I didn't think that way anymore. I had new words for emotions, and the closest connection I could make with this feeling, in English, was *disorder*.

Mom and Dad's decision to adopt again made me think about disrupting the order that was changing me.

After dinner I returned the key to the spot Dad thought was a secure hiding place. Immediately, a pressure escaped down through my spine. I looked through the glass door at my favorite of his guns—a tiny pistol that seemed the only one I'd be able to hold with one hand.

Two years pass.

I go through puberty and I no longer crumple when voices rise.

I take the pistol from the cabinet once a week. It fits me.

As we strolled on the sidewalk in Kiev I thought about summer lasting forever.

"So, high school," said Dad. Mom was eager to see me say something.

The buildings had all-rectangular architecture. This conversation didn't seem appropriate.

We walked around a discarded shirt on the sidewalk, too dirty for even the homeless to pick up. This environment belonged to dreams, ones you woke from wondering where you were, easiest to report to a concerned parent as spider nightmares.

"Whatever," I said.

We were on the sidewalk in front of a political palace and Dad kept walking too slowly, expecting me to go ahead of him. I pulled back each time he did, falling in line, until finally he said, "How about leading, sport?" I looked at Mom and she nodded and I walked ahead and soon it was clear I was taking us back in the direction of our hotel.

"There's a river around here," said Dad. "Let's see if you can find it." He pointed in the river's general direction.

They'd decided on Ukraine over Russia because my homeland was too bureaucratic now. Summer in Kiev was beautiful, yes, but this didn't feel like a vacation. Nor did this trip feel like the rescue mission I'd envisioned Mom and Dad conducting in Russia for me. It wasn't cold. No one was eating flowers to stay alive.

"About high school," said Dad, coming up beside me and then stepping in front ever so slightly as to guide us on a more-direct course to the river. "It's the same school, I know, but you'll still meet some new people."

"Yes, Dad," I said.

"It's about change," said Mom. "This is a time when it's perfectly fine to change."

I didn't say anything and then it got awkward as what I thought was a silent drop to the conversation was just them looking at me for an answer.

"I don't wish to have this conversation in Ukraine."

Later, we drove a rental car on well-paved roads to the orphanage. When we stopped you could still see the taller city buildings among green trees. The orphanage director, a woman whom Americans would call matronly, spoke to us with broken English. Dad introduced me and the woman mistakenly thought I still spoke Russian. I'd lost my first language two years before, but I could still react to questions that sought a *yes* or *no*.

"Nyet," I said. "I don't speak Pa-Rusky."

Children moved around quickly in several directions, positioning for our proper viewing. Some looked away, giggling after waving. Mom touched those who came near on the tops of their heads. They showed her drawings. A few boys played games on cell phones. The environment was predominately cement but clean and painted with bright yellow and light blue. Not all the children smiled, but nothing pointed to abuse. Someone had donated crayons and rulers and stuff.

A memory of boredom—more a feeling, actually—returned to me. I felt the internal weight of being in the orphanage with nothing to do. There were no games back then. The director selected one girl to go home with her on the weekends and live with her family, play with her children and such. She always picked a girl, and yet I always stopped breathing and smiled when she entered the room on Friday afternoon. How could I not believe she would pick me?

An electric bell rang in a distant part of the orphanage and the girls ran to go eat. The director told us they were all happy, yes, but they'd all become prostitutes if they turned eighteen in Ukraine. Mom usually became teary when she heard words like *prostitute*, but she was OK now. Only the boy orphans remained in the room. Mom scanned their faces, looking for a connection to the photos from the online portfolio. She was ready to save one of these boys. But which one? Who was Vasia? I thought to shout his name: *Vasia*! I'd lost focus on the conversation between my parents and the director. *Vasia, Vasia*, I thought.

"A complication?" echoed Dad.

The orphan boys were all watching me.

"The information is not."

The director understood this to be an incomplete sentence once Mom and Dad failed to react in the expected manner. The woman scanned the ceiling and then the ground, stalling as she found more words to explain the clear idea in her mind. "Online portfolio," she continued. "The information is not …." She looked at me and said a quick word in Russian.

"Correct," I translated. "The portfolio is not correct."

I smiled at my accomplishment and was disappointed when Dad continued the conversation, armed with this crucial information because of me, without acknowledging that I'd done something special.

"Ask her what isn't correct, Vladik."

All three watched me as I struggled for words. In the moment before, understanding the director's rapid-fire word choice, I would have said that I could speak Russian once again. Now, as I tried to articulate a thought with words of my own, I returned to functional ignorance.

"You see," said the director to my parents, giving up on me. "Here, you see. Come here, Vasia."

She called the name in a normal voice. And I was startled because such a soft voice indicated immediacy. We'd traveled so far to meet this mystery brother and now he was anonymous in plain sight, within the distance of a whisper.

"Vasia, come here," repeated the director in a still smaller voice, but with more tension.

No one stepped forward.

A moment passed and I only noticed him because all the other boys looked at him. The only boy not looking at another boy was about as tall as the rest, a little skinnier. "Come here instantly," said the director quietly, with a soft tone as though to mask her irritation in front of my parents.

Vasia stepped forward. His shoes were white canvas, his jeans had no stains or holes, and the fabric was tight, as to appear he might outgrow them soon. His shirt had no American writing; it hadn't been donated. His hair wasn't long but looked like it had grown unchecked from his bald scalp, spherically, attended by individuals unconcerned with style. He nodded his head at Mom and Dad once they focused on him, once realizing this boy was their new son.

"Gaylo," he said.

"*Hello*," repeated Dad, already practicing his ability to correct the boy.

The director prompted Vasia to speak a statement they'd prepared together, but evidently he'd forgotten everything. He shook his head. He didn't look as nervous as I thought he should. But he was distracted. "Vasia!" said the director, snapping his focus back to her. She mouthed the words for him to say.

"Vasia," he said. "Theerteen. Very plezed to mee tyou, Moam an Tad."

The director turned to smile at Mom and Dad. The boy stood in place without moving, apparently waiting for a reaction.

Thirteen what? I thought.

"That's quite a difference," said Dad. And then I realized we were talking about thirteen *years*—age, experience, upbringing. The healthy boy before us suddenly resembled a shriveled dumpling.

Dumplings are called pilmeni, I remembered.

The director assured us that the boy was mistaken, that he was in fact nine or ten years old. "Which?" asked Dad. The woman shrugged. The boy's fingers twitched. His aloof attitude wasn't childish indifference but pre-adult protection. How long had he been in the orphanage?

The quality of the director's English improved once she returned to reciting prepared lines. "He has been residing with us for nine months," said the director. "His granny could not look after him anymore."

"My father," said the boy, in Russian, and then he stopped when the director looked at him.

Mom looked at me and smiled as if these were puzzle pieces fitting together. This was my story. This was the story I would share in common with Vasia. His grandmother couldn't care for him. I saw it again, the omniscient perspective in my head of a boy coming to America with a loving Mom and Dad, crying over English ABC pamphlets, blond hair combed by Mom's fingers, lullabies repeated syllable by syllable until they were taken to heart by this precious, pure boy until they represented love. But Vasia wasn't me. He was older—only two years younger than me now. His path into life was further developed; he'd have to backtrack his maturity to fit in with our family.

The boy, Vasia, shook Dad's hand. He nodded in my direction before I left the room. To their credit, Mom and Dad sensed something off with the undergrown boy as well. We left. Mom cried in the car, thinking she'd lost a baby or something.

At dinner that night in Kiev Dad ordered chicken and salad for the table and then we talked about what was possible. I imagined the conversation Mom and Dad had had before adopting me. I'd been six. *Troubled* was the magic word in my portfolio. Mom and Dad had taken a chance and now claimed I'd turned out OK. Mom said I couldn't say no. Saying no to Vasia would be like saying no to myself. If anyone should love Vasia, it should be me. The table felt like legal space. Mom said I needed to be strong. She never gave advice like this; it sounded like a challenge, almost a threat.

They waited for me to speak while I waited for them to move on in the conversation without me. I mentioned the possibility of disorder entering our lives.

Mom frowned and exhaled deeply. She looked at Dad.

"Some day you need to grow up, Vladik," Mom said. And her voice had been soft, so I'd put up no defense to this assault. I wanted to spit on the floor to demonstrate that my mind and body rejected those words, and I suddenly remembered the Russian word for *bitch*.

Dad didn't say anything, which let me know he agreed. It hurt that he agreed.

"He's thirteen," I said with great force.

Dad nodded. What I'd said was true. He didn't say anything, and neither did I, waiting for him to comment on the excessive volume of my voice. (*Only speak loud enough so the people you're talking to can hear, sweet Vladik.*) He wasn't mad that I'd raised my voice. It seemed I'd stumbled on the first time in my life that it was appropriate to speak louder than necessary, using a volume reserved for passionate adults.

"We're a strong family," Dad said. "It'll work."

No one spoke. They waited for me to contribute something else.

And then I realized we were voting.

A week passes while identity documents are created.

Vasia's first time in an airplane was going smoothly. His mannerisms were free of trembles, his blinking was socially appropriate—neither too fast nor too slow—and his questions didn't betray any fundamental lack of awareness. I'd expected him to ask about the food, the time in the air—anything to make me think he was uncomfortable. Nothing about him indicated existential crisis, but he did invade my personal space to lean over and look out the window. With great frequency he repeated this practice, perhaps to increase intimacy with a new family member, asking once what water we were looking at, and then stopping all questions when I said, "Still the Atlantic."

"Still," he repeated.

The mental space felt more negative with each minute that passed without a lean-over and question, as though I'd shut him down.

"Still the Atlantic," I offered, pointing.

"Good," he said, nodding. "Steel."

I thought to correct him, but didn't because I didn't want him thinking everyone did that.

At home Vasia must have thought we were millionaires.

My first impression of the house never became a foundational memory. It was big, with a nice lawn, not too far from the beach, but it wasn't like a castle or anything. That was the look in Vasia's eyes; this was a house for a president or a pop singer.

"Why don't you give him a tour," said Mom.

He watched as I took my shoes off and slipped into my approved house footwear. He accepted his new pair of rubber house slippers— Mom and Dad's first of many gifts. The tour of the first floor included the laundry room, the kitchen, and the living room. He bent his head in the wrong direction when examining the titles of the leather book collection. Vasia said, "I think very pretty," three times. But in the study upstairs he finally stopped and prepared a complex thought. He pointed to Dad's gun cabinet.

"For hunting," I said to him in English. He didn't get it, so I said "Bang, bang," and he nodded.

"Gun?" he said, and then another word in Russian that I didn't understand.

Upstairs I showed him his new room. Vasia in the house meant we no longer had a guest room. He sat on the bed and said *Very pretty*. He looked more or less content. He noticed a collection of books on the desk, more modern, more touchable, and he went over and did touch them with a single finger, separating them so he could see the titles. They were English-language materials to help him out. There was also a new laptop in the drawer loaded with *Rosetta Stone*. He spread the books apart and picked up the only one with Russian writing—a bilingual dictionary. He flipped through the pages in search of something specific. This looked important. He was going to communicate something profound to me.

"Crime," he said, looking for confirmation in my reaction. "Gun crime in America?" he asked.

I said no.

"Gun crime in school," he said. "I know."

I said there wasn't.

He nodded.

"Let's see Mom and Dad's room," I said.

We left the room and he still had a little red backpack over his shoulder.

"No," I said. "This is your room. Leave your stuff."

He nodded but he didn't take the backpack off his shoulder. I reached for it and he recoiled and in this movement I felt a connection to the boy.

"Steel," he said. "I keep."

Later, after the tour, we went to the beach. He was braver than I thought. He might not have ever seen the ocean up close, but he had no problem jumping in the water. He kept his T-shirt on, which I thought would have been a problem. I'd tried to keep my T-shirt on too when I first arrived in America. But Mom made me peel off my wet shirt and show the world the belt marks on my back. "Scars aren't for hiding," they'd said, and, always, like a commandment: BE PROUD OF WHO YOU ARE.

I wondered if Vasia had scars on his back like me. And if he did, depending on the pattern, I wondered if I could guess what instrument had made them.

A month passes.
Vasia walks in on me.
"Why?" he asks.
"There's nothing wrong with it," I explain. "It calms me."
Vasia goes to his room and I put the gun back in Dad's cabinet. Then I think about brotherhood and sharing, and I call out to Vasia, who returns.
I show him where Dad keeps the key.
We'll go to school next week. I wonder if he thinks the building will look like a palace or like a small disappointment like it is for me. And, I think, come to think, the schoolhouse isn't entirely unlike an orphanage.

I wasn't bad at soccer.
I could move in space and kick the ball off the ground and whatnot. Everything else bypassed me in those formative years of athletic adolescence—even hockey, which I loved. I knew when someone was playing it well, but I couldn't recreate the movements because I never had skates. It was like art—that's the analogy someone gave me. I knew what a masterpiece looked like, but that didn't mean the electricity coming out of my brain formed brilliance. Football and tennis and basketball and any other sport you couldn't recreate with a small, bounceless ball of twine were not programmed into my blood.

So high school gym class was awkward. And it's not because gym class was where you gained respect—no, in fact no one cared about gym class, and those who tried too hard were ridiculed silently, but knowingly; but rather gym class was where one, and really one of the only places, where one like me would be in close proximity to girls wearing short-shorts.

So, anyway, first gym class of the year and I was pretty keen not to look like a fool. I'd gotten a bigger body than the year before and I was getting some big muscles. Regarding sport, I might actually *try*.

The middle schoolers were still in the gym and there was Vasia just tearing up the basketball court. It helped that no one else was really trying, but he was really not bad. Stealing the ball and running by people was not that impressive—again, when no one else cared—but shooting the basketball with precision and actually making it in was pretty cool. This kid had some skill. I was happy on a basic level because Vasia was wicked small—even compared to the middle school girls—and there was an underdog factor going on there, just visually. So that made me happy. But then I got this feeling like I was connected to this success—it was my brother making these baskets—and that little bit of happiness turned into pride.

His little chicken legs were swimming in his gym shorts. They'd been my gym shorts two years before. When he slowed down you could see the markings on the backs of his legs. Scars across both calves. Even. Red. Prominent. The girls in my class noticed. They were talking with cupped hands and looking at his legs like I was.

The gym teacher waved the middle schoolers off the court.

Vasia waved when he saw me, bouncing me the ball.

"You know him?" asked a girl in my class that I knew but didn't really like.

"Yes," I said. "My brother."

"He adopted, too?"

I waited a second and then nodded.

"Didn't mean to offend you."

"You didn't."

The girl in my class stared at me and everyone stared at me and I wondered why the hell everyone was staring at me and then I realized I was holding the basketball. I threw it to the middle of the court and everyone started playing.

After school at home, before Mom and Dad got home, I dug through my closet and found some even older gym clothes that Vasia might fit into better. I went into his room—after knocking, of course—but he was somewhere else, doing his homework or something. So I went into his closet to drop the stuff in a pile. But then I thought Mom would get upset—everything was so neat in the house that he'd probably get in trouble—so I went to stuff it all in a backpack on the floor of the closet. Dad had bought us matching North Face backpacks for school. This backpack was the little red one he stepped off the plane with and wouldn't let me touch when we first got home; it was full as though it were packed with newspaper. I opened it up and inside were all types of girl clothes, laces and flowers and light colors.

I knew instantly what this was.

Vasia was stealing. I knew this because I'd stolen like this before. Pens. Coins. Single mittens. You saw what you had never had and you took it. But girl clothes? Pink T-shirts and tiny, tiny shorts. He must have gone into the girls' locker room.

Cute, I thought.

And then a tremendous memory overtook me. I was eight years old and I'd just been caught stealing *Legos* from a kid's model science project. Mom picked me up from school and had to come inside to get me from the principal's office. And when I got home Dad was waiting for me at the kitchen table.

Three months pass.

Winter comes and Mom doesn't force us to get haircuts.

I like this.

Vasia didn't want a haircut and he was still in that fragile stage where Mom and Dad didn't want to push him. I remember basically getting strapped to the barber's chair when I was first here. Everything was wrong about the capes and the scalding hot water and the little machines that did the cutting like they were mowing your head instead of safely removing it with the measured clips of scissors.

"Different things aren't scary," Mom liked to say. "Just different."

So, now, I enjoy this new freedom but, also, I'm like:

What the hell? Why is Vasia so special?

We were on the bus and it was too late. I hadn't noticed before we left the house.

The heater on the bus was going full blast and we were starting to sweat in our winter gear. Vasia's jacket was off and the shirt he was wearing to school was pink. Wearing pink—that was one thing—but the stolen pink shirt of a classmate was sure to bring the attention that would get him in trouble. I looked closely and saw the stitched design on the chest was a bumblebee. *Very recognizable.* It actually fit him quite well, size-wise.

So I told him, *No, this was wrong*, and he said, "Why?"

"You've stolen a pink shirt."

He didn't understand that form of the verb until I explained the idea three different ways. To rob. To steal. To have taken without permission.

"No," he said. "I do not take without permission. This is my."

"Mine."

"This is mine," he repeated correctly.

I assumed this would eventually lead to a well-lighted conversation about stealing and lying, and, really, maybe that's what Vasia needed.

I let it go. I wasn't his parent. I'd told him it was wrong. What more could I do?

Kids getting on the bus definitely noticed his pink shirt.

"Nice," said a boy my age that was neither a bad nor a good guy, just someone I'd once talked to without conflict.

"Thank you," said Vasia to the boy.

Vasia could tell the boy was talking about his shirt, but he couldn't tell the boy was talking about his shirt sarcastically.

"It calms me," said Vasia.

The boy giggled and that pushed him into bad territory in my mind. In the future I probably wouldn't be able to talk to this boy without having to talk about how my brother wore pink shirts with cartoon animals. If he insulted me, I wouldn't back down. I was older now and that's how I'd changed.

The next day Vasia wore a yellow turtleneck with blue ribbons on the shoulders—very Ukrainian and, also, very feminine. He probably stole it because it reminded him of something. His closet was deep, I thought. This wasn't going away.

Another month passes.

I watch out for bullies.

Vasia makes the middle-school basketball team.

One day Mom and Dad were already home when we got back from school.

This wasn't right. They were sitting at the dinner table. The hairs on my neck moved in a way that reminded me of bad things. But I was bigger now. I was not scared. We sat silently for dinner. I waited for the announcement, the punishment, whatever. I was afraid for Vasia because he'd never really caught it from them in this way. *He must be terrified*, I thought.

"Would you like some desert, Alexis?" said Mom.

"Yes, please," said Vasia.

Dad stared at me. Mom stared at me, too, and then went into the kitchen when I didn't say anything. My first thought was injustice: I remembered the conversation when I was younger about my name. Mom and Dad had explained patiently, despite my protests, that Vladimir was a perfectly good name. (BE PROUD!) And just because I had a new last name didn't mean I would get to change anything else. I'd wanted to be a *Michael*.

At the table Vasia didn't look scared. He looked like he was about to eat cake. I inspected my brother. His eyes were dark. He was wearing makeup. It looked correct, like somebody had helped. His eyes popped.

Three more months pass.

During this time it's Alexis at home, Vasia at school.

Snow melts.

High school girls get sent to the principal's office for trying to wear spaghetti-strap shirts. The punishment for each infraction is a one-hour detention.

After school I was in the principal's office. I hadn't been there in a while, not since the year before, and the receptionist even said something about that—like, *Been a long time, Vlad*, or *Fancy seeing you here*. I don't recall the precise words.

"Mom and Dad would like to speak with you," I explained to the principal. "No, it's not urgent. I think they just want to talk on the phone, not to make a big deal about it."

"Is everything all right?" asked the principal. The man sounded like he was afraid. He picked up the phone and asked me to wait and be present while he called. "You've had a good year," said the principal while the call connected. "Good for you."

My mom answered her phone at work. From the distance of a few feet her voice sounded like a miniature version of herself. The principal looked at me while speaking to her and said, "Oh."

Something baked into my blood told me this was wrong.

I could imagine with greater clarity how the scars had appeared on Vasia's legs in Ukraine.

That night an e-mail was sent home so that parents could talk to their sons and daughters. Mom and Dad's cell phones both cracked to life at the same time.

I'm awake.

I won't be sleeping.

I question if all rescue plans must involve sacrifice.

The next day Vasia wore a dress to school.

Evidently his name was Alexis Thompson on the attendance list. *Such a normal name.*

In first-period biology I fought the urge to vomit. Nothing had happened yet, but it was like I could read the future and someone I knew would soon die. The teacher talked about Darwin—it was a lecture day, apparently—and that calmed me. The teacher recommended books he hadn't been allowed to read in high school, and I wrote those titles in my notebook but no notes about Darwin; I just liked hearing about him.

In second-period English the teacher had us discuss *Casablanca* as if it were a novel. The teacher made me talk. I had him repeat the question and I touched my finger to a note I had written in my notebook when watching the film; when we first see Rick he's playing chess by himself. "Let's explore this metaphor," said the teacher.

Someone in my English class must have known.

We'd been at school for three hours and a boy in the middle school was wearing a dress. If it weren't my brother, I'd have said something to somebody by now.

I was sweating.

In the retrospect of ten minutes, I was impressed I'd been able to come up with an answer when the teacher had called on me. During the discussion, while another kid was talking, the teacher motioned with his waving hand for me to stop audibly pumping my foot against the floor. "Take your backpack off, Vlad," he said in a friendly manner. "Get comfortable." I didn't take it off. I said I *was* comfortable.

During third-period Spanish I heard a whisper. I heard my name. Lots of people whispered in Spanish class because if you spoke in real volume you had to do it in Spanish. So perhaps it was nothing. Perhaps high school kids didn't care about the middle schoolers, boys dressed in ball gowns or not.

I didn't go to lunch. I sat in front of my locker, waiting for time to pass. By now people were talking. How could they not be? The boys and girls on my bus had diffused into the rest of the building, sharing the stories of Vladimir's brother in a dress. No one said anything, not even a passing hello, as I sat in front of my locker. I must have looked like I was concentrating.

Last period was gym class.

I walked in a little early and the middle schoolers were in there playing floor hockey. Vasia was doing well—like, really well.

"She's really good at basketball," said a boy over my shoulder. I knew this boy; he was in a class of mine, math, but I couldn't recall a time we'd conversed that wasn't part of group work. The boy was talking about Vasia. My hand-me-down clothes billowed in the wind produced by fast running and strong slapshots. The game reset after another Vasia goal. I wondered where Vasia had changed into gym clothes. Was his dress hanging delicately on a hanger in the gym teacher's office? Was it avoiding wrinkles?

"Do you think they'll let her play on the girls' team next year?" asked the boy.

I didn't respond, but the boy talking to me didn't see this as negativity.

"That's the dream, isn't it? Take all that skill and play on the girls' team. Vasia's going to dominate, right?"

"Alexis," I said, and it was the first time I said it outside the house. The boy apologized. "I'm being supportive," he said.

I nodded. The boy backed away slowly as if I were a bomb—my face must have told him to do that.

I left before the middle schoolers were off the court. I had to walk by the gym teacher on my way out, and I was prepared to tell him I was sick and going to the nurse, but he didn't stop me.

I ended up outside on a bench, not far from where my bus would arrive to go home.

You could see me sitting there from the main office. And after the bell rang for last period to start, when I didn't move, someone must have said something to the principal. But no one came out to talk to me.

I hadn't skipped a class since my first year at the school. Sixth grade. I'd been threatened with suspension if I ever did it again. That was after I'd lit a fire in the boys' bathroom with a ball of tissue and a book of matches from the Chinese restaurant downtown, and after I'd cut my thumb on purpose on the band saw in shop class, and after I'd spit on the hallway ground on the first day of school. Everything I'd done had been necessary at the time; just like the year before, when I'd wrestled a boy to the ground in the cafeteria when he tried to cut me in line. I'd been strong then; I hadn't crumpled. Everything had been necessary.

Now, as I thought about Vasia, nothing I could do for him felt necessary.

How is everyone OK with this? I wondered.

I finally moved to get some chips from a vending machine. Normal feelings like hunger returned. I was tired, too, and I wanted to be away from people. I took a walk into the woods behind school and found two older kids smoking. They offered me some and I declined. They looked at my backpack and I tensed, afraid they might try to take it. When I ran they called after me to come back.

Vasia found me on the bench after school.

"I had a good day," he said. He was holding his backpack to the side so it wouldn't crease his dress. It was the red backpack he'd brought all the way from Ukraine.

A breeze caught everyone's hair and clothes, not just Vasia's. He instinctively held the bottom of his dress in place. My heart was racing. There were a lot of kids around. Groupthink might take over. A mob might form. Words might be spoken that I couldn't pretend not to hear. I was breathing quickly, sweating a little too much for such a mild spring day in Maine.

Vasia asked if I was OK.

I lied, claiming high school classes were stressful.

We got on the bus. When the engine grumbled with life I felt like I'd escaped something. The bus departed and the day was over.

We got home and Vasia headed up to his room.

I went into Dad's study. I opened my backpack and removed the small pistol. I looked at the safety and put my index finger on the trigger. I squeezed and squeezed hard, knowing it wouldn't fire. The gun had been in my backpack since the night before. Energy left my body. For the first time all day I felt nontoxic.

I reached under the windowsill and only felt dust. I got down on the floor and looked up. On my back, posture like a plumber inspecting the bad spot, I saw the key was gone.

"Vasia!" I screamed. "Vasia!"

Small footsteps approached from the hallway.

"I take it," said Vasia, holding up the key. "In the morning so you don't make gun crime."

I grabbed the key with force.

My little sibling didn't crumple. "My name is Alexis," said Vasia.

I nodded. "OK," I said. Vasia left the room.

I felt anger that wouldn't go away. I put my finger back on the trigger, unlatched the safety, and made a perfect hole through the glass window in Dad's study. I might have hit a tree.

Vasia came running into the room after hearing the gunshot. I pointed at the hole in the window. A beautiful spider web radiated in the glass.

Just then the garage door opener came to life and Vasia sprinted away to see which one of them had arrived home first. I concentrated on my lungs, counting while I held my breath, and soon I was calm. This was about me, now. It was time to see what they thought of me. I returned the gun to the cabinet, replaced the key and walked downstairs. In the dinning room I flipped on the chandelier light and took my preferred seat at the table.

It was Mom.

I smiled because she and Vasia wore matching dresses.

Sara Graybeal

POINT BREEZE, 2015

in the amazon, tourists marvel at the size of leaves
        eight times my hand, four times my feet
                let them come to philly
where plants burst like prayers through concrete
        a patio paved, uprooted
                faster than we'll ever be
inside the mice eat greedily
        forgetting the ancestors, necks snapped
                stretching for squares of cheese
        young entrepreneurs: *this is our time*
                clear nests behind the stove
across the street, new condos sold
        wine & cheese soufflé
new cars
        false teeth
                fill each gap
        on this tiny street
new neighbors set out tins of food
        so they come howling, emaciated
        bloody fur blown skyward
four stories steal the sun
                congeal the world in yellow
        young entrepreneurs: *this is our time*
                eight times my hand, four times my feet
do not let them come to philly

those who can will move eventually
those who cannot will fight
cats
property taxes
parking permits
each other
those who cannot
necks snapped
eaten alive.

Sara Graybeal

WHERE ELSE FOR MY EYES

Just now
again in silver
predawn light
a black boy
gunned down
in my dreams
this time
my seventh-grader
last week
his hand broken
from fighting
this must be why
he was the one
when I slept past
my alarm
his best friend's screams
Ms. Sara, Ms. Sara
he's just
lying there
we have to
take him
we have to
move him
but when we knelt
beside him

a blood silhouette
that bookbag he never
took off
that crooked smile
gone
we could not
lift him
we could not
hold him
the stopwatch
started
how long
will this one
remain
in the street
will the die-in
block traffic
on the Parkway
will we remember
to hashtag
his name
until the T-shirts
with his picture
wear thin
blue swallows silver
through the blinds
where else
for my eyes
but the sky
on this
second time
I have had this dream
the first boy
has already
died.

Melissa Boston

THINKING OF RAIN: LAS CRUCES

—for my brother

Toward the beginning of February
I thought that it rained here

I thought that I rose from
the bed
that I had been avoiding
for weeks
with the TV off

I went to the window

     *

As a child
in Ohio
I was warned at school
not to cross rising water

As a child
I was told
high water is
not trite
in southern Ohio
not trite along its river

     *

Thinking of Rain: Las Cruces

They say on the news
Boston is under
three feet of snow
three more is to be expected

A young man in Missouri is declared
dead in his home eight hours
after being released
from the ER
It will be 62 degrees

And I
will listen to each of my alarms go off

Mike Nagel

PINK PLASTIC FLAMINGOS

I was waiting for the shot the doctor gave me to kick in. She explained it to me like this. I can't remember. I said, This is going to help things? My pants were down. The nurse said, You should feel the effects in twenty-four to forty-eight hours. That was twenty-four hours ago. Since then gay marriage has become legal, the man who invented the pink plastic flamingo has died, and the extinction of life on Planet Earth has begun. This isn't the first extinction of life on Planet Earth. There have been five other extinctions. This is the sixth. The website where I read about the sixth extinction of life on Planet Earth had a logo I didn't trust. A cartoon beaker bubbling over with hearts. But they had twenty million Facebook followers so I didn't know what to believe. Probably it was real. And anyway what difference does it make?

I hoped that this shot would make my skin glow with honey-colored health.

It was—can you believe it—my twenty-eighth birthday. I didn't have plans. I'm not a planner. I drank bourbon on my couch while watching *House of Cards*. I turned off my phone. You might think that drinking bourbon on your couch while watching *House of Cards* sounds like a depressing way to spend your twenty-eighth birthday, but you would be surprised. We are all our own best company if we just give ourselves a chance. At some point, around 10 p.m., I started my twenty-ninth year on the doomed planet, Earth.

I've never owned a pink flamingo, never seen one in real life, but still I took the death of its inventor as a loss. The death of American kitsch as we know it. What were we supposed to do now, take ourselves *seriously*?

In the days after the legalization of gay marriage every brand on doomed Planet Earth scrambled to incorporate rainbows into limited edition gay-pride versions of their Facebook profile pictures as a way of saying hey guess what everybody we've secretly been gay-proud all along. As a result it was impossible to tell who had posted what to Facebook since everybody's profile picture looked—or was—exactly the same.

More and more I can't tell people apart. Early stages of prosopagnosia. (Was that what the doctors were trying to fix? My ass still hurt where I'd been stuck.) And was it just a *coincident* that at the exact same moment I was leaning over a table getting stuck in the ass the Supreme Court was deciding that being gay was just as normal/perverted as being *anything else in the world*? American legislation works in mysterious ways, my friends. Who can say what tips the scales?

Thomas Bernhard said that when one thinks about death, everything becomes absurd. Well what about extinction? Extinction is not just the end of the future. It is the end of the past. Unless some other species has been taking really good notes this whole time (looking at you, horseshoe crab!), we might as well have never existed. And after all this work.

Luckily Carl Sagan thought ahead and sent a time capsule into space. Sounds and pictures cut into golden records. Let's just hope the more advanced species has a Crosley®.

According to Wikipedia, 98 percent of all species are already extinct. 99 percent according to the National History Museum. We are working with some pretty slim pickings. And they're getting slimmer. Scientists estimate we are losing a hundred forty thousand species a year. Among them: the Tasmanian Tiger, the Caribbean Monk Seal, the Baji River Dolphin, and men with big giant balls re.: complex social issues. One hundred thousand is one thousand times higher than the normal rate of extinction. And it might just keep on increasing. To as much as ten thousand times if we don't do anything about it. (Just kidding there's nothing we can do.) Most species will go extinct before we know about them. And I was lying earlier when I said the sixth extinction (the Holocene Extinction) started this week. The sixth extinction started ten thousand years ago, right around the time human beings started spreading themselves across the Earth.

Themselves: ourselves: myself. Part and parcel of the whole thing.

Not to get all *according to Webster's* on you, but the definition of extinction is a sharp drop in diversity. A worldwide homogeny. A global case of prosopagnosia.

Originally the pink flamingo was used by the lower class to make their front lawns look beautiful. Then it was used by the upper class to make fun of how the lower class made their front lawns beautiful. Then the pink flamingo disappeared altogether, but the idea of the pink flamingo remained. "The real plastic flamingo is in a sense extinct," filmmaker John Waters has said. "You can't have anything that innocent anymore."

The pink flamingo was originally meant to add diversity to homogeny, but then it became a symbol of homogeny itself. Twenty million made and sold. I'm not sure what that means exactly. It's just funny how our intentions always backfire.

The horseshoe crab has been around for 445 million years and survived four mass extinctions. We could all learn a thing or two from the horseshoe crab. Like how to hunker down and just fucking take it.

On Saturday morning I felt a tingling in my spine. The shot, whatever it was, had started working. The tingling spread to my fingertips. I took a jog. I jogged the same distance I always jog. So I guess jogging wasn't the point. My cuticle health appeared unchanged. My big toe toenail was still yellow and brown. My eyelids were still dry. My ears were still too big. My purpose on the doomed planet was still unknown. Whatever this shot was doing, it was doing it with subtlety and tact. And if I couldn't tell what it was doing, was it doing anything? I liked knowing it was doing *something* even if I was never going to know exactly what it was doing. Placebos are just as effective as real medication for the first couple of days. I could make this shot do anything I wanted. If I just believed hard enough.

In light of the sixth extinction we have all been given coupons for ten dollars off Bulliet Bourbon, redeemable at your local Seagal's Liquor Mart off Greenville Avenue, just north of Lovers Lane. I took a shot and I waited for the shot to kick in.

I didn't turn my Twitter icon rainbow colored, but that doesn't mean I'm not gay-affirming on the inside. Like most things I just don't give that much of a fuck. I can only give a fuck about one thing at a time. And the thing I am giving a fuck about right now is a book called *Thelonious Monk: The Life and Times of an American Original* by Robin D. G. Kelley, a topic I won't be returning to, but that is no doubt influencing these words in deep and undetectable ways.

T H E E E L L L L O N N N N I I O O U U S S S MOOOOOOOOOOOOOOOOOOONK!

The office eight floors below mine has pink flamingos in the windows. I'd never noticed them before. Someone pointed them out to me. "Are those pink flamingos?" they said. We were walking back from lunch. "Oh," I said. "Yes they are. The last of their kind." It was 107 degrees outside. Almost unlivable for human beings.

Of all the extinction events, only the causes of the last two are "known." The rest are published with question marks. Volcanoes? Climate change? Deep-ocean anoxia? This is a your-guess-is-as-good-as-mine field of study, my favorite corner of academia.

The only extinction event I was allowed to believe in as a kid was the Flood. God's attempt to wipe us off the planet. Building a boat was some real horseshoe crab thinking! Still though, it was a close call. I don't know if we can pull that off again. And not everyone thinks we should. The Voluntary Human Extinction Movement (VHEMT) believes it's in the planet's best interest for us to go ahead and die out. "Each time another one of us decides not to add another one of us to the burgeoning billions already squatting on this ravaged planet, another ray of hope shines through the gloom."

More than anything I wanted this shot to give me a transcendent nonchalance about my fate and the fate of doomed Planet Earth. A holy indifference. An unshakable sense of ¯_(ツ)_/¯. But had they developed the technology???

I went to a party and got forget-all-of-this-the-next-day-but-not-quite-blackout drunk. It is possible I reached a holy indifference, but I obviously can't remember so don't ask. And what was the Grand Revelation I was going on about? The next morning I could still taste the beer. I brushed my teeth, but I could still taste the beer. It had *soaked in.*

I Googled "How long do we have?" and Google said that Planet Earth has a habitable lifespan of 7.79 billion years. We are 4.5 billion years in. So. Mostly done.

In attempt to differentiate myself from our increasingly identical species, I changed my Twitter profile picture to a pink flamingo.

But of course no extinction has ever been completely successful. Eventually the tingling went to my head. A constant buzz. I wondered if the point of the shot was the tingling. Or had the beer finally gotten into my brain? Soaked into the gray matter. Found its way to the *memory zone.* I walked in semi-straight lines. I couldn't remember anything. What was I worried about again? What was I saying? Oh, right. No extinction has ever been completely successful. Evolution has never had to start from scratch. There's always a little something left over. That last line of dust at the dustpan. The whole planet PTSDing pretty hard. Nobody really learning anything very interesting. Everyone just lucky to be alive and walking around. A massive rainbow stretching from one side of the sky to the other. God's way of saying, *Never again, I promise, never again.* The horseshoe crab rolling its ten beady eyes, shaking its tank-like body, trying hard not to laugh.

Shawna Ervin

BEYOND FACTS: TRUTH IN ART

An artist, Daniel Sprick, stands near a bench in the middle of a gallery at the Denver Art Museum and tells a group of writers I've come with about his perspective on art. Art is more than facts. It carries emotion, he says. As memoir writers we are concerned with the truth and the accuracy of what we write.

Sprick's show is called *Fictions* and includes a series of portraits that first appear so real they could be photos. Stepping closer, I see the brushstrokes, the texture of the canvas. "It's a painting," someone says across the gallery, a rectangle of space on the second floor of the museum built as a series of triangles. A small LED light shines on each painting. The walls are painted a forgettable shade of tan, the floor a soft, dark wood that absorbs the sounds of footsteps. I imagine being in the open space with my daughter, slipping out of our shoes, running and sliding across the gallery. I grin, stifle a giggle.

How he portrays each model begins with accuracy and expands to the essence of the subject's likeness, their personality, the moment, light and dark. His work is multi-dimensional, as is truth. He tells us that although he's been criticized for a lack of accuracy, it's not the facts he wants to convey. He wants to tell the truth.

"This is Katie," he says, nodding to his right. "She was the person I had to pick up at the airport and why I was a little late." My group of six memoir writers, plus me and two instructors, stands in a small semi-circle. Museum visitors join behind us. I don't like sharing this experience, yet I am proud to share it. "She's in the paintings over there." He waits while we look. "A little different, huh?"

The group titters, tries not to be obvious as we collectively and individually stare at the Katie in front of us. She bites her bottom lip, crunches her shoulders forward a little, relaxes them. She is tall and thin, long arms and legs that are crossed tight like a ribbon run tightly across scissors. I notice her open-toed high heels, skinny-ankle jeans, and sleeveless turquoise shirt. A folded jacket hangs from her arms like a trouser rack. It is November.

Sprick talks to our group about his process. The creative process is work for him, he says. He works eight hours a day. His straight, brown hair is highlighted with gray, parted in the middle, and flops in front of his eyes each time he looks at the floor to gather a thought. The glare of the light above reflects in his glasses when he looks at our group. I stare at a hole in his worn, faded jeans, notice how the fringe covers what I imagine are pale, scrawny legs under the too-large pants that creep down as he fidgets. He hoists up the jeans that are held by a wide, light-brown leather belt, stuffs his red, button-down shirt deeper into the well of his pants, puts his fists into his pockets. His fists look like baseballs, I think, and imagine him as a little boy coming home from adventures with pebbles, sticks, or pinecones and laying them on the counter, excited to recount the adventures they represent. I picture him placing them in a special box, taking them out to remember, the tangible reminding him the experience was true.

I didn't understand art as a child, but longed to be a part of the world the rest of my family shared. My mom played the violin and piano, had a knack for sewing and crafts. My dad led music in several small churches, his tenor voice popular for funerals and weddings. My younger brother enjoyed drawing and often huddled over his desk designing race cars. It was I who lacked the fine-motor control to fully belong in our family. I thrived in a world of absolutes—math, spelling, and science.

In art class in first grade, I hoped to find a medium in which I could gain entrance into my family. I studied the color wheels, small reproductions of famous paintings, and quotes papering the walls around and above doors and closets. To the scent of the kiln, tempera paint, permanent markers, clay, I daydreamed about an art show featuring my work someday, a way to express the colors and personality I saw in the world and how they made me feel.

In first grade I made a pinch pot. It was a small lump of clay, a pinkish brown that I rolled into my hands, dripped water into the hole where I pushed my seven-year-old thumb. I pulled the sides up, one side higher than the other, the thin middle buckling. To me, it was beautiful, my masterpiece.

After school I scurried to the art room to pick it up. My teacher bent over a long table with dozens of pots, her waist-length hair cascading over them. One by one she flipped them over, looking for a name etched on the bottom. Other kids wiggled in line behind me, peeked into the doorway.

That's mine, they shouted. The one with the orange or blue or pink. She handed my pot to me, told me to be careful. I nodded, a hush of reverence coming over me as I looked into my cupped hands at my pot.

I walked slowly both blocks home. Across the crosswalk, then another street, up the small hill to our front door, through the front hall, and into the kitchen, where my mom was preparing a snack, I held it like an egg. Every few steps I peered through my fingers to make sure it was OK, brushed my thumbs over the smooth glaze. I wanted to give it to my mom to keep her jewelry in, something precious.

She would hug me, tell me how proud she was of her little artist, gush over my talent and what I'd made. I would belong.

Years later I found the pot stashed among my other failed art projects in a cupboard. My failure as an artist had become a frequent joke in my family. My pots caved, paintings were grotesque in their obscurity, drawings scribbled in colors that weren't right. I hadn't only failed art, but my mom, too.

"At least you're good at other things," she said after she tucked each project away to prevent guests from seeing what I'd made.

At the art museum Daniel Sprick asks if there are questions. I should listen, I tell myself. His even voice lulls me into looking at a large painting directly behind him. The other portraits are painted on an ivory background. This one is painted on black. The subject, a nude woman, tucks her legs up and turns them away from me. Her skin reflects a light above her.

I quickly examine the painting to see if I can see anything I don't think I should see. It is discreet. The woman's hands rest, one over the other, relaxed, just below her shoulder. Her breast and a nipple are exposed. Cold, I think.

I wrap my arms tighter over my chest and a notebook I brought in case I think or feel something that needs to be set down in ink. No one else has brought a notebook. I want to be like the rest of the group, to be able to remember what the artist says. I know I won't be able to.

In the painting the woman's brown hair drapes over the edge of the black bench she lies on. Her hair is the same color as mine, her skin nearly the same color. She could be me. I want to turn away, but I want to appear like I'm listening. I want to cover her, to help her up. I shiver.

The group laughs at something the artist said. I hear myself laughing along although I missed the joke. We clap quietly and thank the artist. The group disperses, oozing toward the artist and the portraits of Katie. I need space to understand what I think I'm beginning to see in Sprick's paintings, so I move toward the back using my small size as an advantage. I slip between the beginnings of conversations, slide through narrow gaps until I find a quiet space beyond the group. There are a few people mingling through the exhibit where I end up but no one I know.

I pass a series of paintings—a man the artist said had done some work on his roof, a homeless man, the artist's ex-wife. Then a woman in two portraits.

I stop. Her name is Ketsia, the small sign by the paintings says. I try saying the name under my breath—Ket-seeuh, Ketsha. I like it. Her skin is dark brown, a color like rich Midwestern soil. Her hair, woven into long corn braids, is tied up in a messy ponytail, brush strokes that appear unfinished at the top edge of the painting accentuating the coarseness of the bun at the back of her head. She faces to the right, tilts her head up gently, one cheek lifted slightly higher than the other, letting the light fall at the base of her cheek, on her chin and her eyelid. Her eyes are closed.

Ketsia's long, thin neck makes me envision her dancing, the beige and ivory obscure brush strokes at the bottom of the painting what she is wearing for a ballet performance or a way of covering what she wants to remain private. I admire the trust in her relaxed face. If she wasn't upright I would think she was sleeping. I raise my hand slightly to touch trust, put it back down.

A classmate comes up behind me. "That's my favorite," she says softly.

I agree with a nod, say I can't stop looking. My classmate moves on to another painting. I look back to Ketsia, to whom I now feel a loyalty. Growing up in the religion that employed my dad, I was trained to see my ugliness and shortcomings, to see beauty as dangerous, yet another way to fall outside of God's love. Ketsia gives me the freedom to believe in beauty, both hers and mine, to believe in their truth.

"Beautiful," I say under my breath. I notice Ketsia wears blush and silver eye shadow.

"Let me put your makeup on," my friend said at her house. I was in high school, went to her house to discover what was forbidden at mine. She unzipped a large makeup bag and set out blues and greens, beiges and pinks on the bathroom counter.

My mom would pick me up soon. Would the early dark of a Colorado winter night help me hide my disobedience? I wanted to find out if makeup would make boys pause as I walked by, make them forget what they were talking about, want to know me.

"What's the best eye color?" I asked.

"Blue. Don't worry. I know all the best colors."

She patted and brushed, insisting I keep my eyes closed. She told me about the boys she had gone to dances with, a boy she was dating now, but another boy she thought she liked more. I hadn't dated yet.

"Do you want to look? If you want to brush some off, you won't hurt my feelings."

The blush was dark pink, the lipstick deep red, the eye shadow bright blue. The doorbell rang. I wiped at my face with toilet paper, tossed it on the counter, a long white strip strewn with color.

I walked behind my mom to her car, the cold stinging my bare legs under a knee-length dress.

"You look like a floozy," my mom said into the darkness. "What got into you? My daughter would never do something like that."

The exhibit has quieted. I nod farewell to Ketsia and head over to Katie's portraits. The model has gone but I hold her image in my memory.

In the portrait Katie sits, her face plain, gray in a shadow. Her knees are bent. One arm rests on her shin; the other arm wraps around her daughter. Katie holds Lulu's shoulder tightly. Lulu, the daughter, around ten or twelve, burrows into her mom's chest, the top of her head against Katie's chin. Katie appears to be pulling away or weary. Katie looks to her right, down, with a look of grief or regret, a sadness that prevents her from being able to give all her daughter needs. Lulu's eyebrows are furrowed, her lips squished together like she's trying not to cry. Katie's hands remind me of the hands in the large portrait of the nude, the tone of her skin about the same. Her knees look bony and large for her legs. She wears a sandbox brown dress. So does Lulu.

In the portrait I see myself as both the mother and daughter. I think I understand some of my mom's motivations to push me toward the concrete and away from the subjective, how she might have believed if she denied me the privilege of beauty she would prevent the inevitable hurt that comes with loving. Maybe she hoped if she rejected the most tender parts of me that I wouldn't offer them to anyone, and be able to keep them. My mom risked love with my dad, lost herself, forced herself to live in the loneliness in a marriage that failed many years before they divorced.

I think of my daughter, how at four she still wears bits of baby fat in her wrists, her round cheeks, the folds of her neck that are pale against her ochre skin. I want to pull her close, brush her hair out of her eyes, hold her until I stop hurting. At four, my daughter often crawls into my lap when she's tired. She asks for me to rock her, tucks her chin into my chest.

It's the vulnerability in a private moment that draws me to Katie, I realize. It's the needs, trust, and freedom that draws me to the paintings. I see into their experience, who they were at that moment, what they felt, feel it, too. It's the shared experience of being human that wraps its arm around me. I belong.

I want to go home and teach my daughter what I've come to see that day: that beauty means the risk to be vulnerable, to share the shadows. That I belong and she does too, not because of how our pinch pots turn out, or if we can color in the lines, but because we feel and experience the truth. It's not only about the facts, what is right or all that could go wrong. It's about being who we are and translating that through our various art forms so others can join us.

Later I will take my daughter to the long mirror on the outside of our coat closet in a narrow hallway. I will look deep into her trusting eyes and say, "You're beautiful."

She will twirl, place her hands on her hips, do what she calls her fashion-girl pose with her tummy pushed out, her face lifted toward me, her jaw dropped slightly.

"I know," she will say.

"Mommy is, too." The words feel like glass in my mouth.

"Yeah, yeah." She already knows.

I will stick my hands in my jeans pockets, push my fists deep into the seam. I will wish for a pebble, a corner of canvas, the smell of the kiln or tempera paint to remind me of truth, its limits and its expansiveness. I want something I can touch to remind me when I forget.

My daughter will twirl again, her arms outstretched, her fingers brushing against the walls.

"Careful," I will almost say. I won't. I am ready to catch her if she falls but let her turn around and around to feel the beauty of that moment. Her eyes are closed. She smiles, spins faster, her small feet almost tripping over each other, the rhythm of her wisdom making me smile past the desire to make the moment serious and layered with deep realizations.

"Spin with me, Mommy."

I will. I keep my arms in, turn slowly, feel my face lift, my eyes close, a smile sneak onto my lips.

"Wow! I'm dizzy." I'll stop and watch her.

"Do you feel it?" she'll say, still spinning.

I will nod. "I do."

Jim Daniels

THE MANY DOORS

Western Penitentiary, Pittsburgh

After my poetry reading, a prisoner
says, *I thought you were a brother
when I read your poems.* I'm here
with my clearances and creased papers
from the outside where I'll never pass
as black—it'd be a joke, but that guy
can't walk out of here.
                The prisoners
sit split—men on one side, women
the other, guards between.
He and I stand, between.
                Back home
in Detroit, Eight Mile is that split—
black on one side, white on the other,
six lanes of traffic between.
                I can't say
what he saw on those Xeroxed sheets
of my words set on those streets. *Shit,*
he says, but stretched out, wistful.
You just some old white guy.
                *I've got
credentials for that,* I say, flashing
my temporary badge. A guard's
here to bump him away now,
the room draining of color
according to schedule

as I'm led out through the many doors
to the safety of the street by my well-
meaning host/sponsor.
                            We all mean
well, don't we? At least sometimes?
She takes that guy's comment as a good sign.
I who am always looking for good signs
drive off into God's good morning
with the Devil's bad attitude.
                            Brothers.
It's a good sign I'm not in there.
It's a good sign that I got out
with a story to tell that someone out-
side might laugh at.
                            They will never
rename Eight Mile Road after a person—
or two people. Too much traffic
on that road. Too many guards
at that border.
                            What I'm trying to say
is that the last thing in the world I might be
is a brother. Across all those lanes of traffic,
I wouldn't stand a chance.

Jim Daniels

THE SECURITY OF CDS

Certificate of Deposit.
Collection of Debris.
Compact Distress.

13, going on __, my son gave his life-size
baseball trophy to his cousin,
sacrificing his own childhood in favor
of long brooding behind closed doors.

*

I spent my thirteenth summer inside,
avoiding friends to see if they'd care.
They congregated under the streetlight
on bicycles, as usual, swearing and spitting
while I peeked out windows
and twiddled my own unhappiness

until finally one steamy August day
I rejoined them. No one popped a wheelie
or asked where I'd been.

*

He doesn't want to hear the easy ooze
of my story. Or that he's normal. He's passed me
in height, so one night when he explodes
into tears he can't or won't explain, he must bend

down to my shoulder. I've got him in my arms
when a car alarm blares out front. He jerks away.

He takes another shower instead of taking
out the trash. Playing one-on-one in the yard,
I shove him into the fence. He laughs
with stunned fury. I beat him, or he lets me win.

*

Candle of Darkness.
Chest of Desire.
Christ Damnation.
Civic Duty.

His birthday card to me
took five seconds to scrawl.
I love you Dad. I'll take that
over the old crayons and glitter,
rubber stamps, scissors and glue.

Cold Duck.
Cuteness Denied.
Curses Detailed.
Coins Dropped

into the well, wishes unspoken,
though if he'd asked for a penny
I'd give him all the pennies
in the world. Wouldn't I?

The map to the treasure
fades blank or is shredded.

*

At thirteen, I hid in the weeds behind the garage.
Even my dog snorted. My father
had slapped me for mouthing off.

I'd given up dreaming of the big leagues
and took up the avid pursuit of photographic
evidence of naked women. If my parents
were giant marionettes, and I had cut their strings,
why did they not fall? Why did they not
leave me alone?

My father took me fishing, and he never fished.
My bullhead wouldn't die till I smashed it
with a hammer. Why is that funny? he asked.
I buried it behind the garage.

                *

I've been practicing my shrug and deep breaths,
using then filing away clichés
so I can use them again. When love
becomes a shove, what else can you do?

Circles of Despair.
Cancellation of Debts.
Redeem? Roll over?
Rates incalculable.

Collect Dust.
Call Dad.

I'm saving the birthday card.
Terms unspoken, undefined,
subject to change without notification.
All the pennies in the world.
Wishes plop into the well.

I wish I could tell you more,
but then nothing will come true.

Andrew Cox

SOMETHING MOVED IN THE ATTIC AND IT'S BIG

A number system etched on the pills you take add up to the golden mean of your wants and needs. Outside the wind gets testy and everything twitches with the fact that we are confused about our current status. How pleasant when your eyes dilate and you wish this moment were the skyscraper you see rising into the sky to lord it over the city. Warning: These drugs may cause excitability in adult children. You and your pharmacy know the pills are not driving the car, you are—the pills read the map. Do not take these drugs as a substitute for talking as if we need someone to speak for us. You have no problem when your fears become children on the street begging for change. Side effects may include the urge to bring forward something that has lived in the background as if it knew it would be checked off the list.

Stephen Jarrett

RUPTURE

No one understood why Adam moved to a trailer park in Loysville, why he married Becca Stilton, why he repaired septic tanks for a living, why he became the guy at Ruth's Diner who ordered a bacon cheeseburger with French fries, why he left a six-dollar tip for a seven-dollar meal, why some days he charmed everything he touched and other days his hands shook so wildly that he couldn't bring a bottle of Coke to his lips. Frankly, after all that had happened, the world expected his body to wash up on the shore of the Susquehanna, to be discovered by two drunk fishermen, who would call the police, appear on Channel 9 with reporter Sarah Boeing, and share their tales with the patrons of fifty-cent taco night at Shooter's Pub.

Adam's trailer was nestled in a grove of healthy-looking elm trees on the gravel edge of the Paradise Valley Trailer Park. He spent many mornings cleaning up twigs that had jettisoned during overnight thunderstorms, landing as wooden bundles on the grill above his fire pit. He slept on a pull-out couch, hung discarded, koala bear bed sheets as drapes, and kept his wardrobe respectable, buying plain T-shirts and Levi's from a KMart thirty miles down the road. He looked seasoned, but clean. He found that shaving daily and briefly acknowledging the presence of others left this impression.

He was responsible for the subterranean upkeep of the Paradise Valley Trailer Park. That means he was responsible, as owners Bill and Beverly Middleton put it, "for keeping track of the shit." So, he did. It's doubtful that any park in the nation hosted so dutiful a septic administrator, and Adam's toolbox—a pristine, aluminum contraption painted firehouse red—was an object of envy amongst the park's tool-fetishizing populous. Adam relished his work, approached it with sobriety and intelligence, in a delicate dance of wrench and torque, causing many of the park's retirees to joke that maybe Adam, you know, maybe he thought the septic system was the Hoover Dam or something.

Still, they liked that their shit never seeped through the ground, their toilets flowed like Amazonian waterfalls, and they could rely on Adam to keep their vileness contained. And Adam was content to do so. He wanted them to have their microwave dinners, to get wasted on low-grade tequila outside of the communal laundry room, to attend church services under a wooden pavilion and shout, "3 nails, 1 cross, 4 given!" at the behest of their gangly, correspondence-course minister. Have your world and I'll have mine, he thought.

Adam loved that he could toss old newspapers into the fire-pit and look through his binoculars at the clear constellations above his trailer. He loved that he could burn incense and listen to New-Age-infused Native American flute CDs while he took long showers. He loved that he was known only as "septic guy," or among the less restrained: "The Shitman"; it meant that when the day's work was done, no one would interrupt him while he whittled Saharan animals on his porch, listened to the cicadas, or read from a leather-bound copy of Seneca's *De Vita Beata*. He loved his early-morning bike rides, identifying Pennsylvania songbirds with his perfect twenty-twenty eyes, and marking new sightings in his notebook. He loved hearing the Amish play horseshoes until three in the morning, how sometimes he'd catch the features of their faces lit by the temperamental luminescence of firefly swarms. He loved going to Ruth's Diner and using as much ketchup as he wanted on his fries. He loved throwing Frisbee with Bill and Bev's Labrador after work, letting the dog lie on him afterward because it didn't want him to leave.

During his first Paradise Council meeting (a mandatory social), he attempted to undermine plans for the park's Fourth of July celebration. He didn't understand how firing an anti-tank missile at an abandoned barn with the word "EVIL" scrawled on its doors would register as homage to John Locke-inspired Sons of Liberty. He fumbled through his carrying case and read from a photocopied Erich Fromm passage on mass hysteria. He passed a highlighted excerpt around the hall and a woman accused him of harboring Nazi sympathies. When he tried to explain that Erich Fromm was, in fact, "a dedicated scholar of the Talmud, and a vocal anti-Fascist," a group of large men rose to settle the dispute, one carrying what looked like a bedpost. Bill Middleton intervened, wielding his sway at the moment physical violence was imminent:

"The Shitman meant no offense!" Bill's comment followed by an en masse thump of re-seated butts. In Paradise Valley, like every other chasm of human history, big fires were relished and those with brains were best suited to silence.

Gradually, Adam adapted to the presence of decapitated deer heads on front lawns, to the open-windowed viewing of hardcore pornography, to the ten-year-old brothers who would dismember then eat daddy long-leggers on a dare for a quarter. Their father, drunk and instigating, would cough up a coin once he had confirmed full digestion and watch the boys run to the gumball machine near the laundry room. The brothers would let a rainbow of calcified sugar cascade into their palms and yell "Shit!" when a few gumballs landed against the cement, resounding like firecrackers. Adam didn't want to forecast their futures, but when he did, out of some cruel habit, he wished for his total inaccuracy.

He met Becca at the bimonthly Mennonite bake sale located three miles outside of Paradise Valley. Becca, a failed astrophysicist, had only recently withdrawn from her doctoral program at MIT to pursue what she considered a promising small-business idea: a clothing line named Plaidypus Fashions. Adam was examining a cartilaged loaf of carrot bread when Becca's hand grazed his to reach for a bag of chocolate-covered raisins. An elderly Mennonite man responsible for the table knew what was happening before they did. He grabbed the rungs of his overalls and shook his head in disapproval. When they walked back towards Adam's truck and Becca tripped over a horseshoe, Adam caught her and loved the way it felt. The feel of her hair as it grazed his arms reminded him of a tenderness he'd thought extinct.

They watched the sun descend through a line of ribbed, wooden fences. The Mennonites packed up their tables as kids hoisted plastic bags over their shoulders and parents activated their high beams for the drive home. Becca and Adam stayed in the truck as the night turned indigo. He leaned his head backwards into her chest. She didn't mind that he moaned into her shirt, a moan of relief and gratitude.

For the first time in years, he accepted the caress of a woman's hand, the support of a stable body. Her arms reached around his shoulders like cucumber tendrils, and their torsos rose and depressed in unison motions of breath. Through some effort, she slipped a chocolate-covered raisin into his mouth. He pawed backwards in an attempt to locate her face in the darkness, and she laughed as he tried to reciprocate, pressing a chocolate-covered raisin against her stomach, then her shoulder, then her cheek. They laughed, and Adam soaked in the synaptic electricity.

The darkness reminded him of his grade-school trip to the Dunkirk planetarium. His entire class had stayed the night, and they were permitted to lie on their sleeping bags during the instructional movie in the Omnitheatre. He and his friend Chris had used their flashlights to make amusing faces to each other and, later, to communicate with the girls in Morse code. Eventually, "F R A N N Y L I K E S A D A M" made its way across the void. Adam was skeptical of the luminous blasts, waiting for the final, confirming "M" to arrive, doubting Franny's sentiment until the last character was delivered. When the "M" registered, Adam felt like he was living in a different body.

Adam made Franny a papier mâché dolphin the following week. Franny gave him a bulky dracanea plant, which he kept and maintained well into his teenage years. They kissed and held hands beneath Ben Hannon's trampoline while the other kids harassed a rented birthday donkey. Franny carried Adam's books when he broke his pinky on the diving platform in swimming class. She left school abruptly in the seventh grade, paper dolphin in tow, tears in abundance, and when she did, Adam felt like he was living in a different body.

Becca's gapped bunny teeth clanked against Adam's united front row. He slid his lips along her bones and suckled the marrow. He didn't like the way she kissed him: in repeated, localized pecks devoid of moisture. She didn't like the way he kissed her: in slow, intentional diving motions. He didn't like that her knees curled like fishing hooks. She didn't like that his biceps were smaller than hers. Still, they groped for each other's bodies, grateful for any part they discovered in the indigo texture. As Adam cradled her rib cage, she curled her stomach upwards, and he looked outside of the truck, doubting the authenticity of his experience, waiting for a new, gigantic, ethereal "M" to arrive.

The clouds above them broke and the moon revealed its neutral incandescence. The sight, which he normally relished, lit their faces in full detail: the blackheads, the hairline scars, the galactic irises. They looked at one another only through the blurs of physical motion, squinting their eyes more and more, narrowing their lids to simulate the original dark, which hid them until the light was undeniable. Adam knew, somewhere in his body, that their union was tarnished.

In time, he adapted to her kissing and learned to think of hers as a sort of endearing, hummingbird's love. He found himself placing his right hand under her left kneecap when they made love and toying with her right while they lie in bed reading. He convinced himself that no other kind of knee existed, and if it did, he didn't want it. She asked him to start lifting weights, so he bought a weight bench. She asked him to stop kissing her like a veritable Don Juan, so he attempted more sporadic, detached kissing methods. He asked about her life and she, sensing his apprehension to divulge, didn't ask back. Mutual absolution was the policy. They were married by George the Notary, a man who issued marriage and fishing licenses like borrowed Tylenol pills, with an equal degree of nonchalance.

When Bill and Bev Middleton caught wind of Adam's emerging romance, notified by the grammatically butchered marriage announcement in *Daily Paradise*, they made an effort to communicate their concerns.

"She's got a bad reputation," Bill said, as he tucked his turtleneck into a pair of high-fastening salt-and-pepper jeans.

"What does that mean, exactly?" Adam asked.

"It means she's a crusher of souls. It means she will turn your heart into gunk."

"She will turn my heart into gunk," Adam repeated, staring at Bill.

"We've seen it too many times to count," added Bev, a woman whose advice on love, born from the diligent, cataloged taping of *The Days of Our Lives*, Adam questioned.

"What do you suggest I do?"

"Drop her," Bill said.

Bev left the two men alone, strolling down towards the communal man-made lake.

"That's not going to happen," Adam said, returning an object to his toolkit.

"Adam, I wonder. What are you doing here?"

"Shouldn't be hard to figure out," Adam said.

"Oh, my mistake. You're here for the sights, I guess. To survey Loysville's natural splendor." Bill expanded on this statement by moving his palm in a salesman gesture towards the horizon. They looked upon a hairy sunbather whose body, surrounded by potato chip and candy bar wrappers, formed a snow angel of waste.

"Something like that," Adam said.

A married couple drove up the hill in an old golf cart. The man stepped out, unwrapped a lump of newspaper, and began to gut one of three carp over the family's firepit. The woman went inside to grab foil and cooking oil out of their trailer; she prepared to fry the fish on their kerosene grill for dinner. While they worked in grimaced silence, a little boy called for the man from their front door, saying "Ba Ba" repeatedly, rapping his left hand against an aluminum panel on the door. The father looked back once to verify the source of the sound and ignored it before returning to his task, tossing entrails over the hillside.

"You know it's within my rights to get a background check on you, Adam."

Unbeknownst to Bill, a penal system flourished in Adam's chest. It punished him for every unkind look he gave, for the days he walked too confidently, for his lifetime mispronunciation of the word "indefatigable," for his failure to comfort Franny, for his failure to protect Herb Martin (who got his ass kicked in gym class: kicked until his ears bled black), for his moments of inappropriate laughter, for the carrots he'd double-dipped at school banquets, for every word he had meant one way that was taken the other, and for all the wrong ways he had lived.

"Of course, I don't think you've done anything, Adam. I'm well aware that you're a veritable Aquarian child. That's not my concern. You just need to let someone in," Bill said, placing his hand on Adam's shoulder.

"I'm trying to let someone in," Adam said.

"Almost everyone here is an idiot. Maybe I'm worse because I take their money and make a life out of it. I have my reasons. Bev got pregnant when we were teenagers. I was certainly an idiot then. I needed to come up with something fast. A pyramid scheme. Idiocy compounding idiocy. I needed to be here. But you, your interest in this girl. It's just a way for you to round out this delusion you're sculpting."

"You've been here, what, six years?" Bill asked.

"Yes."

"Yeah, and you've run the same god damn routine for six years, Adam. You remember that poem about the girl who paces around her room until she digs a track into the floor? That's what you're doing here. What's worse is that you think you're in paradise. Don't let the name fool you. This is hell. Death Valley, maybe. Valley de Purgatorio, or one of those transitional layers Dante described."

Bill paused for a moment before saying, "I named it Paradise Valley because the lie felt better."

Bill's eyes sunk as he spoke, and the silence between the two men suggested that Bill had confessed to a heavy sin, expecting Adam to reciprocate.

"I don't want you to stay here anymore. I don't want to listen to the waitresses at Ruth's make fun of you behind your back. I don't want this place to become your home. These idiots don't even see you. They're bats with 20/6000 vision, shitting all over the floor. Oblivious with a capital 'o.' You shouldn't be living here, laying pipework, eating overcooked meat in a diner five nights a week. You should be enmeshed in the world."

"Are you asking me to move, Bill?"

"I'm naming your affliction."

"Well, thanks for the prognosis. Unfortunately, I don't think geography makes any difference at this point."

"Adam. What are you doing here?"

"Nothing more or less than anyone else."

Bill huffed, and then, as if to an invisible witness, said: "'Nothing.' That's the first straight answer you've given me."

Adam walked to his truck and slammed the door. He turned the key to the ignition, pressed on the accelerator, and the gravel outside of Bill's trailer hissed. That morning, Becca had complained of an earache, so Adam drove thirty miles to the KMart to buy her a selection of ear-irrigating devices. He bought one with a blue clown horn for "vanquishing accumulated wax!" He bought one with a pen-like syringe filled with diluted vinegar. He bought ear canal wicks that turn neglected wax into taper candles. He stood in line for twenty minutes and helped an old man carry his groceries outside. When he returned to his truck, he stuffed the bloated bag of ear goods into the trunk, moving aside two boxes of plaid blazers he'd been selling out of his truck in an effort to salvage Becca's business.

When he opened the door to his trailer and announced with gentle emphasis, "Becca, I have your EAR-igation kit," Adam found Becca screwing George the Notary on his pull-out couch, their moans resonating against the cheap metallic walls of his home, the windows open, inviting his ears to find them.

He wanted to think that she was a terrible woman, but he was overcome with memory, and the understanding that all of those memories, lodged in the wrinkles of his brain, would now be compromised. He had loved her mind as much as her body. He loved that when they drank four cups of jasmine tea together, she asked him: "Do you have the largest bladder in the world?" He loved that she would read *Newtonian Mechanics* in the kitchen while he listened to the *Best of Baroque Lute!* on the couch, how he never acknowledged how warm it felt to have her in the other room, how she never acknowledged how warm it felt to have him in the other room. He loved that he had trusted her so completely. He loved that she would play Chopin funeral marches on cloudless Saturdays, that she would pack a kiwi and a spoon for him in his lunch pail every day, that they could talk until their brains stalled, until Magritte clouds burst through the windows and they risked the onset of epileptic fits. He loved that she had trained her brain to be a professional swimmer with a regimented, Olympic workout while his was a modest, cross-country runner who stopped for a plum at the quarter-mile mark. He loved that he could bring her disciplined brain to a state of rest, could calm her into a state of silence, that they could do that for one another, that they could both wake up shaking and within a minute of holding one another, lie in place like hibernating animals.

He didn't ask or demand that they leave. They left quickly without saying a word. He dragged the couch out of his trailer in one swift Herculean motion and chopped it to pieces with an ax on his lawn. He poured kerosene over the flower-patterned fabric and set the couch on fire. The smoke billowed, and he looked up at the moon, which lingered above him like a bulbous stage prop. The trees showed ash stains on their trunks for weeks. A rectangle of black grass sat adjacent to his trailer until the spring. George the Notary mailed him the paperwork for the divorce and Adam pretended that he hadn't seen George's grotesque, crooked cock penetrating Becca and his sheets were not marked in blood and semen stains, which he had to burn in an oil drum. Adam signed the documents and returned them, barely legible.

In high school, Adam's bedroom was littered with awards: holographic "Choral Laureate" plaques, Mathlete ribbons that made Miss America look like the recipient of a sixth-place pie-eating prize, sultanesque Judo championship rings, and a six-foot Quiz Team trophy for clinching the regional tournament with the answer to the question:

"What infectious disease claimed the lives of more soldiers during the American Civil War than battlefield injuries?"

[Buzz] "Gangrene."

[Accolades]

It began at age five, at the "We Care 4 U" preschool, when he played a papier mâché fiddle in the talent show, and parents decided that he was adorable, his mimed bowing was authentic, and his nonexistent tone was, in fact, quite rigorous. It snowballed as he proved his kickball prowess in grade school (his calves were monstrous), as he mastered piano by 13 (melodic minor scales in four octaves by age 4, for example), as he learned to foxtrot from a library book (the girls responded), speak Hungarian fluently (inspired by Cold War spy films), as he baked pecan pies sprinkled with brown-sugar asterisks (recipe available in the June 94' issue of *Pastry International*). At 17, he won a prestigious Pelton Grant for designing a sensor-laden playground that produced energy (electricity) as children teetered on the seesaw, bounced on the cushy red grid, or pinned their favorite victim(s) against the monkey bars. During recess, it could power an entire middle school. The contraption thrived on contact, friction, and mayhem.

During this period, what some would call Adam's "Golden Age," Adam's mother was dying of cancer, which had spread from her colon, to her uterus, to her breasts, and then to her brain. Towards the end, he found her naked in the kitchen, trying to cook eggs and bacon on the floor. He learned to cover her with a bathrobe, take her to bed, and mop the floor. He removed envelopes from the thatched laundry hamper, ten-page letters she'd written to God, letters he refused to read. He learned to scrub the words "birds," "salvation," "deliverance," and "agony" from the kitchen table with steel wool and diluted soap. He learned that she didn't know or respect where a page of paper ended. He wondered all of the time where her organs were: where they had put her colon, her uterus, her breasts, where they would put her brain when that failed, too.

He wanted to bury them in the back yard with the goldfish she'd bought him as a boy, the one he'd fed so much that it imploded. He didn't know that could happen. He wanted to bury them next to the burnt London broil they tried to cook when he was eight, next to the time capsule they agreed not to open until 2051, next to the box of notes he'd received from volleyball star Melissa Kowalski, whose blonde bangs bobbed an affirmative "No" when he asked her to the Dunkirk Spaghetti Social. He wanted to bury them next to the Virgin Mary statue they bought at the Westland Flea Market, the one they'd left four feet in the ground for future "conquistaliens" inquiring about the religious iconography of Homo sapiens. He wanted to know where she would go, to where she was dissipating, where all of the memory-laden wrinkles of her brain were moving. He wanted to squeeze the pain out of her.

He wanted the receptionist at the DMV to understand why he needed to rescind his original offer to be an organ donor. He didn't want to scream at her. He didn't want the others in line to stare at him. He didn't want to fill out six forms in triplicate, his hands shaking profusely as he carved black ink into the empty slots. He didn't want to write, in response to the question:

"Why have you decided to alter your organ donor status?"

Because I can't surrender my body.

He meant that his brain, the one that had contemplated the significance of the number zero the night before Mr. Morowitz's algebra exam, the one that had written a twelve-page paper on Emiliano Zapata, the one that had composed his first piano concerto, in conjunction with his heart, an organ that leapt for Melissa Kowalski's dry humor, for her curiously large, spike-enhancing biceps; the one that had crawled into a ditch when his father called him from an Army base in Germany and said, "I'm not coming home"; the one that had quivered when he looked through a telescope at his first solar eclipse, the one that retreated to its natural, subdued pulse when he'd sat under the slide in grade school—it was his. The two lungs that had breathed the air on Asateague Island as he placed a horseshoe crab shell over his head and claimed to be an Anglo-Gascon knight, the nostrils that had breathed his mother's favorite laundry detergent for seventeen years and mistaken it for her natural scent, they were his, too. The stomach that had processed the nutrients of his favorite meals, the tongue with its taste buds that relished the four or maybe five shakes of garlic powder, the electrons in his amygdala and pineal gland, the ones that felt any morsel of pleasure, joy and hope—they were his, too.

He had promised to take her to Agropoli on the southern coast of Italy. She had been there once as a young girl with her father and two sisters. They'd picked lemons off of the trees as they walked along the coastline, and her sisters thought it strange: how she could peel off the yellow skin, add some sugar, and eat the fleshy orb in a few casual motions. They spent their nights with relatives who couldn't speak a word of English, but exuded love so palpably that she felt cloaked in it for the rest of her life. She had loved the ferry rides, taking note of the small islands and inlets, wondering if anyone ever lived on them, if any undiscovered plants or insects called those spots home, if anyone ever bothered to explore them despite their apparent insignificance. And that's what Adam wanted, too: to ride on the ferry with her, to share that same thought for an instant, because he wondered the same thing, if anyone ever bothered. He wanted them to know the same feeling together. He wanted to visit those people who had made her feel cloaked in love, and he wanted to receive some minor scrap, some thread of that feeling. He wanted all of them to be protected for as long as the strands would hold.

She died in the winter after graduation. Adam, by then, was eating two pieces of fruit a day and taking herbal laxatives to shit. He looked in the mirror and questioned the authenticity of his own face. He had no friends, but plenty of suitors: valedictorian Sarah Boeing, the physics department of Yale University, the Parent Teacher Association, the 200K-home-inhabiting citizens of Dunkirk, Pennsylvania, and choral director Janet Bryant, who, during a high school assembly, called Adam "our greatest hope." He wanted none of them.

The Christmas Eve after his mother's death, Adam walked around with a concealed bottle of spiced rum, the hood of his black jacket drawn over his skeletal face. His retinas were pummeled by the artificial light of the lampposts in his housing plan. He watched rosy-cheeked Christians sing "Joy to the World" then crawl into their SUVs peppered with "Support the Troops" magnets. When most of them had gone, he derived some satisfaction in listening to the rhythmic crunch of his sneakers in the snow. As he walked past a gray electrical generator, he saw what looked like a body nestled in the curl of the hillside. The deer was frozen solid in the snow. Its eyes and mouth were slightly opened. He rubbed his hand against the fur of her body. The more his hand grazed her torso, the more he cried. Adam's father, who had taken him hunting only once, had taught him the different kinds of kill-shots. This deer was gut-shot. When gut-shot, he understood, the deer dies from internal injuries and its meat, tarnished by the spreading bile and toxicity, becomes inedible. Its organs are ruined.

That same night, he walked through the grocery store in downtown Dunkirk, looking for toilet paper. "Wishful thinking," he thought, glad that now, perhaps because of his drunkenness, he was able to entertain a comic thought regarding his sphincter. This lasted for less than a moment. He stumbled upon two men, one hunched over in pain, and another, laughing in huffs as he shook a bottle of spray-on Lysol in the "Home Care" aisle. The laughing man was in his late thirties, wearing a flannel, long-sleeved shirt and black jeans covered in baked bean and semen stains. He sprayed Lysol into the other man's hair, onto his crotch, and, as Adam approached, fired a burst into the man's eyes.

"What's going on?" Adam demanded.

"My brother and I are just fooling around here," he said, shaking the bottle.

"Doesn't look like your brother is enjoying himself," Adam said. He watched the man's brother—in his early twenties—bow his eyes, rub his shoes against the tiles, and pick at his cuticles.

"Yeah, I guess that's true. Then again, it's really none of your fucking business."

"I guess it's my business because you're spraying chemicals in his face."

The man's brother rubbed his eyes and curled against the shelves as the men raised their voices. Adam approached him with an outstretched hand.

"Let's wash your eyes out in the bathroom. Just leave them alone for now, OK?"

Adam pretended that the older man had vanished. He created a blindspot. He raised his eyes and focused on the door to the men's bathroom, a door covered in graffiti, knife etchings, and a few pieces of petrified gum. For just a moment, I'll take care of this boy.

The older man grabbed Adam's collar and held his head against a row of disposable diapers.

"He doesn't need your help, you fucking faggot."

Adam struggled against the man's hold.

"No, no. You're staying here, sweetheart. We're going to hang out here for a minute," he said, against a woman's announcement that the store would soon be closing, "and then I'm going to take care of you."

Adam didn't think of the people who had watched the man degrade his brother publicly, who had appraised him a psychopath unworthy of confrontation, who had watched him push his brother into the metallic edge of a stock boy's pallet, who had, as they left the store, thrown some change into the collection pot of a Salvation Army Santa or a muscular dystrophy research canister. He didn't think of the man's friends who would visit on Saturday nights so they could set the brother's hair on fire or make him drink Old Milwaukee until he puked like a Viennese fountain. He didn't think of the man's brother who they locked in a closet overnight, who sobbed into a quilt, who carried his breath in a mason jar, who did everything he could to avoid being seen. Somehow, Adam knew this already. Sometimes, you just know.

Adam allowed the barrier between his brain and his heart to crumble. He grabbed a can from the shelf above him and struck the man on the forehead, the edge of the metal connecting directly with the oversized frame of his skull. The man stumbled backwards into a shelf, but Adam couldn't stop. He wrapped his biceps around the man's neck and added pressure.

The man's heart, which had leapt for no one, and his brain, which had thought only of himself, of schemes to humiliate his brother, of roadside prostitutes he'd wanted to tail and fuck, of every base ambition one could birth, Adam took them all away from him, took his organs out of the world, took the breath out of his lungs, took the scent of cigarettes, cow shit, and motor oil out of his nostrils, took the taste of tobacco out of his tongue, took ahold of his frozen, lead heart and squeezed it into mush, then dust, then nothing. Somehow he knew the full story of his organs and he let those, like the man, die in his arms.

When the couch stopped burning, when Adam subdued the last of the glowing orange cinders with a bucket of water, he walked four hundred feet to Bill Middleton's trailer. He knocked on the door five times. It was three in the morning and the Amish had finished playing horseshoes. There were clouds in the sky that blocked every constellation. The cicadas were silent. There was nothing divine at work. In the morning, there would be complaints of seepage and rupture.

The door creaked open. It needed to be oiled.

Bill was watching a program about the garbage strikes in Italy. "Lemon trees," the narrator announced, in an unfazed, machismo timbre, "have been mutated by the fumes." The still image, which Bill and Adam never saw, was a withered yellow orb, its surrounding, crescent leaves turned inward. A man in a hospital mask pointed to the tree before the shot transitioned into commercial.

"I can't breathe, Bill."

Bill took a sip of water out of his mug.

Adam fell to his knees.

"I can't breathe."

Glen Armstrong

THE BEDSIDE BOOK
OF HOLLOW VICTORY

Some days we're the well-bred couple.
    Some days we're the boxing bears.

In this desolate space we pace
    ourselves,

    enduring hits and jabbing
    back.

By mid-November we know.
    We toast our enemies' downfalls.

Glasses clink.
    The garden stinks.

Sometimes we drink to better times.
    Sometimes we reason

    that slaughter is seasonal.

Sean Thomas Dougherty

LIGHTHOUSE ROAD

Who was the man who strolled the spine
of light inside this city along the frozen lake,
who nodded out in the empty husks
of long-closed steel factories, warehouses,
counted the chorded plumes of the refinery
smoke above the barren Great Lake sky,
the tenements of tar & DT tremors,
a frozen bay where old men perch
with rods over dark holes cut into the ice.
waiting for a tug, far from the gated cul-de-sacs
out past the corn farms, & their giant churches
whose spires pierce up to Christ,
a paler Christ than the icon of Mary
who reaches out from the altar
of the gold-domed Russian cathedral
& the babushkas bending to carry their burlap
bags of beets & cabbages & sausage,
down the East Side block he walks
his brown dog, & the cars that pause
to offer him the tiny plastic envelopes,
he waves his hand & nods
away from the dark place inside himself
& how he arrived a decade ago to teach,
tugging a bad marriage & a small son,
to arrive into this ice & snow to work
the long hours bent over papers alone
& the years of despair that traveled home
with him, until he didn't come back

but hid in the dim light & dark corners,
he made his nest in the last dregs
of a tall glass & the pills & smoke,
at the last stool of the last bar
on Earth the year he lost his job,
he nearly disappeared with all the weight
of moonlight like silver knives
his ex-wife kept in a bureau drawer,
the night he took one out & slit his wrist
for nothing even now he can name—
how the blood squirted up into the air
in a way he did not expect, he grabbed
a dish towel & duct-taped it & raced
to the emergency room, to the doctors

with their questions he could not answer stitched
into his wrist. Now & then on nights like this,
he touches the pale snake of that long scar.
He recalls that other world of laments
he never left behind, a shadow world
that never leaves my side, as the brown dog
tugs him trudging through the slush
down the long road towards the distant light
we call home.

Sean Thomas Dougherty

PSALM OF THE WORKING POOR

It's not that I have nothing.
It's that nothing halves me.

Savannah Johnston

CARRION

Tennessee cut the tongue out of Pop's boot to get the thing off. Blood had seeped through two pairs of socks. At the sight of blood, Jonathan, his husky, whimpered and snapped her jaws. Tennessee shooed her away. She listened, but he had to tie her puppies to his pack to keep them from licking Pop's boot.

Dark blue and black bruises splintered up Pop's calf. His skin was hot, and Pop cried out when Tennessee cut the sock. A bone, thin and graceful like a bird's wing, reached out like a hatchling beginning its escape. Like he'd been taught, Tennessee bathed his father's foot in the isopropyl alcohol he carried. His father screamed then, a scream that startled him, the high whine of a dying animal, before reeling back in the dirt. The puppies yipped along, excited. He bound the foot in strips of white cloth that bloomed burgundy.

His father breathed for a few days more, wet sickly breaths, unaccepting of water or food. Tennessee kept himself awake by pinching his eyelids and pricking beneath his fingernails with his knife, Pop's bow and quiver on his left. Jonathan lay on his right, growling softly, her puppies suckling noisily. At night, the forest came alive around them, the chirps and howls of the wild circling, waiting.

Pop died about sunrise, just as the morning glow washed over the trees and wooded peaks. In time with the changing of the season, the oak and hickory trees cut a river of burnt gold across the mountains. A tendril of smoke sought out the sky from down in the valley. Probably hunters, Tennessee thought. The time was right for them, and they were the only ones arrogant enough to leave a fire burning. They would stick by the creek, most likely, where the soapberry trees snaked alongside its banks.

The night's siege had ended, and now Tennessee broke up the soil with his hunting knife before laying it aside to scrape away the loose earth. He dug like he'd watched Pop dig. He dug until his fingers ached. He dug until the dirt began to cut into his hands. He knew he was strong, but he could be stronger. He knew from watching the tourists that drove them up the mountain every summer that he was stronger, taller, and faster than their boys, but Pop was a tree of a man, nearly twenty hands high. The hole had to be big.

The wind tore across the terraced camp, shuddering pine needles from their branches. A few pinecones clattered to the ground and the puppies tried out their barks on them. Tennessee stopped digging, his fingers cramped like spades. The puppies were too loud, not like Jonathan, who knew better.

Maybe they're hungry, Tennessee thought. His own stomach turned and he felt its emptiness for the first time in days. His father carried the food—too heavy for a boy, he'd said—and Tennessee opened the pack with dirty hands. The tourists had been scarce this year, or they had made themselves scarce to the campers, Tennessee didn't know. Pop chose their routes and had only just begun teaching him the winding circuit they used. The pack held just a few cans, leftovers, things like soups or chowder, a few mini-tins of beans, and about twenty pounds of cured venison they'd just picked up from one of their old camps a few days east. Tennessee broke off a chunk of it and sucked on it until it was soft. He opened one of the mini-tins and dumped it on the ground in front of the puppies. It was beans and hot dogs, something the tourists never seemed to run out of, and a meal Tennessee hated. The beans were mushy and sweet, the meat too soft. The puppies scrambled over one another trying to outdo themselves, smearing the sugared sauce onto their paws and muzzles. One puppy yelped as another bit its ear, tripping over its own tether.

The venison settled uneasily in his stomach, and he took a drink from the water jug tethered to the straps of Pop's pack. He drank in long, loud gulps, something Pop would have never allowed. More water than just enough to wet your throat was a pleasure, a luxury taken after a long day and a good meal. Tennessee took another drink, grateful that Pop had died with his eyes closed.

He pulled out another can from the pack; there was some writing on the label, a red banner above a picture of steaming yellow soup in a bowl with blue trim. Tennessee recognized some of the letters, like the *e*, *n*, and *s* from his name. With his knife, he whittled a hole in the can's top and drank from it. The soup was salty and thick, with a hint of cream that reminded him of the powdered milk they'd had when he was little. He covered the half-empty can with a cloth and set it in the nook of a loblolly pine to save for later. The puppies began to lick one another's paws and faces for the last bit of beans.

When the puppies were born, Tennessee had helped Jonathan along when the fourth and final puppy had gotten stuck. The fourth puppy was fat, much fatter than the others, and when it finally eased from Jonathan, it was clear that the pup was dead. Its sac was filled with water and the puppy was bloated. Tennessee wondered if the baby in Dead Ma's belly would have come out the same. Tennessee had buried the dead pup, but by the next morning, the pup was gone. He hadn't buried it deep enough.

Pop always said a body's got to be buried at least five feet down—any less and something's bound to dig it up. Tennessee was too young to dig when Ma died, but he'd watched. He'd watched Pop scoop away the loam with his wide, thick hands. He'd watched Pop undress her, peeling her canvas coat from stiff shoulders, tugging off jeans she'd lifted that spring. He'd watched her big, round belly, squishy now, not hard like before. He'd sat next to the grave, holding Jonathan's neck. He'd named her that after a story Ma liked to tell. She was buried seven winters ago beneath a woods' rose bush. Pop buried her on the shortest day of the year.

These puppies, now nearly six weeks strong, didn't look quite like Jonathan had as a pup. Their bodies were smaller, longer, and Pop said they were likely coyote pups. He'd wanted to kill them straight off, but Tennessee had begged to keep them. He imagined a pack of hunting dogs, trailing alongside them as they crisscrossed the mountains. He imagined himself leading the pack, their alpha.

His back against the tree, he flexed his fingers until his joints began to move properly again. Jonathan came up from behind and nuzzled his neck with her wet snout; she'd wandered to the creek, probably. He scratched her jaw and pressed his face into her neck. He reached into the pack and got her a bit of venison. She tossed it between her jaws before swallowing it whole, and she pressed her nose against Tennessee's palm. He gave her a second piece.

If it weren't for Pop's body lying between two towering post oaks, their camp would've been nice. The little clearing was on high ground with good visibility, couched against the mountain where the grade steepened. For a holdover camp, it was perfect. For a grave, it'd do. But he couldn't stay here through the winter: the wind would strip the tops of the trees before spring, and there wasn't any cover in case of snow or rain. No, he couldn't stay. Tennessee rubbed his palms together, trying to stop their tingling.

He squatted next to the meager hole he'd dug and then, when his ankles began to quake, he got on his knees. He fell into a rhythm with it, driving the knife into the dirt with his left hand, digging methodically with his right. There was a power in the pattern, and with each stab, he drove the knife to its hilt in the dirt. About a foot down, the sandy soil gave way to a soft clay, and it was cold to the touch.

The puppies whined against their tether, and Tennessee kept digging.

The shadow of a turkey buzzard flickered through the trees. Tennessee stopped and watched for the bird's shadow to pass over them again. The thought of a turkey buzzard's gnarled red head snapping into Pop's belly made him shake. He clenched his fists and kept digging.

By evening, he'd managed a sort of foxhole, nearly waist-deep and about half as long as he needed, but he had to stop for the night. His hands were cracked and the cracks were caked with clay. The sun had already begun to sink behind what Pop had called Mother Lode Mountain. It wasn't the largest peak in the range, but it was closest to a couple of waterfalls so it was popular with the tourists. In the high season during the summer, they'd cut a path through a few scattered campgrounds, taking what they needed. Mother Lode Mountain tourists brought all kinds of things: RVs, generators, clothes, blankets, canned food, tools. They had enough to never miss a few things here and there, Pop said.

Jonathan, too, had come from the tourists. In the story Ma liked to tell, Jonathan was a boy born into the wrong life, a life built around things. As he grew, he began to see how the people around him were bent and twisted by their things, and he cast himself out and learned to live high in the mountains, in the purest air of all. He remembered how her voice lilted when the boy made it to the mountaintop. Tennessee's Jonathan was a little thing when Pop brought her back to camp; a puppy, but not nearly so as her own were now. She had been left alone, tied to an iron stake, Pop said. Tourists didn't know what to do with such a beautiful dog. She would be wasted on them.

Tennessee took the can of soup down from the tree and emptied it, dumping out the last of it for the puppies. Jonathan perked her ears at him, whining, so he used the knife to saw off a chunk of the deer meat. The piece he gave her was bigger than his first, and he knew it'd keep her busy for a while at least. "Stay, girl," he told her. He needed to rinse the cans out so as not to draw any more attention to their camp, and he felt better knowing that Jonathan would be near Pop's body.

He tucked the soup can under his arm and picked up the mini-tin, ducking under a low branch to circle back to the thin deer trail. There were rules to pinching from the tourists: never more than one thing per tourist, never the same camp twice in a season, cover your tracks. Part of covering your tracks meant washing out the cans and stripping the labels. That way, Pop said, the tourists couldn't prove nothing. The creek ran a little more than a quarter mile west, and Tennessee hurried, keeping one eye on the path and the other on the rapidly setting sun. He came out of the trees on a slope and took small steps through the high grass.

The soup sloshed in his stomach. It felt as if his mouth were coated thick with it. It had been stupid of him to eat it so quickly. He'd been greedy. If he were honest, he'd admit it had never set well with him, the canned stuff. But for the seconds it took to eat it, it was the best thing he'd ever tasted. He hoped he wouldn't throw up.

He cut through a thicket of soapberry trees and came out on the south end, at the creek. The water level was low, the creek's silt banks bordering the narrow pass. A bright green bullet casing lay in a clump of grass, and Tennessee picked it up. The casing was cold, and he tossed it into the stream, watching as it bobbed like a cheap cork downstream. A shameful way to hunt, bullets.

He tapped the sand with the toe of his boot until he found a spot that didn't sink. Crouching over the creek, he ran the can under the cool stream. Once the cans were rinsed, he peeled the labels off and crushed them into pulpy balls, tossing each one into the water. Minnows swam near the surface, picking at the paper as it floated downstream. He set the cans on the bank and scrubbed his hands.

He left a murky current, but the coolness soothed the sharp ache that seeped out of his hands. The clay had worked itself into the swoops and whorls of his palms; he shook the water from his hands.

The creek, its current no longer broken, reflected the purple sky as dusk set in. Somewhere in the vast expanse of pine and oak, a coyote howled. Farther out, other coyotes joined the chorus, and their calls reverberated across the range. With every round, some were closer, others farther away. The pack circled. Tennessee shook the cans out and forced them into his jacket pockets and headed back through the thicket.

When he was little, Pop told a story to keep him close. It wasn't like Ma's story about Jonathan. Instead, Pop's story was about a man who wore a long coat. The man lived in their mountains, and he skirted the tourists with enviable ease. He ran with the deer, the elk, the coyotes, the bobcats, and even the bears. For all intents and purposes, he wasn't a man at all. He followed the tourists' trails and when he felt like it, when he found one he wanted to punish, he'd pick them off. Poof. You've gotta be smarter, Pop said. You've got to stay close to camp.

The high grass rustled farther up the slope, and a howl rang out, so close that Tennessee felt it in his chest. He pushed on, cursing himself. He'd taken too long, he'd dawdled. Now it was night and he ran, his footfalls in time with his heartbeat. The cans clanged inside his pocket. In the daylight, he knew the path, but under the thick shroud of darkness, the deer trail was just a sliver of sand, barely traceable. But he did know this path and he let his muscles lead, quick strides that left behind heavy bootprints.

Cover your tracks, Pop said. Stay close to camp.

You've got to bury a body five feet down, Pop said. Or something's liable to dig it up.

He nearly fell as he burst through the pines, but he righted himself and surveyed their camp. Pop was laid up next to the hole, his arms at his sides. His pack was open, and the ground was strewn with shreds of paper. Jonathan had backed up against her puppies, who were scrambling excitedly over Tennessee's pack, their tether tangled around their bellies. She cocked an ear at him and snarled into the dark. He went to her and scratched the scruff of her neck.

"S'alright," Tennessee said quietly. "Done good."

She tossed her heavy head beneath his hand and kept her nose pointed west. He went to Pop's pack, tucking the empty cans in the front pocket. He didn't need to open the big pocket to know the venison was gone. His mouth was dry as he swept the paper scraps into a pile. He hadn't tied up the main pocket; that was stupid. That was so simple, so sensible, as to have never been codified into law. Pop never left his pack untended. The bulging moss-green pack was his shadow, and now it occurred to Tennessee why. His eyes went hot, but he grit his teeth, grateful that Pop had died with his eyes closed.

The howls had quieted for the moment. Jonathan's ears were tucked flush against her head, her teeth bared. The coyotes were silent, but they were there, just beyond the trees. Tennessee could hear the gnashing of their jaws as they ate his venison. He swallowed air as if that would fill him. He had to keep digging.

Tennessee wrapped his hands in the white cloth and grabbed his knife from beneath the empty pack. He kneeled by the foxhole, his breath rattling as he stabbed at the dirt. The knife broke the soil again and again, and he drove it deeper with each stroke. The cracks in his hands opened, rubbing raw against the coarse cloth, but he kept digging. He wished for a shovel, like the one Pop had taken to bury Ma. Pop had left that shovel at a campsite.

Don't carry what you don't need, Pop said.

His stomach lurched and he tamped down the urge to heave. His mouth was wet. He swallowed and kept digging.

Miles down the ridge, a mountain lion screamed. Its shrill, plaintive cry mimicked that of a woman. Tennessee paused, listening; the scream had silenced the other creatures lurking in the night. The quiet was uncomfortable, the only sounds being the scrape and brush of the knife in the soil, the sweep of the dirt. The quiet was like a blindfold. When he and Pop stalked deer, the moment before the arrow's slick release, the moment before the arrow pierced its breast, was quiet; in that moment of stillness, the deer knew.

He crawled into the hole on his knees and, leaving the knife suspended in the side of the hole, used his hands to break up the clay wall. Closest to the surface, the dirt came away easily. Worms and grubs wriggled, reaching out into the air, struggling to right themselves as he swept them into the loose piles of dirt. He'd eaten worms when he was little, curious at first and then just because he liked it. Pop had clapped his ears for that.

Men don't eat worms, Pop said.

He kept digging. Jonathan pawed at the hole's edge. The mountain lion screamed again. The moon climbed overhead, illuminating him through a gap in the trees. He kept digging.

The coyotes started up again and he dug faster, urgently. They circled as they had before.

We know you're there, they seemed to say.

Tennessee's arms quaked when he took up the knife again. The wind chilled him, and on its tail he caught a rancid, hot scent. With another gust it was gone, but he knew that if he could smell it, the coyotes had always smelled it; they liked it. Tennessee wiped the sweat from his brow and he felt the dirt smear across his face.

He kept digging.

As the dark sky began to pale, birds began to wake, and a bobwhite whistled in the pine. The hole was deep and, exhausted, Tennessee found that when he stood, his head was just below the earth's surface. He could almost extend his arms down the hole's length, but it was painful to try. The bobwhite whistled.

The bobwhite is the man in the long coat's messenger, Pop said.

Jonathan began to growl. On his tiptoes, Tennessee saw her crouching low against the ground. From between the pines, a gray coyote slunk into the camp. Jonathan snapped her jaws and barked. She backed up against her puppies.

The mountain is more afraid of you than you are of it, Pop said. The man in the long coat isn't afraid of anything.

Tennessee jumped and tried to hook his elbows over the hole's lip, but the ground gave way and he fell back hard on his tailbone. He got up and tried again. He fell. He screamed, grabbed a handful of clay, and lobbed it out of the hole. He heard it clatter into the grass. Still, Jonathan barked and snarled.

Panic gripped his body as he heard the wet snap of jaws. He groped blindly for the knife. He found it and held it tightly in his left hand; he jumped, jabbing it into the earth, and tried to pull himself out. The effort made him cry out. He kicked at the clay, finding a foothold and propelling himself up. He pulled himself out of the hole and turned, crouching low with his knife in front of him.

Jonathan was in a frenzy, her puppies crying between her hind legs. Two coyotes were on Pop, one gnawing his blackened foot, the other tearing at his wide hands. Their muzzles were speckled with dark blood.

Tennessee screamed and charged, swinging the knife in front of him. He caught one on the shoulder; it yelped and jumped back. The larger of the two crouched low and lunged, and Tennessee stabbed at it, the effort of his swing spinning him on his feet as he missed. The big one sank its teeth into his calf. He tried to shake the beast off, but it held its grip. He slashed its nose and the coyote released him, shaking its snout as it retreated.

The coyotes didn't run, but slunk away just as they'd come. They were confident. The sun was rising, but it would set again. Tennessee brought his legs to his chest and wrapped his arms around himself. Jonathan licked his hand, her puppies yipping excitedly. He swallowed a sob. He clenched his jaw until it throbbed.

Crying is a waste of resources, Pop said.

Tennessee crawled to the pack and rummaged for the isopropyl alcohol. Rolling up the cuff of his pants, the bite didn't look too bad, considering how his leg throbbed, how he could feel it throbbing in his ears. He counted seven good puncture wounds, two of which gouged into the muscle of his calf, but none so wide or deep as to need stitches. When he poured the alcohol over it, he thought that he could hear his skin burning, searing into his leg. There was just enough white cloth left to wrap the worst of his leg. He wrapped it as tightly as he could.

He took a shaky breath and looked to Pop. The bandage on his foot was torn, chunks of flesh ripped away in thick, ragged pieces. His thumb was gone. Tennessee pressed his palms into the grass. Pop's face was slack.

The bobwhite whistled.

Tennessee rubbed his eyes with his fists. His knuckles were wet. He stood, careful, and lifted Pop's ankles. It startled him how much meat looked like meat. The flesh of a dead man wasn't much different than that of a deer.

He dragged Pop to the side of the hole. The body's stiffness was fading, and Tennessee sat him up, his arms barely reaching around Pop's chest. Tennessee pressed his face into Pop's shoulder. Pop's jacket smelled of dirt and smoke, but the smell of iron lingered faintly. Tennessee rocked a little, back and forth, and let out a shallow breath. Gingerly, he crooked Pop's elbow and tugged his arm out of the sleeve. He did the same with the other arm, careful with Pop's mangled hand. He scooted out from behind Pop, pulling the jacket off. Pop slumped forward.

He flipped Pop into the hole. He heard the crack of something inside Pop. He looked down into the hole and saw Pop, contorted oddly in a kind of squat, his legs twisted beneath him. Tennessee's own leg throbbed, but he tried to push it out of his mind. Kneeling beside the hole, the grave, Tennessee began to fill it, scooping heavy handfuls of dirt over his father's body. The splash of the dirt sounded like a hard, sporadic rain.

The sun was in the center of the sky when he finished. He collapsed beside the grave, hungry and exhausted, and tried to catch his breath. Jonathan lay next to him and he ruffled her fur. The puppies slept next to the pack in a pile of soft fur the color of wet sand.

When his sweat had turned cold and throbbing in his leg had calmed to a cruel ache, he opened a can of beans and took a small bite. The food disturbed his empty stomach, and he dumped half of the can onto the ground for Jonathan. The husky lapped it up hungrily, finishing it just as the puppies woke and tousled over one another, eager to join her. Tennessee counted the cans: two tins of beans and two others, both with pictures of orange soup on the label. The dirt that crusted his arms cracked as he pulled himself up.

It would freeze soon, Tennessee knew. The cave Pop had pointed them toward was still five days south, more with a busted calf. He brought the canteen to his lips and drank until he heard the water sloshing in his belly.

The puppies played, still tangled in their makeshift leash.

They will starve, Tennessee knew.

He twirled his knife's tip in the dirt. He could hunt. Pop's bow was a little big for him, but he could manage. But that would take time. The tourists were gone, and the few hunters that still roamed the valleys were dangerous.

Hunters hung the heads of their kills on walls in painted lodges, Pop said. They killed for the sake of the kill. We are not like them.

No, there wasn't time to hunt.

He crawled to the puppies. Gently, he untethered them, unlooping the rope from around their fat paws. They mewled and tumbled over one another, happy to be free of their restraints. They nipped at his fingers.

He took one in his hands, a boy pup, and rubbed the soft felt of its ears. He pulled at the scruff of its neck. He drew his knife across its throat; it fell limp in his hands as its blood pumped out of its body, seeping into the dirt. Jonathan cried in short yips. She barked. She pawed at the ground, her tail between her legs.

Tennessee's mouth was wet. He laid the dead puppy on the ground and slit it down the middle. It was warm, the puppy, and its insides were warm as Tennessee reached into the animal. A little stomach. A liver. The puppy wasn't much of a thing.

He looked at Jonathan and he saw a sadness in her eyes. He looked away.

He would skin the puppy. He would start a fire. He would harvest what little meat the puppy had. He'd be on the move by nightfall. It would freeze soon.

The bobwhite whistled again, and a mockingbird returned its call. The bobwhite was silent.

David Sloan

After the Wash

In the predawn, a dark-fruited moon
ripens to rose and dissolves,
a ribbon at a time. Pond peepers quiet.
In the shed, the chickens
begin to ruffle and cluck, roused
to unease by a shadow loping
at the edge of the woods,
tail flared parallel to the stubble field.

Daylight sifts in on a din of birdsong,
over a hoe left lying between beet
and onion rows, past the empty line
and lilac quivering in the held breath
of early morning, when a type
of mending seems most possible,
to the blanket tossed off in a rumpled V
between them, still bearing the imprint
of night's entanglements.

What compels them to probe too near
each other's mystery? What cruelty spurs
this unmasking, a bare-bulb questioning
that always ends badly for both, as when blades
grind each other into dullness, or like a fox
lured into the coop, only to find above
those tender necks a battalion of beaks
primed to peck at its greedy eyes.

Nancy Carol Moody

A FLINT IN A SLIPPER BURIED UNDER GLASS

I am walking the dog though there is no dog. Pink leash and rhinestone collar suggest poodle, female, but this dog that's not is a Basenji, male. Three days it's been since the house burned down. A candle in the garage investigators didn't want to believe. They wanted wax and flame on a ledge next to curtains, something incendiary begging for climax. But the evidence was bull to the red cape of theory. Blackened puddle on the floor slats, no oily rag or sawdust nearby. The garage not garage. Horizontal bars for training forms to preposterous positions. Mirrors as walls, incineration implying a millionfold of stars. The candle remains a question mark, but when is trouble where it's supposed to be? A sear on the inner calf owns many stories. Likewise the plume on the scent of a draft. Briquettes on the rooftop, wick beneath the door. Inside, the clamoring of a barkless dog. The facts of me are easy if only you would ask.

Sarah Fawn Montgomery

THE LAKE

The Iowa lake came with little warning,
just a town meeting announcing
This land's for public use now
and a map of what the water
would look like when the houses went.

No one protested much
because what could you do
when it came down to recreation
and the finer points of city planning?

The Johnsons were long-timers
so they sold for a tidy profit,
and the Smiths had wanted to downsize
since their son went off to State,
so they got inspired to up and move
to sunny Florida and bigger water.

But Widow Brown wouldn't leave,
kept on gardening like she never heard,
ignoring the signs around town
advertising a new swimming spot,
a dock for shiny motorboats,
and even a summer stand for dipped cones
and dogs with different kinds of mustard.

She disregarded the men in hard hats
and the government paperwork insisting

no one was really asking for permission.
She'd return from grocery shopping
to caution tape around the yard and tractors
alongside her old wheelbarrow and spade.

Eventually they busted the windows and pipes
so she couldn't stay, and built up the land
around her yellow house, pumping the basin
full of water like a backyard mud hole.

Swim deep enough, past legs and rafts,
or the bottoms of those shiny boats,
and you'll see her overturned barrow,
shards of window like a shark's teeth.

Fish swim in and out of the opening,
circling the living room,
walls gone green with algae,
finding themselves at the table
the widow left carefully set for tea.

THE MISSOURI STATE UNIVERSITY LITERARY COMPETITIONS

Moon City Review is a publication of Moon City Press, an independent press housed in Missouri State University's Department of English. To help commemorate the journal's origins as a student journal, we are proud to publish, via an open competition, one piece of fiction and one poem by members of our student population.

This past year, fiction entries were judged by Trudy Lewis, author of two novels, *The Empire Rolls*—published by Moon City Press in 2014—and *Private Correspondences* (TriQuarterly, 1996), and also the short story collection *The Bones of Garbo* (Ohio State University Press, 2003). Lewis chose Dane Lale's story "The Remarkable Face of Arlind Penthurst" as this year's winner. Of Lale's story, Lewis says, "[It] impressed me with its narrative confidence, its deft gender reversal, and its insightful exploration of identity." She adds, "This story always knows where it's going, and yet the author leaves plenty of space for introspection and ambiguity. 'The Remarkable Face' reads like an upbeat cover of Nathaniel Hawthorne's 'The Birthmark.' It's simultaneously classic and contemporary."

The other fiction finalists include the following authors:

Colin Brightwell
Beth Fiset
Zachary Fletcher
Sydney Ingram
Christina Orlandos
Genevieve Richards
Jordan Ryan
Bill Stoner

As for the poetry competition, this year's judge was Sarah Freligh, whose collections include *Sad Math*—winner of the 2014 Moon City Poetry Award—and *Sort of Gone* (WordTech Communications, 2008). She is also the author of chapbooks *A Brief Natural History of an American Girl* (Accents Publishing, 2012) and *Bonus Baby* (Polo

Grounds Press, 2002). Freligh selected Ali Geren's entry "Delinquent Motherhood" for the prize. Freligh says of the poem, "[It] drops its readers immediately into the conflict that launches the narrative trajectory. From there, the poem ripples out, even as it circles back to the triggering episode, managing to explore universes through an intensely personal and particular lens."

The other poetry finalists include these writers:

Mary Chiles
Hannah Farley
Matt Kimberlin
Courtney Price

We are proud to present our students' work to you in the following pages, as we are proud of the work all our students do here at Missouri State.

Dane Lale

THE REMARKABLE FACE
OF ARLIND PENTHURST

Arlind Penthurst was an ugly man, but he had always made the most of it. When he was seven, he played the rat in Mrs. Tyler's second-grade class production of *Charlotte's Web*, and it was then that he caught the acting bug. By the fifth grade he had begun to learn the limitations that came with his crooked, oversized nose, sloping brow, and distended jaw—both in his stage life and his personal one. But it wasn't until high school drama club and getting the lead in the Corman High production of *Richard III* that he realized the unique opportunities available to a unique-looking actor.

Puberty only made him stand out more. He sprouted to a towering six foot four, and even with his tendency to slouch forward, he loomed over his peers and castmates. They called him Lurch, and sometimes Dicknose, but Arlind never felt this was anything more than friendly ribbing. He was well known and well liked, not often bullied, and once, during his senior year, he even got to hook up with Tracy Eustace, the starting center for the Corman Lady Gophers.

After high school, he studied theater at Ohio State, and it was there he learned that acting was more than instinct and passion. He cultivated his technique, hoping to be versatile, striving to do more than just stand out.

The years following his graduation from the program were marked with small successes. He landed a few minor roles on stage and screen, and all were well received. He was a high school bully in a Friday night sitcom, and the casting director remarked that she was impressed with his capacity to convey menace. He was the hapless stepbrother in a teenage party comedy, and the general consensus among the film's fans was that his gawky presence and absurd physicality stole all three of the scenes in which he appeared. He was even a mental patient in a production of *One Flew Over the Cuckoo's Nest,* and a theater critic for *The Columbus Dispatch* had specifically commended his performance for its "captivating wretchedness."

It was this last achievement that motivated him to make the move to Los Angeles. He signed with Distinguished Features, an agency that specialized in men like him, and within five years he had received small but notable parts in almost a dozen films. After ten years, he had become a sought after commodity for any role that required a memorably hideous countenance.

He was sometimes a henchman, sometimes a lack-wit, sometimes a geek, sometimes a monster. His success was ample, his screen presence ubiquitous, and though very few people outside the industry knew his name, his face had achieved household recognition. But in the spring of 2013, just before his fortieth birthday, Arlind Penthurst decided he didn't want to be ugly anymore.

Tom, his agent, took some time to find his words when Arlind told him about the surgery. He nodded and licked his lips. He sat down behind his desk and nodded some more. Finally he said, "Arl, I totally support whatever cosmetic decisions you feel are right for you. You know that, right? But I wonder if this isn't a bit of a misstep." His inflection rose at the end of the last sentence, bringing it to some middle-ground between a question and a statement. He eyed Arlind expectantly.

"How so?" the big man replied.

Tom commenced a new round of nodding, apparently quite impressed by his client's query. "Well …," he ventured. "Have you considered that the Arlind Penthurst brand is largely grounded in your authentic, everyman look? Changing that look might throw people a little."

"I don't look like everyman. I look like the fucking Hacksaw Man."

"And that was one of your biggest films! Everybody loves the Hacksaw Man!" Tom got back to his feet and came around the desk toward Arlind. "Arl, your face is what gets you hired. You want to go and trade it for a new one when it's a hot commodity? Why the hell would you do that?"

Arlind's underbite set his lower lip over his upper one when he clenched his jaw. It made his determination look like a pout. "This is happening. I've already decided. If you don't want to continue representing me, I'll go elsewhere. But this is happening."

They left it at that, and Arlind went home. He lived in a two-story apartment in Franklin Village. Though his name was alone on the lease, he knew he would find Melissa there, making lunch in the granite-countered kitchen or curled up in bed for an early afternoon nap. She was the last one he had to tell, and while he had been able to predict his agent's and publicist's reactions accurately, he was entirely uncertain what his girlfriend of seven months might do with the news.

She was at the stove, stirring wild rice. The steam made her face flush and strands of her dark hair cling to her forehead. She greeted him with a soft, easy smile, and Arlind was struck, as he had often been, by the sincerity he saw there.

They ate on the couch, ceramic bowls perched on their thighs. Arlind waited for an opening to tell her about his decision, hoping she would ask about his meeting today, but Melissa was too outraged by the documentary she had watched that morning to talk about anything else.

"You know, it's exploitation—pure and simple. These people are creating the entire piece. I mean, I've used assistants before, but they're completely under my direction. Hirst's assistants are the talent—*they're* the artists and they're being treated like maintenance guys. You see the difference, right?"

Arlind agreed. And as she went on, he continued to agree. It wasn't that it was a dull topic or that he didn't have any opinion on the issue. Any other day he might have had a lot to say about it. It was just that he had worked up the courage to tell Melissa about his decision, and he didn't know how long his resolve would last. Finally, he just interrupted her midsentence.

"Honey, I need to tell you something."

Confusion, then worry, played across her face in turn. "Well, that's never followed by anything but bad news. What is it?"

"It's not bad. Just big." He tried to find the right words, and when they wouldn't come, he just said the most direct ones. "I'm going to have surgery next week to change my face."

It was not the way he had intended this to go, but once he began to explain his plans, the tension that had been clinging to his spine and shoulders melted away, and he began to feel good. He told her about the procedure, about the recovery time, about the cost. He told her he had been planning it for a while but hadn't wanted to tell anyone until he was certain the time was right. She sat and listened patiently, and, to her credit, she seemed to understand why he had only now chosen to reveal everything to her.

When he finished, they sat in silence. Arlind fingered the ridges of his bowl, waiting for her response. She gripped his hand and looked him in the eye. It was a sympathetic gesture, but it also smacked of concern. "You know I've never cared about how you look. This isn't for my sake, is it?"

It wasn't. In fact, Arlind hadn't had trouble with women for quite some time. He had found that most were able to overlook superficial defects if you could prove you were a decent and successful man. But the way Melissa had phrased it made him realize something. She didn't deny that he was ugly; she only claimed that she was better than caring that he was ugly. Part of him loved her for her honesty. Still, another part was hurt.

Arlind had always accepted his ugliness as an objective truth—a simple physical reality. But he was surprised to discover that he had also always believed that this truth could be refuted in the right person's eyes—not just overlooked, but entirely negated by the subjective gaze of a woman who loved him. Melissa could hardly be blamed for not living up to this belief, especially when he hadn't even known he'd held it, but all the same, the betrayal was there, hard and sharp and unreasonable in his stomach.

"It's not for you. It's for me," he replied, a little too loudly. "I'm tired of getting hired because of how I look. I'd like to be able to play something else some time. Something other than …." He trailed off. He couldn't think of a way to finish the sentence without effusing self-pity.

She dropped his hand and crossed her arms. Her mouth got tight and her eyes hard. The sympathy was gone. "So it's just the business? You need to be one of the dapper leading men? You're going to have doctors cut into your face, break and rearrange the bones, just because you're tired of being typecast?"

"It's more than that. I'm not—."

"I had no idea you cared that much about appearances." Melissa stood and grabbed the bowl of rice from his lap. "I don't date actors because, most of the time, they can't see past their own face. I thought you'd be different."

"And what made you think that?"

She stopped on her way to the sink and turned to face him, her free hand on her hip. "Not … you know what I mean."

"No, really." He was on his feet now. The stone in his gut had cracked wide, and stale, bitter air rose from his throat, seeping into his voice. "When you first saw me, what elusive, intangible quality did you just happen to pull from the fucking ether that made you think I wouldn't care about appearances?"

"You know what I mean!"

"Yeah, I think I'm starting to."

The surgery was the following Thursday. He was undergoing two procedures simultaneously—one to correct his underbite and another to reshape his crooked nose. Dr. Susan Brayer was one of only three plastic surgeons in the country who routinely performed both in the same session, which was why he had sought her out three months earlier. All told, he would be under her knife for ten hours. Still, Arlind felt calm and certain as he sat in his final pre-operative consultation with her. Before she left him to the nurses, she asked if he wanted a mirror to see his old face one last time. He politely refused.

Not a single person in his life had approved of his decision. His friends told him he was committing career suicide, and the people he paid to manage his career said the same with slightly more tact. Melissa hadn't been to his place since their fight, and the text he had sent her earlier that morning remained unanswered. Even his mother was upset by his determination to change his face, but then, she had never seen what was wrong with it in the first place. She only ever watched his romantic comedies and frequently suggested he play the leads rather than the belligerent boss or the weaselly roommate, never understanding why he couldn't. All the same, as he lay on the operating table, sinking into the thick, saturating fog of drugged sleep, he still could find no regret or anxiety about the procedure within his own mind.

When it was done, he spent two days in the hospital before he was strong enough to move to the Healing Haven Recovery Spa. There were several of these places in and around LA. They provided a discrete and peaceful environment for anyone with the means who wanted to avoid the stress of their busy lives or, oftentimes, the scrutiny of the public eye while their swollen skin settled and their scars mended. Healing Haven was just west of Pasadena, less than a mile off Ventura Freeway. It was one of Hollywood's more remarkable monuments to unnecessary opulence, boasting amenities that included a library, a twenty-seat theater, and, perhaps most needlessly, a sixteen-by-thirty-two-foot swimming pool. It employed five massage therapists and two chefs, maintained three separate Jacuzzis, and operated a shuttle service to the offices of a dozen plastic surgeons in the area.

Arlind spent his first day there lying in his room, taking his meals through a straw and trying not to suffocate on the blood that congealed in his nose and pooled beneath his tongue.

His healing jaw was held closed with a splint that made trying to speak a futile and painful experience. It would be weeks before he could talk in more than grunts and gurgles, and longer still before he could chew food. He didn't sleep well, and oftentimes, when he woke up, he would forget about his condition and panic when he couldn't open his mouth. Arlind had never been claustrophobic, but being trapped inside his own head, barely sucking breath through the putrid morass behind his clenched and aching teeth, was enough to send him into frequent bouts of terror and despair.

Melissa asked if she could visit on his third day at the spa. He had messaged her before leaving the hospital, letting her know that he had made it through the surgery, but this was the first he'd heard from her in over a week. She arrived at midmorning, just after he had slurped up the protein shake that was his breakfast. He was sitting on the edge of his bed, still dabbing foamy, white drool off of his bandaged chin, when she knocked on the open door to his room.

"Arlind?" Her hair was in a tidy half-braid and she wore a sleeveless, blue-and-orange patterned sundress. She looked stunning. "Can I come in?"

He dropped the soiled towel to the far side of the bed and waved her in. He tried a smile. It was tight and strained, but she smiled back in that soft, familiar way, and wrapped him in her bare arms.

"I'm sorry I didn't come sooner." There was a shimmer collecting in the corners of her eyes. "I was mad at you for springing this on me, but … I don't want you to go through this alone."

He tightened his arms around her.

Last night, he had had a dream about running from his alter ego, the Hacksaw Man. When the hideous, blood-stained monster had inevitably caught him, he hadn't begun dismembering him, as was his tendency. Instead, the madman pinned him to the ground, with one meaty, calloused hand clamped around his mouth and nose. The Hacksaw man smiled, twisted and malicious and gleeful, and Arlind had known, even as his lungs throbbed with the need for air, that he was transforming—that his face was draining into the grisly mitt that closed around it, losing all features, becoming nothing.

He had woken gasping through his teeth, sputtering and trying desperately to wrench his mouth open.

Even when he had realized where he was, he could not slow his breathing or calm his panic. It had taken the resident night-shift nurse forty-five minutes and a powerful sedative to settle him back down. Before drifting back to sleep, he had lain in bed for another hour, stroking his own arm, focusing on his breath, and thinking about Melissa—the heat that came off her skin as she spooned him, the deep, tuneless hum she emitted in the dark. He had missed her more in that hour than he could ever remember missing anyone.

Now, with her standing over his bed, looking down at the sodden bandages that encased his face, he mostly just felt embarrassed. He knew he was a sad sight at the moment, and the inability to speak—to make a self-deprecating joke or half-assed excuse—was a frustration he didn't know how to handle. The awkward tension mounted in the room as Melissa searched for something to say and Arlind struggled with his voicelessness. Finally, he grabbed the pen and pad of paper he kept on his bedside table.

Thanks for coming. Sorry I'm such a mess.

She shook her head with a benevolent smile. "Oh, no, sweetie. It's fine. You know I don't care how you look."

He looked up at her for a slow, sad second. She was so beautiful. But her eyes were brimming with undisguised pity. He gave an appreciative grunt.

I'm so grateful. I can never tell you how much. I ....

He stopped writing. He wasn't sure what else to say. He *was* grateful. She had never hesitated with him. Never held back any part of herself in the seven months they had been together. She was kind and giving and unabashedly human, and it was all open for him to enjoy. It may have been all he ever had any right to hope for.

But he wanted more now. He didn't want to be loved in spite of his face. He didn't want some generous soul to accept him for the way he was. He wanted to look into an open heart and see something more than kindness and understanding. He wanted to see longing, rather than acceptance, in his girlfriend's eyes—the kind of stupid, wretched desire he had felt for her since their first date.

He was done making the most of things. He had earned the right to be genuinely wanted with thirty-five years of wearing his ugliness like armor, selling it like a stockbroker selling junk bonds—convincing the world that his deformity was actually character.

Just thank you, I guess. He finally scribbled.

She laughed and pulled him into another hug.

After she left, Arlind went into his bathroom and approached the mirror over the sink. He looked at his swollen face, swaddled in gauze and plaster, and he tried to reconcile it with the face he had seen his entire life in mirrors and movie posters, in strategically lit head shots and on the expansive canvases of movie screens.

He had been considering the surgery for longer than he could remember, and the face he had envisioned in all that time was not the one he could imagine was behind the bandages now. And staring himself in the eye in that moment, he realized he didn't recognize anything about who he was. He remembered his dream, remembered his face being sucked away until it became featureless—a blank slate. He closed his eyes and thought back to his beginning acting course at Ohio State.

"We start by becoming nothing," his professor had told the room full of young, green performers. "You can't be anybody until you've learned to be nobody. I don't care what you put into your character; it's still you at the center unless you strip that away first."

Arlind kept his breath steady, remembering the exercise and peeling away the shreds of himself, one at a time. When it was done—when he had lifted the last, lonely stone of being from his mind—he looked up at the face in front of him.

Ali Geren

DELINQUENT MOTHERHOOD

At seventeen, I bought a pregnancy test
for my friend Jennifer, who had been having sex with her
quarterback boyfriend. If one in ten
of the girls in my class hadn't needed one,
or hadn't had sex with their quarterback,
running back, forward starter, ten-point-shooter
boyfriends, perhaps I might've been more
concerned, but to me, she was just one delinquent
among twenty-three others in our class who made a bad decision
that spawned a slew; Jennifer dropped out of school
and moved out of her mother's house. My mother
said that if I dared be as fruitful as the young parents in my class
she would beat me black and the lesson stuck.
Jennifer is married now, to her quarterback boyfriend.
One baby has become four more and though
I think of a mother of five as fat, and ugly, overworked and haggard;
Jennifer is none of these things, a blonde beauty still,
with beautiful children and her quarterback boyfriend-turned-husband
who works at Eyemart now, seventy hours a week,
so that Jennifer can stay home and make children and raise children
and there is no shame in that. Not for Jennifer.
Not for my mother, either, who had four children
and now asks me for grandchildren. *Your ovaries,*
she says to me as we fold laundry and gossip about
beautiful Jennifer and her five children, *are going to dry up
and fall out. Like raisins.* I haven't ever responded well
to scare tactics, and my flippant *I wish they would* only serves
as exasperation for my mother, who was married by younger

than I am now. I do not tell her that I kissed a girl.
I do not tell her that I liked the way her lips felt against mine;
I do not tell her that I kissed her again, and again, and I do not
tell her that I never want children, not in so many words,
and I do not tell her that my plans involve, for the most part,
this girl and lots of cats. I tell her none of these things;
instead, I fold my father's athletic shorts, and my lineman brother's
t-shirts, and my mother looks up from the ironing and says
I think Tanner and his girlfriend are having sex and all I can think
is that my brother's girlfriend is blonde, like Jennifer, and a part of me
wonders if she is destined for motherhood,
if someday I will buy eyeglasses from my little brother,
if his girlfriend will be as lovely as Jennifer is, a mother of five and still
that high-school-cheerleader beautiful. The thought does not concern me
as much as, perhaps, it should.

John Davis

BALANCING

And my daughter was watching
Mister Rogers' Neighborhood with me
on the couch
And I was balancing a beer
on my belly after working a sixty-hour week
And my daughter was running off
to play with the dog
who injured his paw
who growled with a ball in his mouth
who scampered around the house

And my beer and I were watching Mister Rogers
making a sandwich
slicing fruit into banana smiles on bread
My beer and I were riding
the train to Make Believe
but could not follow the storyline
of the king and queen picking and pawing
with puppet hands
My beer and I were holding on
to couch cushions like deck furniture
on the *Titanic*

And my daughter was pulling off
my shoes while Mister Rogers
was putting on his sportcoat and saying good-bye
saying you are the best at being you
And I was watching the screen

turn gray then black when my daughter
shut off the TV
And my beer and I were empty or full
And my daughter pulled me to dinner
and my wife arranged the peas
on my plate into smiles and frowns.

Mark Irwin

What did you do today? How long will it last? Will you remember?

Time, trying to name what has no name. Your mom's
death. Where were you when it happened? You say Rome,
trying to capture its monuments, Caesars, churches. To say *now*
and know that nothing remains between you and sky. When
we had new bodies and eager mouths. When you said *cow, truck, horse*
with the entire force of your body, pushing, wrapping names around
things.—The rope of language and all its fraying strings. *Will you,
please, will you?* To return to a childhood house no longer *home*
and be haunted by that word.—To forget words when only the body
moans and the town seems all dust under new snow.

Andrew Koch

YEAR OF THE TEENAGE WITCH

In the span of a summer, all of Martha's friends discover their dads are terrified of them, every lipstick shade rounded up as contraband. The rebellion that began at the sleepover spreads to the backs of station wagons, the library stacks. Streaked in glitter and magic markers they swear unholy vows over sneaker feet. Geometry is something to do in the woods at midnight with gel pens, penknives. Geology is measured out in basements, the depths of thimbles and tablespoons, two quarts of weed-killer. Stolen spray paint conjures tornadoes, dark magic behind dumpsters and drug stores. If you leave a thing underground, they discover, it will eventually disappear.

Katie McGinnis

THE FOX WOMAN
AT KARACHI GARDENS

One Tuesday, on the first morning of the first week of spring, you decide to take your daughter, Fidda, to the Karachi Zoological Gardens. Fidda lies in bed and feigns sickness. You feel her head and find no fever, but she insists that her stomach is in knots. You place a hesitant hand atop her stomach to feel for rumblings. You discover none. You understand that the past few weeks of school have been difficult for Fidda, that she is being teased about the separation, and you offer the zoo, which you cannot really afford, as a momentary distraction.

But it's not even a pretty day, says your daughter, turning away. She looks out the window and massages the pink ball of her foot. Her hair is slick with oil and twists in a braid like a tangled root.

You go into the kitchen and consider the expense of calling a doctor. You consider the expense of medication. You consider how the doctor would need to touch your daughter with his hands. You decide that there is nothing a doctor or medication can do that the sun cannot. When you return to her room, she shuts you out like a dog. You insist: Open the door. Now, Fidda.

I'm tired, she says.

It's time to get up. Get moving.

I'm dying, she insists. I really am, Papa.

In the kitchen you snack on a plate of oranges sliced into thin waterwheels as your daughter readies herself. The waterwheels have been sitting on the counter for sixteen hours and are chewy and pliable. You do not enjoy the texture. You do not enjoy oranges. You eat them only because they are cheaper than apples and because when you cradle the waterwheels in the palm of your hand they look like little orange suns and this to you is something close to power. You turn on the radio but the batteries are dead so instead you imagine your daughter's progress.

First, she combs out the accordion of her dark mane. Now she adjusts a hijab the color of a bruised poppy in a mirror's reflection. She reaches into the drawer for something you try to imagine but cannot and clips a polka dotted bra over teacup breasts. Although you have never witnessed any of these things, you believe in them. Outside a car honks. You stand in front of Fidda's door and encourage her to hurry.

The Karachi Zoological Gardens is less than a ten-minute walk from the Empress Market. Admission is listed as 10 pkr for adults and 5 pkr for children. Your daughter barely qualifies as a child and you are grateful to save 5 pkr. The man at the ticket booth passes you a photocopied map of the attractions on waterlogged paper that is fringed with black mold. He reminds you that you will need to return it at the end of your trip. The map smells of cigarette ash and as you pass beneath the gates you realize that everything carries the odor of ash. The zoo is heavy with fecal fumes and rot. Your daughter does not notice. Her eyes flit from path to path and you notice a thread of rose in the loom of her cheeks. She orients herself in respect to the map. She sickles her feet duckishly. You look down at your own. Your toes are yellowed with a thick coat of dust.

Where to?

The aviary, Papa, she says.

The domed bars of the aviary are painted a powder blue. You imagine that this is so the birds will believe they live in the sky. The birds squabble and squawk and catch their feathers in a vice of beak and beak and pull them taut to preen. You watch them tenderly and wish you could understand their language. You are convinced that they are speaking. You do not know the names of these birds or their native lands or any fact that you might impress your daughter with because the laminated letters on information signs are weather-beaten and worn. You can only be certain that the birds are an assortment of colors: yellow, red, ochre, purple. That their feathers alight with an oily sheen. Your daughter grips the side rail and leans as far forward as she can.

They'll bite off your nose, you warn.

No they won't.

I've seen it happen.

Quiet, Papa, she says.

A little ways up the path a man is selling colored sweets out of a cart. These sweets are specific to Karachi. A woman has poured the liquid syrup into molds in her kitchen for over thirty years and so far, as you can determine from the color, the recipe has not changed. You recall a tart taste time-blunted and roll its memory with your tongue. You look away. You look back. The man is dressed in a linen waistcoat soiled yellow at the armpits and belly. His arms are comically thin. You cannot nor have you ever been able to see the physical manifestation of sunshine, only its luminance, but as you study the man you come to appreciate his posture, the way he bends away from the light. You imagine a stalk of milk thistle held against a flame. You buy a handful of the sweets for your daughter. Fidda eats them greedily. She licks her fingers in careful succession. She shoves the sticky wrappers into your pockets. Her mouth is a rainbow that she wipes off onto her sleeve.

Your daughter leads you from the aviary, up a cobblestone walkway and to a white bridge traversing a pond. The bridge is clean and well maintained. The wooden planks groan beneath your weight. There are other children on the bridge, perhaps five, six years of age, all boys, and they throw handfuls of brown crusts at the ducks that swim in circles to avoid themselves. Your daughter lets go of your hand and for a moment you believe she is lost forever until something in the water captures her attention. She stops. You stop. You are startled by the ghost of a man standing at left of your daughter's shoulder. You realize your own reflection. Your daughter points to the gray, bloated bodies of fish hugging the shoreline. You are quiet. You are familiar with the dead fish at the harbor. You are at peace with the sight of their silver bodies frying on the afternoon pavement. But the sight of fish decaying in water unnerves you.

Are they dead? she asks.

Very.

The boys behind you break into laughter. You suspect that the laughter is at your expense. You have no reason to think this. You are reminded of your wife. She had laughed at your inability and taunted you with the name of the neighbor's young son, a boy who had only just grown into his underarm hairs. You could not understand the access point of her knowledge. That night she slept alone in the living room with her pillow and yours. Your daughter takes a candy wrapper out of your pocket and crumples it and throws it into the pond. She is surprised when it floats. You look back at the fish. You can still make out a bit of golden gill speckle.

I want to go home, Papa.

Why?

My stomach.

You're hungry?

No.

Then what?

I don't know. I feel sick.

Nauseated?

A little.

We should go see the fox woman.

In the palace?

Yes.

It costs extra.

We have 5 pkr.

The fox woman lives in an ivory palace at the far end of the zoo. There she reclines on a bed of polished mahogany and accepts visitors for 2 pkr apiece. A sign explains the fox woman was born thirty years ago in Africa to a Bedouin tribe. She is immortal and speaks every language in the world. She wears a hijab for the sake of modesty; she claims to be an honest woman. You are under no such illusion. You know that the fox woman is not actually a fox woman because fox women do not exist. Instead, the fox woman is a hired boy who paints himself with a woman's colors and fits on a hijab and sits below a platform and guides his head up through a hole cut into the wood. To the left of the hole the zookeeper stretches a twenty-year-old thinning fox pelt, fixed with levers that, when pulled, makes it jiggle in a way that is not at all lifelike.

Visitors greet the boy in Urdu, Sindhi, and Balochi. The boy dressed as a fox woman will answer appropriately. You first visited the fox woman when you were a teenager, and at the time it was unclear to you if the boy was a linguist. You tried to trick the boy into a mistake of speech but couldn't and the contradiction between his apparent youth and wisdom disturbed you. Even now, as the boy dressed as a fox woman greets your daughter in English, and then, at your request, Swedish, you search for hesitation in his lips. You cannot find any.

The boy's lips are very red. The lips of the women you've known have been shades of pink, peach, and pale vanilla, but never red. The boy's lips curve with a fullness unique to your expectations. A red circle rests painted between his eyebrows. You recall how your wife guarded a redness between her thighs; hers had been a wet, gaping thing. You and your wife discovered a mutual dissatisfaction with it; she claimed she was defective, but you suspected your own culpability. She suggested: treat me like a man. You refused, the very suggestion abhorrent. She threatened you with a frying pan but returned to the kitchen and set two handfuls of chicken dumplings into sizzling oil. The odor was nauseating and you could not eat. She reiterated after dinner: this is a mutual dissatisfaction. The next morning she left to live with her sister in another city. You wonder how she is doing. It is a passing thought and does more to upset you than to excite you. You feel warm. You look away. You look at your daughter. Her eyes are big acorns.

What do you eat? she asks the fox woman.

Cake, fruit, juice.

People, too?

Never.

Do you sleep here?

Yes.

Are you happy here?

This palace is very comfortable, says the fox woman. At night my master opens a hatch in the roof and lets the moon silver my fur. The temperature is always cool and never too warm. I am very blessed.

Your daughter grips the guardrails so tightly that her knuckles whiten. She bends forward, grinning a toothy grin, and her teeth are like that of an animal. The boy dressed as a fox woman pulls on a lever and the arms and legs and tail of his pelt jiggle. Your daughter squeals in delight. The noise upsets you. You wish you could smother it out of her. You notice a menstrual stain escaping her inner thigh. A moment passes. You recognize its boldness and you worry that others will see it, too, and that they will mistake her raw sex as a reflection of your own. You reach and tear off your daughter's hijab. She shrieks.

Papa.

You unfold it and shake it out like a blanket.

Papa.

You tie the hijab around her hips. Your daughter is weeping. Others look. Others are looking. You shield your eyes. You wonder: What am I doing, little Fidda? The boy dressed as a fox woman looks. The fox woman parts her lips. You hush your daughter. You hush your daughter Fidda and she begins to sob. Quiet, Fidda, you command. Oh, Fidda. You lead her outside of the ivory palace into the sunshine. The sunshine stings your eyes. You shrink.

Susan Taylor Chehak

FELICITY

There was a fire pit behind the trailer, in a circle dug into the ground and lined with stones. Tinder had been gathered from the woods that ran up the hill and over, toward the creek. These were branches downed by storms, lightning-struck trees, or just some clearing of brush that the farmer did. The real farmer, that is. The man who worked the land and lived in the real farmhouse. Not to be confused with my husband, who owned the land and worked in the city two hours away. It was our farm, but we lived like tenants in the trailer because mostly we weren't there. With the memorable exception of that summer, when I brought Del out of the city and Harry commuted to and from his office on the weekends. It was supposed to be a vacation, like summer camp, except we didn't go anywhere and there was only us: the farmer and his family in the house and me and my daughter in the trailer and my husband in his car, coming or going, depending on what day of the week it was.

We sat in camp chairs after dinner as it got dark, the three of us. A little family low to the ground, poking our sticks at the flames. Contemplating something. Drink in hand. Me in a blue cashmere coat because it was chilly even though it was summer. Or maybe I'm remembering it all wrong. Maybe it wasn't summer. Or anyway not high summer. June more likely. Early, when the weather was still unreliable and the true heat of the season hadn't yet come on.

My bare legs poked out from beneath the coat. I was wearing shorts, olive green, and a sheer white blouse and high-heeled sandals. I'd spent some time polishing my toenails, deep red. I'd made supper for us, too. Too fancy for the trailer kitchen where I had to cook it and the Formica table where I had to serve it. When a steak and a potato would have done just fine, I'd made instead a beef bourguignon. Meat from the cows that were raised on that farm. Not cows. Steers. The cows had the calves and the calves grew up to be steers and the steers were killed and cut up into the most gorgeous pieces of meat you've ever seen.

The trailer had two bedrooms, one in the middle and another at the back, with a very small bathroom in between. The walls were thin, so there wasn't much privacy. I suppose Del could hear our every word, cough, sneeze, fart, sigh. She must have known what we were up to in there, her father and me. This was before there was such a thing as headphones or portable music players. She only had that little radio, and she turned the volume up high so we had to listen to it, too.

The new calves were close, in the field on the other side of the fence. They crowded at the gate, bawling for their mothers, but there was nothing we could do to comfort them. It was all part of the plan, the farmer had explained: babies must be weaned.

The yard light by the main house popped on. We doused the fire and went inside our trailer. Me to my book. Harry to his bottle. Del to her radio and her bed.

I wonder now what in the world that other family must have thought of the three of us. The man was big, with white hair and a blue shirt and dirty jeans and boots. His wife was short and plump and rosy in a way that made you think you liked her, soft all over like a biscuit. There was a teenage son, too, and a baby. Some kind of afterthought, I guess, or maybe there had been a bit of tragedy in between.

One night they had some sort of crisis over there. I don't know what it was. Just that all the lights came on and the four of them spilled out of the house into the yard. The man first and then his wife with the baby in her arms, while the boy hung back in the doorway, a simple silhouette. There was an argument under the yard light, and they looked like puppets moving about. She was throwing wild punches. Their voices clashed and rose above the moaning of those calves. Then they all piled into the truck, the baby screaming like a little pig, and drove away.

I didn't hear them come back, but in the morning the truck was right there where it should have been, so maybe I'd imagined the whole thing, or dreamed it. Nothing was mentioned. I thought it would be rude to ask.

Harry and I didn't fight. We kept it civilized, cold and calm and private, just between us.

Moving to the city in the first place was supposed to be an adventure, but I never quite fell into it with the joy I might be able to bring to such a project now. Harry had worked hard to make it so, and then the farm was supposed to be a bonus, ice cream on the pie, a place to get away to. Why couldn't it have been a lake house? I wanted to know. Somewhere with other people at least. Instead of only cows and all that mess in the barn and that family in the house. Del didn't like it much, either. She was full of complaint and resentment, too old anymore to buy into her father's half-baked dreams. She'd be going off to college in the fall and she had reveries of her own.

We'd shopped around, looking at several farmhouses with land. Harry's idea, but I went along. There was money from somewhere. I didn't pay enough attention to know what or how. A death, maybe. An inheritance. I didn't have much energy then. Or willpower, either.

We looked at two places first. Both were very remote and isolated, in what seemed to be a completely different world from anything we were used to. An old couple still lived in one of the houses. They seemed sad to be leaving. The wife had her place all set up at a TV table in the living room. Her body was bigger than her chair. The other house was unoccupied and infused with a gentle yellow light. I loved it. The empty rooms seemed to hold a promise of some kind. Woods and a creek out back. A sunny room, with a pine floor and many windows, for Del. I could picture us there. And I wanted it. Ached for it. But there was a hog farm close by, and so in the end Harry nixed it.

Leaving our old neighborhood in the suburbs and moving into the city, from a house on a street to an apartment on a floor with a view, and then a farm, too, not just some country retreat but a real farm, with a trailer for a home—it was a change, to say the least. Harry insisted that what we had was really the best of both worlds. If you got tired of one, you could pack it up and switch over to the other. Which was better, the city or the farm? Which was worse? Each was lonesome in its own way. But the farm was also remote, and maybe that was why Harry put us there. Everything was new, and that was both terrifying and enthralling. An idyll at first, I guess, until Harry had to leave us, the Mercedes winking in the sunlight at the top of the long drive, then gone.

Del and I had no car of our own to use while we were there. I don't remember how it happened, but we must have planned it that way, and I must have agreed to the plan, though it does seem now, looking back, that it was a way for Harry to keep me, hold me there.

That day the wind picked up and blew my hair out of its 'do. I fought it with my hands and scurried inside the trailer. Del followed and found me in the bedroom pulling the whole mess up and twisting it into a hard knot at the back of my head, securing it there in a way that pulled my face tight. Red lipstick then. A touch of rouge. I was wearing pink capris and a yellow blouse and green flats. I had lovely feet then, long and smooth. The diamonds on my fingers, in my ears, at my throat, glittered. The wind rocked the trailer, and our eyes met in the mirror. There we were.

He called every afternoon at the same time to see how we were doing. Did we need anything? Was everything all right? There had been a storm in the night. I'd lain in the bed and listened to the thunder rolling off away from us, mighty and loud, as the lightning brightened the windows and the trailer shook and trembled on its blocks. The next morning the yard was mud. The cattle had moved away from the fences. The babies were huddled together in a corner, bawling.

I put on boots and tiptoed carefully, picking my way down the path to the farmer's house. Del followed but hung back. The boy answered our knock. He stood framed in the doorway—in his white T-shirt and blue jeans and bare feet. He held the screen open with his big hands and looked down at me, the hint of a smile on his face and a sweet little crumple in his brow to express his concern when I told him we were all right and to tell his mother so. I didn't want them to worry about us, I said. He looked up and past me at Del. I turned and she turned and together we picked our way back through the mud to our own yard and the trailer there.

When Harry's afternoon call came, I didn't mention the storm. Everything was fine, I said. We'd stayed inside all morning, playing cards and drinking tea. After I hung up, I made myself a drink and then that became the routine. His call was a signal: the day was done.

Two drinks and then I'd make dinner and after that Del and I would go outside into the yard to watch the sky go dim over the trees behind the farmer's house. And that was that.

I was a beauty then, and I took care of myself, no matter what the circumstance. Carefully applying makeup, though I didn't really need it, and curling my hair, styling it myself. I was good at all that. Moisturizing my skin. Polishing my nails. My body was a treasure, I believed. It was my most valuable asset, by far, and I carried it like a trophy for others to admire. I was a frail flower—my own description and only half ironic—so I counted on Del to be the strong one, the rock upon which I could rely. But mostly I left her alone, and that summer Del seemed to revel in the unexpected freedom, though she must have also been fighting off the loneliness that went with it, hand in hand. She'd been practicing all her life, and that summer she mastered it, being on her own. I pampered myself, read books, played cards, drank my gin, and slept, while Del wandered the farm and spied on the farmer and his family. The horses. The cows. The boy.

The calves cried for their mothers. Kittens played in the barn. It all seemed very safe, like something out of a storybook, really. We came upon an osprey by the creek, and he lifted up dragon-like and huge, scaring Del. My diamonds flashed in the sunlight. The horses roamed the pasture. I made us pancakes for dinner and grilled cheese for breakfast. I lay in the hammock, reading novels I'd found in a box in a closet in the trailer—big fat romances, with torn covers and flimsy pages, that I wouldn't have wanted anyone to know I read. Del and I took walks down to the creek. I found a round rock that I insisted she carry back. Maybe it's a geode, I said. We'll crack it open and inside we'll find a jeweled cave. You'll see. She didn't believe me and left it where it was.

There were wasps nesting in the gutters of the trailer. Watercress thrived in the wet manure at the bottom of the hill.

Pretty soon I couldn't remember anymore what we were doing there, and so when Del looked at me like that, fire in her eyes and her mouth curled up nasty in the corner, the pretty dimple that had charmed us all when she was a baby and then later as a girl toddling around and laughing at everything, clapping her hands and spinning with joy—now it was a sign of her resentment boiling up. This farm. The mud and the mess. She stopped brushing her hair, let it go all wild and wore those shorts—cutoff jeans with fringe and pinching her in private places—tugging at the hem. Also a big T-shirt, one of Harry's. She was small and so she swam in it. Tied it in a knot at her waist. Flopped around in sneakers, too. She was trash outside the trailer, lying on a plastic chaise, trying to get a suntan, swarmed by flies. And no, it did not take long for the farm boy to notice her. Or for her to see that this was just another way to get to me. I think I'll go down to the barn, Mom, to play with the kittens there. And didn't I know exactly what she was up to, following that boy, in his boots and his jeans and a torn T-shirt, too small for him—they should have traded, those two—and the next thing you know she's sitting on the fence and he's standing there, chewing on a length of straw, and now the dimple is flashing in her cheek in an altogether different way.

At first I thought I'd intervene. Good parent and all that. The woman in the doorway watched them, too. What did that boy dream of, I wondered. Staying put and taking over when the old man got too old and sick to tend to it all himself?

And in the book that I was reading, this girl named Felicity got herself into a bind with an older man, in a bar at the top of a building, with a view of the city spread out below, and she was still believing that everything that happened to her was like a dream come true. You knew from the way she touched her hair that before it was all over, she'd be dead.

And it would have gone on like that. Me in the hammock lost in someone else's story. Del inside the trailer, sleeping or eating or talking on the phone. Or slipping down to the barn to watch that boy at work. Or wandering around down at the creek, following the trails through the woods or across the pastures. Watercress sandwiches for lunch. Sweeping the steps and trying not to look beneath the trailer, not wanting to know what might be hidden there. The dogs running around the yard, chasing each other. Nothing wrong with it, any of it. Harry working in the city, and his Mercedes showing up at the top of the drive.

But then I got sick. Whatever it was, I don't know. Cow shit on the watercress, maybe. Or just an ordinary flu bug. Me locked in the bathroom, letting everything go, then padding back to my bed to languish there. The fan in the window, turning. Del doing her best: warm water and a wet cloth. She'd learned her mothering from me, but I only got worse. When Harry called, he told her to go down to the farmhouse and knock on the door and ask the family there for help.

The yard light was as bright as a full moon and the boy was a silhouette in the doorway, calling to his mom. The dogs barked and a cat twined at her ankles. The farmer was asleep in his chair, whiskey bottle at his feet.

I don't know. I saw none of this, of course. But I have a memory of it anyway. Del, fiddling with her hair, her voice so low she has to say it twice. "My mother's sick." The woman follows her back to the trailer and on inside to my bedroom. She stands over me, considering, then pulls me to my feet and walks me outside to the truck, where the boy waits.

He drives me straight to the hospital in town. I have the cashmere coat on over my good silk nightie and a pair of pretty sandals on my feet. If you didn't know I was sick, you wouldn't know. The nurse has dark hair and a mole on her chin. Someone must have told her she was beautiful once.

It wasn't serious. I wasn't going to die. Dehydration, they said, and gave me a shot. Some pills. Firm instructions.

He was waiting in the truck. His mouth was tight. The cab stank of sweat and mud and boots. Logs rolled loose in the bed. When all the lights were behind us, I told him to pull over. And when he did, I moved in close and kissed him. "You will not touch her," I said. And "Go on then. It's all right. It's fine. Touch me instead."

When we got back to the trailer, all the lights were out. The calves wailed by the gate and their silent mothers huddled helplessly in the field beyond the barn. I covered my ears and wanted to scream but held it back and let him set me down on the sofa like I was a precious china plate or a crystal figure all aglitter on a shelf in the sun. Del emerged from the back, rubbing her eyes. He didn't return her smile. She fixed a glass of lemonade and my cigarettes and an ashtray and turned on the TV and brought me my book to read. And water and another pill and an aspirin and then some toast to nibble on and a box of crackers. She called Harry and told him what had happened and that I was all right.

I fell asleep there on the couch, and she didn't even move me to my bed. But later I heard the door squeak and her footsteps on the gravel, crunching, and I guessed she'd gone out into the night to meet the boy, but by then I was just too worn out and tired to go have a look. Anyway, I knew he wouldn't be there.

The cicadas droned in the twilight. The sky was spangled with stars and the bright moon illuminated the heaving backs of the cows in the field pressing against the fence.

In the morning I saw what she'd done: opened the gate and let the babies go.

The farmer and the boy had a real time of it, getting the calves back where they belonged. There was plenty of yelling and cursing, along with Del out there crying in the yard. What did she think? They'd leave them be? That she could somehow change the way things go?

Harry's Mercedes was winking in the sunlight at the top of the drive. He built a fire in the pit again. We sat up late, poking at the ashes and staring at the flames. Del didn't join us. She was inside the trailer, curled up on her bed, all alone. We let her be.

In the morning we packed up to go with Harry, back to the city where we knew we all belonged. He wore a dark suit, white shirt, blue tie. I had on a yellow dress, a sheer green scarf, lipstick, and heels.

The farm family had gathered on their front porch to see us off. The calves were gone. Their mothers wandered the pastures looking for them. The creek ran clear. The osprey soared overhead. Del stood in the grass and scowled. Harry took me in his arms. There wasn't any music, but anyway, we danced.

Sarah Browning

THE FORT

He is small, not a man.
Not even a young man.
He is a boy. He knocks
one sister down in the
tall grass. *I'm going*

to have you, he tells
the girl lying silent
at his feet. *Have you
and then burn you*.
In the fort the sisters

built two blocks
from home. *Go get
matches*, he tells the
other sister. Boulder chair,
boulder TV. Chipped plate

from home. Bent spoon.
Run and go get matches.
He is small. Not a man.
The sisters silent, the
younger runs toward

home as if toward matches,
calls at last to the men
on the porch. But she left
her sister in the tall grasses.
She left her there, in the grass.

Sarah Browning

GRATITUDE CHALLENGE

1. Tequila: sharp kick into oblivion

2. Cigarettes: ratching pull on the lungs, breathless on the escalator

3. Envy: green canopy over the generally generous heart

4. Vodka: cool, indifferent; colonizes bloodstream

5. Sloth [insert arresting image here]

6. Bourbon: wintry interior

7. Cynicism: this list, Q.E.D.

8. Despair: take me, flay me, lay me on the couch

9. Self-loathing: after #8, above

10. Prosecco: haha in a bottle

11. Contempt: *strivers, whiners, entitled little twerps*

12. Gin: juniper juju

13. Shame: this body, ungrateful

Sarah Browning

A Christmas Story I Want to Tell You

That time in high school, when, after
caroling, Roy Reynolds and I offered

ourselves to make the egg nog. The other
boy and my sister stayed in the living room,

regaled Roy's parents with caroling tales,
families inviting us in for fruitcake and punch.

How Roy and I went straight for the pantry
and kissed, how good Roy tasted. We found

a cookbook, then, and began to beat the eggs.
How next, the nog half made, the whites not

yet stiff, we lunged back into the pantry
to grind our untried hips hard against

each other. Eggnog is long in the making,
so no one raised an eyebrow when at last

we entered, bearing the bowl high, bourbon
and brandy redolent of our kisses.

Or maybe we smooched just a short time
in Roy Reynolds' dark pantry, Christmas,

1979—one evening out of all those
awkward years just sweet and hot, illicit

with nutmeg and milk. And I want to give
it to you, this story, my lust, how it was,

that once, free from worry and shame.
How it might be, again.

Alex M. Frankel

WHAT A SAN FRANZISKO LIFE

My Giannini, near the sea and the seagulls, the fog and the foghorns, and the fog-drenched, fog-dripping Monterey cypresses! A.P. Giannini Junior High—it's a few blocks from Ocean Beach, which on most days resembles a dying British resort instead of what people commonly think of as upbeat California. Not long ago I went back to the old neighborhood. As I walked by my alma mater, I wanted to go back in time, transplant my middle-aged mind into my pubescing body, see if I could stand up to the bad boys and maybe even become popular. How did I survive there for three years? The school was like a gigantic snake coiled up in the heart of the Sunset District, ready to rise and wreak havoc on the Sunset and then the world. And children passed through that snake and somehow emerged from its innards, but we could never get the stink out of our systems.

While my peers inhabited the well-known coastal city of San Francisco, I existed with my parents in the forlorn German-Jewish city of San Franzisko. I was fourteen, tall, awkward, shy, greasy. Ninth grade started (the last year of junior high), and Mrs. Palmer assigned me a desk in the back of her class.

Lorraine Palmer had been employed at Giannini since about 1944. She had scarce hair, colored brown and held down with an abundance of pungent spray. She wore thick glasses lightly powdered with an intriguing white substance. Sometimes, when she lectured on history, she put one hand on her hip and scratched her scalp with the other while gazing out the window at the immense expanse of schoolyard; this was her harried-public-school-social-studies-teacher-no-nonsense pose. Whenever people hear I come from San Franzisko, they think of Telegraph Hill, cable cars, the Golden Gate Bridge, and ask me why I left. Whenever I think of San Franzisko, one of my first thoughts is of Mrs. Palmer and her social studies class. She especially loved the Chinese boys and girls: "I love you!" she'd say, or "You're beautiful!" Because I sat near the back, I had Fry right behind me. He was allied with Kevin and Chuck nearby. I usually couldn't pay much attention to Mrs. Palmer because Fry, a tall boy, kept poking me in the back. One day he called to his friends (in the middle of Mrs. Palmer's lecture), "He's got this big zit on his ear and it's about to bust!" I felt a flick of his middle finger on my earlobe and heard Kevin and Chuck laugh. The pimple burst overnight, and the next day I had a Band-Aid on the wound, and still he flicked his finger at it and reported everything he did to his friends. My acne had gotten worse. It was especially bad around the neck and earlobes. Mrs. Palmer was lecturing about the Russian Revolution, and suddenly she asked me to repeat the point she'd just made. I couldn't, because I was trying to fend off the blows from Fry and control the snickering of Kevin and Chuck. She shook her head and the Chinese students turned around and stared at me. I was already in her bad books for failing the quiz on Ethiopia. I went home, where I inspected my face, a sick mess of pimples that had recently burst, ones about to burst, and ones still in the making. Beyond them I had big, ominous raised areas—potentially mammoth pimples—that could rarely get to the point I could successfully squeeze and heal them.

I was already counting days until graduation. Soon I'd be, Gott willing, moving on to Lowell High (the "academic" school), a halcyon world of high windows, sunlight, freshly mowed lawns.

Mrs. Palmer must have had good reasons when, a few weeks after the bursting of the earlobe pimple, I was placed together with Fry, Kevin, and Chuck at the start of our field trip to the Japanese Cultural Center. We didn't take a traditional yellow school bus but went in private cars chauffeured by teachers and staff. I sat in the front seat of a car driven by a lady I didn't know, accompanied by Fry, Kevin, and Chuck in the backseat.

The lady at the wheel chattered away and didn't seem to notice how badly Fry was jabbing at my neck. Halfway to Japantown she got lost and left us to ask for directions at a gas station. The jabbing got worse. Fry, Kevin, and Chuck knew how to hit, knew where it hurt, and I heard the usual terms: faggot, fag, sissyfag, queer, queerbait. With our chaperone gone, the three built up the hitting and the bad words like the crescendo of a fireworks show.

I still have my A.P. Giannini yearbook. I can see pictures of the three of them. Fry was tall and oafish, Chuck an urchin who couldn't stop squirming, Kevin freckled and boorish. At the time I could hardly see them as individuals, just a three-headed hellhound, but now I look more carefully at Kevin's picture: Under the long seventies haircut, his face at first looks "gayer" than anyone else in that school. But this may be because he was told by the photographer to smile; it's what they call a "Pan-Am smile": curled lips, but nothing happening in the cheeks, and the eyes unnarrowed and uninvolved. A manufactured smile. I cover Kevin's lower face with a bookmark: no hint of a smile. I have to move the bookmark far down almost to the lips to see where the small smile attempt begins. I once again cover the whole face except the eyes, which are so grim I would never guess that he was trying to appear pleasant. Then I search for him on the World Wide Web and find out he went on to Lincoln High. His graduation picture there— yes, the whole yearbook is online!—shows a smile just as fake as the one from junior high, and thin, severe lips (thinner, more severe than mine). Under his name we can see the caption: "To own a profitable business and fly down the highway in my Porsche Turbo." Kevin was the meanest and the worst of the three. I look again at just the eyes. Dour, unforgiving eyes.

It was San Franzisko and it was the Sunset District in the seventies: All the races and religions and ethnicities you could think of were found in my chaotic A.P. Giannini Junior High. Some last names from a single homeroom in the yearbook: Tablan, Wong, Mendoza, Drocco, Tso, Miller, Schunck, Mafarreh, Dean, Cueva, Takeyama, Yu, Li. And yet all the boys behind me were white. Whites seemed capable of an extra level of malice.

"He thinks he's cool cuz he's riding with us!" said Chuck.

"Marcel, what a name for a fag!" observed Kevin.

"Check out the zits on his neck," Fry said.

"I saw him in the locker room yesterday," said Kevin. "He has one muscle on his whole entire body!"

Chuck laughed. "He walks alone in the yard at recess scratching his asshole and humming to himself!"

Were Fry, Kevin, and Chuck real? Was Mrs. Palmer real? Sometimes I wondered if all of "life" wasn't just an ambitious scientific study—of *me*. Maybe NASA-like technicians had my image up on some huge screen, where they probed my reactions to sorrow and joy.

In Japantown I wandered around in the wind, peering into restaurants and souvenir shops. Only seventy-four more days till the end of Giannini! Then I heard the Noon Sirens—like a motorcycle tearing along the freeway, only a more sustained wail. Tuesday twelve o'clock! San Franziskans have known that siren call since World War II and will know it for generations to come. It doesn't mean the Japanese or the Russians are minutes away with their bombs and missiles; it means the plush comforts of home, a dog wagging its tail, soft-boiled eggs, muffled gramophone records, fog, school, Mami and Deddi, wind rustling through leaves on a rare sunny day.

Mrs. Palmer chose a few of her favorite Chinese students and introduced them to the pleasures of hibachi steak. As she left the restaurant, looking pleased with her meal and the company she kept, I worked up the courage to approach her. "Is there anything you can do?" I asked. "Please, may I go in a different car?"

Lorraine Palmer: I've Googled her and discovered that she died some years ago, in her eighties. Decades of dedication to Giannini but, besides the obituary, there is no mention of her. I knew, though, that she came out of the forties and fifties. That was her era. She knew her history, knew her constitution, knew how to write a quiz and score it.

"Please, may I go in a different car?" I asked. "Fry and his friends won't leave me in peace."

My teacher, a moment ago so full and happy after her hibachi meal, looked exasperated. I noticed the white particles on her glasses and again wondered what they could be. Dandruff? Probably, but she never seemed to wipe those glasses clean. Mrs. Palmer scowled, placed her hands on her hips. I can still see her face as if it were right in front of me. It was a strict little face that knew what it wanted in life, knew what it liked and what it didn't. By that age I was already tall, but I keep visualizing her talking down to me as if I'd been little.

My Mrs. Palmer—it would have been so easy for her to help me, but she had no time. It is strange: Math was always my worst subject, but I never get bad dreams about it, only history, social studies, English. In these dreams I'm always near graduation but without the credits that I need to finally get the diploma. There's some assignment that's slipped my mind, some exam I forgot to study for. I don't want anyone to think that my Mrs. Palmer was a bad teacher. Our textbook looked imposing and felt heavy in my briefcase, but it was elegantly written; she lectured effectively, and I was learning. I seemed to be heading for a B or B-. But I can't stop remembering all the praise she lavished on the Chinese boys and girls (especially the boys), whom she arranged in the front rows. I can't help remembering the angry, strict look on her face that she went through most of life with. I can't help remembering the dyed hair and sagging face and ascetically schoolmarmish wardrobe. She looked down at me and scowled. Didn't she know about my perfect dog and my protective parents? Hadn't anyone told her about my successful, splendid bar mitzvah? Hadn't anyone told her about my luxurious room, with its tigerskin rug and seven unique clocks and maps of Paris and reproductions of masterworks by Renoir and Degas? My Mami told me, "If anyone bothers you, report him to the teacher." But you wouldn't help, Mrs. Palmer, when you so easily could have reprimanded the unkind boys or put me in a better car. You weren't a bad teacher, and I don't want anyone to think so. On our first day in class, you gave us an essay prompt: "Communication Is the Key to Understanding." I went home and tackled the project with dumb gusto; next day I submitted my best ideas and prettiest handwriting. As soon as we turned the papers in, you took the batch and, maybe based on penmanship alone, chose my essay to share with the whole class. But as you read, I saw disappointment begin to cloud over your face. Even the first sentences seemed a bit off: "I was walking through a zoo in Israel when a sweaty young man came up to me and said *mayim* which means water. I was able to point to the drinking fountain because I know a few words of Hebrew. Yes, communication may well be the key to understanding …." But my words didn't seem to sit well with you, and some of my peers were already snickering. I think we got off to a bad start, Mrs. Palmer. What happened? You stared at me from your teacher height. You could have so easily used your power to put me in a different car. Instead, you turned and walked away, shaking your head. You said something sharp and disapproving—it contained an exasperated "should!" or "ought!" or "must!"—but you were in such a rush to get away from me that you spoke already with your back turned, and I couldn't catch the words.

The ride back to Giannini was worse.

The lady teacher I didn't know—a short, plump person a few years younger than Palmer—seemed unaware anything was the matter. She went on about Japantown: the shops, the food, the authentic Japanese architecture, the clean, helpful clerks. She went on about her love of Giannini and particularly Group One. I was part of that group, the "gifted" group, though most of us were not in the least gifted. I still don't know what hidden administrator or bureaucrat put me in that group for my last year of junior high, and I don't know why. Who makes those decisions, and what do they mean? And then they affect your whole life. Seventh grade I belonged to Group Five, eighth grade to Group Three. Why these changes? Giannini had fourteen groups altogether, and by the twelfth, thirteenth, and fourteenth group, no one seemed to care about the kids anymore. In Fourteen over half the students were black. In my group just under half were Chinese. The two cohorts never talked. Group One was nurtured, praised, encouraged, allowed an occasional field trip. Group Fourteen was patrolled by employees who were just glorified security guards. And this apartheid would continue: The boys and girls with great grades were bound for Lowell High; the riffraff ended up at Abraham Lincoln High School, not much better than the county jail. But soon I was leaving, soon I'd be going on to Lowell, where they based admission on a points system. The highest possible number was forty-eight, but the cutoff to get in varied from year to year: Sometimes it dipped to a low of forty or forty-one, or rose to a high of forty-four. I had forty-two points. Soon I was leaving Giannini forever, but what was going to happen to me if I didn't make Lowell?

"Did you see how cute?" said the nameless lady as she drove. "The way they bow to each other? The Chinese don't bow, you know. I'm so jealous of their skin—I heard Orientals have an extra layer!" The boys snickered and the lady chattered. And then of course she got us lost again and left to ask for directions.

Fag, zit-face, goon, freak. Fingers and keys in my neck from all three of the boys in back, and laughter. Mrs. Palmer, please help! But she is far away. She can't help.

"I wonder how he ended up with that name!"

"See him trying to play basketball yesterday at recess?"

"Look at that shirt, he dresses like a old man!"

"Don't get close, his hair stinks!"

"Why does your hair stink?"

"What's with the accent? Why's he trying to sound like the Queen of England?"

"He never uses the shower after P.E. He's afraid we'll see him with a hard-on!"

"I bet he's got a hard-on now from sitting close to us!"

"You got a hard-on, faggot?"

"You ever seen his parents? They're like grandparents—it's gross!"

"Why is he even in our group?"

"You got a hard-on, faggot? I asked you a question!"

"Ever watch him in algebra? He just stares out the window. He's fucking dumber than we are."

"Look me in the eye, fag. I'm talking to you!"

I don't know why I brought along my big brown briefcase that day. I must have forgotten about the field trip. I had it stored between my legs. Suddenly I grabbed our social studies book and turned around and looked Kevin Svensson in the eye and with both my hands brought the big book down on his face. I couldn't help myself: It was just automatic and unthinking, a rage to destroy life. I've felt it only a few times, quick, overwhelming, ecstatic. He let out a little yelp like a puppy when you accidentally step on its paw. He covered his forehead. I'd gotten him above the left eye.

The others went quiet, stared at Kevin and then at me and then back at him. When he lowered his hands, we saw a swollen redness half the size of a strawberry above the eye. I turned around and I looked straight ahead, panicked. Oh my Gott, you couldn't see much of that eye anymore! What if …? Should I apologize? Pray? Run to a phone booth? Run away?

"Does it hurt?" Fry asked.

"Not really—*you* know," said Kevin, trying to laugh it off. "It kinda does."

"What'd you do that for, fairy?" said Chuck.

The lady I didn't know got her directions and returned to the car and drove us back to Giannini. Kevin did not advertise his wound, and the lady didn't notice. I still felt Fry's bumping on my back, but less. Now bumps came half-hearted. At the end of the trip, the three just scattered in different directions, with Kevin probably going home, or going somewhere, to nurse the hurt I'd inflicted.

I walked home and faced the medicine cabinet mirror. I was tall, sweaty, weak in front of that mirror. My mother was smoking and chatting on the phone in German. Another afternoon in the Sunset of the 1970s. Except that I'd just disfigured Kevin Svensson. Would I be summoned to the principal's office tomorrow? Would Fry and his friends be waiting for me before or after school? I hated the way school days and home days battered me. Why did they have to be this bad? Others seemed to be doing all right, looked content, looked as if their faces had reasons to be doing genuine smiles—for example: the quick, popular learners who sat in the front rows of Palmer's class.

That year my father sold his '59 Studebaker and bought a used Jaguar that was never to lose its potent new car smell. That year we began to attend the opera on Saturday nights, instead of formal Tuesdays, because no one had to be up early on Sundays. That year my mother opened the front door a crack and our terrier, Terry, who must have been planning his escape for years, ran between her legs and was run over by a truck. He wasn't dead. We took him to the emergency vet and, since it was Saturday, arrived at the opera just in time to hear the opening bars of *Il Trovatore*. I cried and slept and cried in my middling orchestra seat. Terry survived with a limp, which soon disappeared; he lived until old age. That year the cleaning woman came in twice a week; my grandmother visited on Sundays; the spiderwebs proliferated in our back yard, and the fog rolled in at the start of the summer and stayed put for months. We were lucky if we got a bit of wind and sunshine in September before the rainy season began. That year (or a year like it), I gave up watching TV but heard from my room as my parents watched the seventies go by in their den. I didn't sit with them, but I heard the blare of tacky saxophone solos and trumpets from endless sitcoms and crime dramas on our old RCA solid-state TV. My Mami and Deddi had survived the Holocaust and overcome statelessness and poverty only to find themselves, in their fifties, lounging in faux-leather recliners contemplating *Charlie's Angels*.

A few days after the field trip to Japantown, one of Giannini's administrators, a heavy little man with a car salesman look of dress shirt, tie, and no jacket, walked into social studies armed with a list. The cutoff for Lowell High had been forty-three points. Out loud he read the names of boys and girls accepted by the "academic" institution. Because of my recent D+ in algebra, "Frankel" did not appear: I was going to be sent to Lincoln, along with Fry, Kevin, and Chuck. People clapped when they heard their own names had made it on the list. Relief and jubilation swept through the smart rows like a warm wave.

Marcia LeBeau

Why I Skipped
My Poetry Workshop
for Blow-Drying Boot Camp

No one is dying for lack of what is found
at the Anthony Garubo Salon on Maplewood Avenue.

Wine and cheese and a free hair product are offered.
This does not happen at the Paterson Public Library.

In comfy swivel chairs, the torque of the ultimate blow-dryer
is discussed, not the merits of the latest literary journal.

Alligator clips are being passed around, not a single sharp-
toothed barb. All the hot air in the salon has a purpose.

Looking in the mirror at our strawberry-scented wet hair,
none of us pretend we know what we're doing.

I'm feeling called to take on aching arms and burnt scalp
instead of writer's cramp. My goal: round-brushing

my hair into stick-straight submission. A submission
I accept without hesitation.

Marcia LeBeau

A Car Called Poem

I know a poet who named his car Poem.
When he asked, "Don't you love my little Poem?"
his friends would rack their brains trying to think
of the last thing he had written and if it indeed
was short and if it was any good, for that matter.
And there would be an awkward silence as the Poem
passenger was trying to figure this out, whereupon the poet
would start feeling quite melancholy, first about his car
and then about his latest piece that was in fact quite long
and wasn't really getting much traction in the poetry world.
This is how he began to think it was time to take a different
route with his work altogether. Not that anyone would notice
or care, but he simply needed to feel better about his oeuvre.
Yes, he thought, time to go short and sweet. He might just park Poem
at the local Walmart and write with the radio cranked
while tired, overwrought shoppers walked by peering briefly
at the loud shaking car, but ultimately not really caring
what was going on inside, since they had dry rods of spaghetti
at home waiting to be boiled.

Tricia Asklar

DROP DAY

The small spice bowl with chili powder,
cumin, crushed red pepper and sea salt
slips out of my hand. I already know
this will happen. The woman at the grocery

drops her coupon book. "It's a drop day,"
she sighs. The cashier drops stickers
from the promotional giveaway, the pet
store shopper drops a credit card.

"It's my back," she says. "Can you reach
that?" And I do. All day. People drop
and drop. The day of the Paris attacks,
we're unhinged before we know the rest

of the story. The black beans simmer
with kombu. I've cut the kabocha
and wait to sauté onions and garlic,
to add tomatoes, mirin, and miso.

I pick up the spices I stirred together
ten minutes before, not to include,
but to move them closer to the pot.
The next thing the steel bowl chimes

against the tile, my socks blanketed
in dark red. The floor, too.
The dust spreads,
sifts and separates,

like atoms, like falling leaves,
like the spray of casings—
all of those containers
that bind powder.

Michael Don

FOREVER TWENTY-TWO

Because we had been printing and pooping a lot, we were low on ink and toilet paper. We weren't actually all that low, but we were feeling antsy, like we hadn't been out of the house in days, though just two hours ago all four of us went on a seven-mile run. We ran together every morning to activate endorphin production, to encourage the digested to exit our bodies, and most importantly to build morale both as housemates and coworkers.

We raced down three flights of stairs and out of our apartment building. AJ, our Director of Human Resources, pulled a fifty-dollar street-sweeping ticket off the windshield of his little Acura sports car, crumpled it up, and flung it into the street. "Sweep that," he said. We crammed into his vehicle and sped over to Target, our knees touching, our heads pushing against ceiling.

In the store we split into pairs. AJ went with Frog, our Director of Acquisitions and the only one of us with a six-figure college loan, to acquire ink, and I, our Director of Operations, went with Gabe, our Director of Communications, to procure toilet paper.

When we reconvened at checkout, Frog grinned and placed a silver library bell on the conveyor belt.

"Another impulse buy?" I said. We had been buying a lot of silly appliances: a bottle opener with GPS, a digital clock that looked like a banana, a waffle iron in the shape of Massachusetts. We figured in the near future we'd be in the black.

"This one was well thought out," AJ assured us. "Frog has a plan."

"What about our budget? Who's in charge of our budget?" I said.

"Gabe?" AJ said, looking at Gabe.

"Gabe?" I said.

"A bell can do many things," Gabe said. He hated getting into it with Frog. We all did. "Probably worth the investment," he added.

When we moved in together, we signed a contract promising not to apply for outside jobs in the first six months; we would remain patient and together we would succeed or fail just like we did as teammates on our college swim team. Our company—Twenty-Two Thingvalla Ave.—was only in its first month of existence, though we already had a few promising business ideas. First, a website called *pleasesendusonedollar.com*. If enough people were willing to send us one dollar we could have a very respectable income with very low overhead. Then came *pleasesendusonemilliondollars.com*. The beauty of this business model was that we'd only need one client every five years or so. Another idea was to send random invoices to big companies. Surely we'd slip through the cracks every so often. We considered creating a website that gave sex advice and reviewed sex toys, though none of us were particularly good at sex, nor were we having sex. We had made a no-dating pact that wouldn't expire until the company earned its first one hundred dollars. In two weeks we would have a company-wide meeting laying out all our ideas and voting on which business model we would grab by the horns and ride into the land of profitability.

When we got back to the apartment Gabe took the toilet paper into the bathroom and Frog set the bell down on the kitchen table. Then we went into our respective offices, which were also our bedrooms, and buckled down.

Just a month ago we graduated from a fine university a few miles down the road. Our mascot was an elephant named Jumbo, which we took pretty seriously. If it weren't for Jumbo we wouldn't have these really cool T-shirts with a print of a baby blue elephant eating from an acacia tree. On the cold misty day that was our graduation, we were lauded by the President of Greece. He said we were some of the brightest and most talented twenty-two-year-olds in the country and that this meant we'd be presented with opportunities to use our education selfishly and unethically but at all costs should refrain from succumbing to such temptations, and in turn make contributions that will improve the lives of others, not just our own lives. We heard the president loud and clear and wanted to do exactly as he instructed, but we had loans that weren't going to pay themselves, and our degrees were in philosophy, sociology, religious studies, and art history.

☾

The next day I woke to the ding of the bell and Frog announcing that he'd moved his bowels. I rolled out of bed and loped into the kitchen.

"What time is it?" I said, squinting.

"6:47," Frog said, looking up at our new banana clock.

"Then it's back to bed," I said. "See you at eight for the run."

Frog dropped to the floor and did a series of crunches, then popped up, dinged the bell, and announced, "Ten crunches." He flashed his big childish Frog grin, the one that usually meant he'd woken up feeling hopeful, on the verge of catching a break.

Frog had turned down full scholarships for swimming to various Division I schools so that he could become a Jumbo. No one in his family had ever attended a private university. His parents, who dropped out of college when Frog was born, were skeptical of the cost of his degree in relation to its real-world value and had all but told him not to bother returning home until he gave up his elitist lifestyle. Frog became Frog because of his freakish talent in the breaststroke; we'd never seen such springy, powerful, lean, agile legs. And because he rarely responded if we called him Nathan. AJ, Gabe, and I all had some family cushioning and could afford to flake it up for a few months. There weren't many jobs available for us liberal-arters, but we figured we were smart enough and creative enough to create our own. Hadn't the President of Greece said exactly that?

I was working out the details of a theme-party company. We would take a van full of decorations and props to the customers' apartment or fraternity and set it all up. I was imagining a locker-room-themed party when I heard the bell ding, followed by Frog announcing he successfully purchased the domain name *22thangvala*.com, we of course already owned *22thingvala.com*. An hour later, another ding and AJ announced he posted an ad on Craigslist for a Twenty-Two Thingvala Ave. unpaid internship. Later in the day, Gabe sounded the bell for designing an invitation to a banquet in three months where we would divulge our quarterly numbers. Frog hit it again for a bowel movement and I finally got in on the action for creating a flowchart of our workflow.

We continued on like this, dinging the bell for our runs, our bowel movements, for washing our hair with shampoo, downloading a new pump-up song, adding to our business ideas Google Doc, anything the bell-dinger considered productive. All the dinging had Frog in an excellent mood, which had all of us in an excellent mood. We felt light and fast on our runs, we were eating healthy, and we were growing our list of feasible business ideas, some of which the President of Greece would have approved.

One afternoon I paused outside Frog' office while he was on the phone and I listened to him declare that in a few months he'd be putting dents in those loans and in a year he'd return home with a big surprise. I shook my head and exhaled, then proceeded to the bathroom where a half-sheet of notebook paper Scotch-taped to the mirror read, *All employees must wash hands before returning to work.*

A day before the big meeting in honor of defining our company's mission, Gabe squealed from his office, then called an impromptu company-wide meeting. We were all dressed in our brown work slacks and Jumbo the Elephant T-shirts. "We're like a family," Gabe started off. "No, fuck it, we are family. We've known each other for, what, almost four years now? And we've been through a lot, right? The good: Montreal, a conference championship, the hot seat, the Swinging Johnsons, Taco Tuesdays, Wine Wednesdays, Poor Life Decision Mondays. And the bad: breakups, shoulder injuries, shrunken Jumbo T-shirts, last place at NESCACS our freshman year. And through it all we've treated each other like brothers. Never afraid to say you're being a dick or I love you. Well, you guys are dicks and I love you very much and I got a job. I'm giving my two-weeks notice. I love you guys."

We didn't know Gabe had been applying for jobs, but it turned out we all had been applying for jobs. All of us but Frog. AJ and I got up and shook Gabe's hand. Then we hugged him. We were feeling hopeful. If Gabe, the Art History major, could land a gig, our time would come soon.

"We'll get the paperwork sorted out tomorrow," AJ said.

Grinning wide, Gabe went over to the bell, pressed down on it, and called out, "Got a real job!"

Frog followed Gabe into the kitchen, picked up the bell, trotted into my office, which looked out over Thingvalla, lifted a window, and hurled the bell into the street. Before it bounced and then skidded along the asphalt, we heard it ding.

"Threw the productivity bell out the window," Frog announced.

"Asshole!" Someone called up from the street.

Frog came into the kitchen, pulled the banana clock off the wall, and smashed it on the floor. He took a deep breath, then looked at Gabe and muttered, "Thank you."

We made a circle and put our arms around each other. Silently, we swayed back and forth. We went on like this until someone's phone rang and we decided it was time to get back to work.

Gary Joshua Garrison

NEGATIVES

1.

We saw the wreck outside of Ernakulam, Roger and me, on a twisting highway that led to the mountains.

We'd been driving for most of the morning, or since the early afternoon. They were the kinds of roads that buttered your brain: quick and claustrophobic with trees, everything blurring by so fast it's impossible to focus on anything but the pink of your jaw reflected in the window.

It's generous to even call it a road, Roger said.

I marveled at the jungle. The green and overrun. A civilization squirming in the roots and press of progression.

It's like Eugene, Roger said, *or the place where they filmed Star Wars*.

It was around then when we saw it. The car wrapped around the stay of a hulking tree. As we came up on it our driver honked and I winced at the urgency of the sound. The two men beside the car looked over slowly, to our small sedan, and did nothing but watch us pass, their faces pained and smeared and streaking to memory. The whole scene—the men with their hands on their hips, looking over from their smoking wreck, with its metal nose socked to a U around that tree—from curtain to curtain, lasted for a breath, for the short burst of our horn, and was over.

That was outside of Ernakulam somewhere, but not past Munnar, amid a hundred thousand square miles of green and overrun.

2.

What I'm getting at is that I can't help but think of the children. All along that stretch of jungle road we passed busloads of them.

There were men and women too. But what I saw was the children, their bodies commas from bus windows and mixed among the luggage on the roof, waving, laughing.

On a ferry to Fort Cochin we watched a barefoot boy dangle out over the water to run his fingers through the wake.

It's like a fucking bomb shelter, Roger said of the ferry, running his hand along the corrugated steel shutters that pulled down over the glassless windows.

I said, *Maybe like a tank that floats.*

And he said, *No, like a bomb shelter that floats. And that kid will be vaporized in the fireball. That'll make him important. He'll be burned to a shadow on the hull. Like a negative.*

That's terrible, I said.

Nah, Roger said, chewing at his lip, *cause he'll be forever like that.*

3.

Outside of Prague we woke on a train. Roger peeked his head out the window and whispered, *It's like West Virginia.*

I liked to tell him his head was too full for anything to be new.

For him, the south of France was like the Canadian Rockies. Jakarta like Bangkok. Dutch like English; the Mississippi just the Nile with trees; my new apartment like his grandfather's after the divorce with fewer model trains; everything like something, like a movie he barely remembered, like a place he'd never been, like the space between his mother's breasts.

Eventually, I cornered him in a cafe some place unimportant.

What's the point if it's all the same? I asked.

Listen, he said, *we're all just looking for our fireball.*

So I loaned him some money so he could hop a train to the World's Fair. Later, he'd tell me his weekend there was like the year we dropped acid in the damp-earth basement of my sister's townhouse.

4.

What I'm getting at is that I learned something.

I learned that one car against a tree and one car flying past, safe, is a busload of children thrown from a small cliff. The slightest glance from across a bar is a heart overrun, a small and undeniable love.

I haven't figured out the math of it yet.

But by the time I got home from Kerala I was telling strangers that I'd seen a school bus flip longways into the jungle. And I'm not wrong. There are piles of child bodies. There are mountains of the devastated. War happens. A bus of children toppled from the road. Why wasn't I there to see it? What's the difference if I feel the horror of the witness in some lonely corner of my chest?

The fingers of warm sympathy over my wrist. Isn't everyone in love with me somehow?

Aren't we all just negatives? Aren't we all just waiting for our fireball?

5.

Years later Roger and I are having drinks with women we have known for decades. We are at a bar, in the town we grew up in. And the woman who is the one who used to love me turns to Roger and says, *Does it still haunt you?*

She means the child bodies.

The ones I made myself a victim out of. The ones who gave me sympathy and sex and so many small undeniable loves.

Roger looks to me and sighs, heavy and exhausted. There are gray hairs around our ears now and pains behind our eyes and in our knees. The woman who is the one who used to love me is drunk and her fingers are loosely cinched around my wrist. And there is hope that she will love me again, at least once more.

Listen, Roger starts. There is only a sip left in his glass, but he drinks it. The women are all ears and breasts and beautiful.

The fingers tighten on my arm.

When I look at him he bites his lip. I am a negative chasing down another insignificant fireball.

He puffs his ruddy cheeks and opens his mouth where I can see a small spark—a flame, a permission, the blinding light of another reckless infinitude—and says, *It was like nothing I've ever seen before. They were mashed like peaches against the trees.*

Andrew Collard

KID GLOVES

the lake is cold for June / ice
        still thawing / as we keep

skeletons sewn
into our newborn's mattress

I'm old enough to know
I hurt things / young enough
       to think it off

while walking
at the waterfront / afraid

to step inside

         ***

the birth was hard / and I can't seem
       to tell her that I cried

she asked me / once a spider
on our bedroom wall

        she wanted me to crush / I left alive

         ***

a washcloth is darkened
with hard water / who

      will change him / how long
         can I hope

she'll ask me
      have I hurt you / can
         I fix it

       ***

I never learned / to swim
         so what

could I carry
      in the cresting

his fingernails
came out sharpened / only

within reach of his
       own skin

Andrew Collard

I Knew a Man

Before I named this sickness, I knew symptoms: his finger tracing
    patterns around
the A/C dial, sentences wavering like a boy on stilts.

The purpose of the conversation's hidden, turns to *missing things:*
    when I could leave
the house without explanation, when he had fun

without me, when I was fun. We pick at wounds like flies dive
    drunkenly about rot,
impossible to un-explain as headlights flash to tell us *Watch*

out where you're going. Our house is running out of room, and soon
    the yard's curtain
will part on how we live: watching for whose

hand will open first, practice for receiving or for letting go. The
    fever's gone too deep;
its vagaries leave spaces wide

enough to hide in, contagious and contracted by speculation. *I miss*
    kissing, he says. *I*
miss when the phone rang urgently

and we both still answered, so much to say. Well, I say, I miss when loss
    had higher
stakes. I miss silence in the car,

I miss music; I miss every street and ride we took but this one, futures
    ripped like
branches from the passing trees.

Laura Bernstein-Machlay

CLUTTER

Because I live in Detroit I drive all the time. To and from my daughter's school in the suburbs, to visit Mom in Birmingham, another suburb, to grab groceries from the Trader Joe's/Westborn Market circle either side of Woodward Avenue. Or down Woodward the other direction, deeper into the Cultural Center of my city, to the art school where I teach.

That's just the outline of course, the tacks on the map. There's bank and vet and friends and pharmacy and mall—all the destinations that make up a day, a decade. That speed miles onto my Nissan Versa with its flashing airbag light—something else to fit into this already cluttered week.

My Versa's pretty down-to-the-bones, no Bluetooth, touch-screens, parking assist, passive entry, heated seats, rain-sensing wipers. No satellite MP3 equalizer, whatever that means. No GPS so I'm always lost.

I listen to the radio, to the classic-rock station, which recently added Bowie and the Clash to their playlist. Or the new-rock station. I sing along, loud and off-key as a tornado siren, because I'm so often driving alone—this being Detroit where everyone so often drives alone. And when ads come on for drug rehab programs or music festivals I can't afford, I change the station to NPR.

In early evening I like *All Things Considered*, that news show my friend calls *All Things Liberal,* which works for me. I like *Morning Edition* for the same reasons and listen after I drop my daughter, Celia, at school. In this way I collect odds and ends of world news, medical breakthroughs, statistics about our enormous, dying planet, and I pull them out like vacation souvenirs to punctuate points in the classroom. I especially like *This American Life* because it makes me feel quirky and interesting, and *Science Lab* because it makes me feel smart.

Recently *Science Lab* dedicated its hour to sleep, something which interests me in a gut-deep sort of way since I, like nearly everyone on my mother's family line—Bubby and Zaidy and Mom, the Aunties, the great Aunties, my daughter, all of us—have such a fiddly, tricksy, sort-of relationship with it. We all discuss it all the time, sometimes first thing when we speak.

Celia: "Don't talk to me. I'm too tired. Too too too too tired. I couldn't fall sleep last night for anything so I went on Tumblr and talked to my friend in the Netherlands."

Me: "I can't hear you. I'm a slug today—woke up no fewer than seven times in the night. Seven times! Then I slept through the alarm."

Mom: "I'm extra-alert. Got a whole four hours!"

Bubby and Zaidy quit sleeping at some point before my childhood. Worry, maybe, or guilt? About their children, about whatever poor choices they'd made decades before, about their parents, dead and buried. As a child I loved spending weekends at Bubby and Zaidy's, not least because I knew when I shuddered awake at midnight and felt the walls breathing, I could skulk down the hall to their door, see the friendly strip of light beneath it, and know I wasn't alone in the universe.

I wish now I could go back, tell my younger self to knock on their door just once, ask them about it, that addiction to sleeplessness, ask when the insomnia began, the long hours of reading and sorting buttons and cleaning behind the ancient refrigerator while the sky languished, dark as dirt, outside the windows?

If I could, I'd like to know when they gave up, stopped trying, what I have to look forward to. Then again, *better life through chemistry*. With a little pharmacological voodoo, I function well enough.

But here's the thing. According to *Science Lab*, sleep matters for lots of reasons, one of them being to wash the clutter from our minds. As the scientist said in his Scottish accent—probably Scottish, I was tired when I heard that story—sleep somehow softens neurons in our brains to well-washed gauze, so superfluous details—petty, piddling ones—simply float away like dust motes in the breeze, and we're left in the refreshed mornings with only what really matters.

But what, I wonder, about the rest of us, the crappy sleepers? Are we doomed forever to the muddle, the stray thoughts and superfluous details, the endless stuff of life filling all the rooms of our brains so we can't take a step without tripping over pizza boxes and dime-store tchotchkes and scraps covered with unfinished love poems and whatnot?

My husband Steven falls asleep in a wink, slumbers like a brick. Nice for him.

Once I drove cross-country in my battered Chevy Vega, the one I scored secondhand from a customer I'd grown friendly with at the bead shop where I worked. The Vega, which had belonged to the woman's stepson, retained a faint smell of pot—just a whisper behind leaking motor oil and exhaust—all the days I owned it.

I put off the drive so long my grad school was set to start in less than two weeks, so in five belly-wrenching days, I drove across two mountain ranges, through more states than I'd previously visited in my lifetime: Indiana, Illinois, Wisconsin, Minnesota, North Dakota, Montana, Washington, all in this car held together by duct tape and rust and prayers for clear skies—my wipers working only sporadically.

What's more remarkable is how I bundled my life into the back seat and the pocket-sized trunk of the Vega. How I mercilessly purged all the stuff of my childhood, families of plastic horses, stacks of LPs, hundreds of band fliers, years of clothing—all phases from fat girl to Madonna to forties classy to bag lady. The stuffed Bigfoot, the mannequin in her sxities housecoat—Gerty—whose loss I still lament.

"Are you sure?" asked best friend Vera. "Are you sure you want to let go of Gerty?" And I did. I was resolute as a standing stone.

"Only what's necessary," I said. "Only what's essential for survival."

This included books and books, rain gear, two umbrellas—car and I were aimed toward damp Seattle. I brought hippie clothes, a couple of lamps to study by, an inflatable matress, a battered boom box, 657 mixed tapes. That's about it.

And as I nomad-ed about Seattle, as I moved place to place, my volume of possessions remained relatively constant. I'd lose some, gain some, a houseplant abandoned with one roommate balanced by a painting I got in a breakup. Somehow, in those few years I achieved that most coveted of kingdoms—the monarchy of equilibrium.

Which went right to hell the moment I returned to Detroit, the moment Mom decided to fill up my new house. The moment I met Steven with his cheerful pack rat tendencies—Steven who gave me permission to gather, to collect, to keep stuff just because I liked it.

It's years later, and once again Steven and I are talking about moving, leaving Detroit. It's a regular threat and maybe one day we'll up and go, though I have my doubts. In the meantime I'm trying to clear the detritus of two decades, and smacking headfirst into roadblocks.

"What about these corduroys?" I ask Steven, holding up pants he's owned since high school. "Can these go to Salvation Army?"

"No." He is aghast. "Celia might wear them one day."

"They're bell-bottoms," I say in return. "There's an embroidered peace sign on the butt."

"They're vintage," says Steven. "My mother got them for me."

"She gives you things all the time," I try again. But no go. The peaceful corduroys return to their home in the dresser, the extra dresser in the basement.

And, "What about this basket of stuffed animals? You haven't looked at them in three years."

"No." Celia is aghast. "I used these to play race-team with Arlo, back when he was Amy."

It's been like this for weeks now, and I'm no better. While our house appears merely eccentric on the surface, twitch one painting out of place, one framed photo of Bubby and Zaidy, one Buddha, Aunt Martha's lace doilies, some stranger's childhood teapot, and it just looks cluttered.

I spend long summer days sorting photos, boxes of prints I amassed till we went digital, the digital images now cluttering the computer. I sit on the floor until my back locks into a question mark and stare at album after album, at loose photos heaping the floor around me like autumn leaves. Cities I've lived in, countries I've hitchhiked and Eurailed across, statues and buildings and faces I can't remember beyond the mirages in my hands. A thousand photos of me pregnant, thousands more of Celia's first weeks, baby Celia in rash stage, toddler Celia in never-gonna-nap-again stage. Pictures and pictures.

And cards, years of birthdays and Hanukkahs and Christmases and anniversaries and Mother's Days. RSVPs from my wedding, RSVPs to other people's weddings which I forgot to mail.

And Celia's drawings through the years, scribbles to stick figures to robots with bellybuttons during the robots with bellybuttons era. Her end-of-year schoolwork, unopened sacks of squiggles become letters become cursive become sentences. Every math problem ever.

This is one small room, a storage space really, off one of the upstairs closets.

Like collectors everywhere, my Bubby saved for lots of reasons. Because of the Great Depression, because of WWII, because of self-recrimination and a hodgepodge of fears that Bubby clutched close to her heart: social anxiety and agoraphobia, snakephobia and spendingmoneyphobia. Because of these and probably lots more reasons, Bubby was a hoarder, but only of certain, very specific things.

She didn't hoard like hoarders on TV, being too contained, too ashamed, for such extravagant hoopla. Instead, she was a secret collector, much like she was a secret eater, a secret sneaker of Kahlua-sips from her secret stash in the kitchen. She was collector of old clothes from the 1930s on, a thrift shop of old clothes straining the closets, clothes in a hundred sizes of too small so I could never use them for dress-up—Bubby being four foot ten on her tallest days and tiny as a wren.

Of buttons, the big tin of buttons, carefully removed from years of shirts and dresses and coats which finally, irreparably, gave up the ghost. Bone buttons and coral and glass and wood and Bakelite and plastic. Shaped into circles and squares and triangles, cowboy hats and flowers. I'd go straight to that tin every time my mother brought me to Bubby and Zaidy's house, pry open the top, carefully, so buttons wouldn't slosh over the sides, let them slide like rubies and emeralds through my fingers.

And the oldest clothing and sheets, the ones un-sewable even by Bubby, which she tore into rags to clean the house, and when those got too shredded, she tore them into strips, wound them into a great ball brought out when Zaidy needed to bind roses to their stakes, or Bubby needed to tie up garbage bags to put on the curbside.

Spools of thread heaped in drawers, every possible shade so when Bubby sewed up Zaidy's shirts and socks, you could barely notice. The story Auntie Ellie tells about playing in those spools as a child and getting her finger caught: the more she pulled, the tighter the noose.

How she ran crying to her parents, and Zaidy said, "Hold still," and went to find scissors. And Bubby said, "No, no," and grabbed Ellie's hand, carefully unwinding the thread one tiny loop at a time. Waste not, want not.

In fact, Bubby and Zaidy lived minimally, without frippery, without treats, because they were hoarders of money. Zaidy might have liked to go to restaurants, eat a good meal while out on the town. He might have liked to take a vacation—and he certainly earned enough on his 1950s teacher's salary. But Bubby wouldn't have it, was too locked in her *what ifs*. What if the stock market crashes again, what if prices shoot up and up like bottle rockets, what if the neighbors turn on us and we have to make a run for it, what if the sky falls like shards of broken glass? What if what if what if?

So my mom and her sisters went without. Without new clothes, without luxuries of any sort, while Bubby used lipstick—definitely a necessity in the fifties—down to the bottom of the container, as far as she could, then dug out whatever remained, whatever was stuck in the lid or wedged on the sides. She'd melt it down in a saucepan with other leftover lipsticks so the different shades of red merged like oil paints on a pallet. And when the hybrid lipstick went liquid, Bubby scooped it into bottle caps, let it harden and applied it to her mouth with her finger.

"She really was ingenious," I say to Auntie Ellie when she tells me this story, and I can hear her shrugging over the phone.

Or maybe *ingenious* isn't the right word. Maybe the word is desperate? And since desperation is as much an inherited trait as insomnia, we all—her daughters and granddaughters—got it, too.

Auntie Ellie, the youngest sister, the one who married well, lives in comfortable splendor in her Mediterranean mansion, replete with a zillion whimsical antiques arranged just so. The oldest sister, Malka, has had a fraught existence; at one time, her house was cluttered full of trash and feral cats, but now Cousin Shayna has her in assisted living and her tiny apartment is empty as a mirror.

Mom, meanwhile, sells old silver-plate and jewelry on eBay. But she mostly buys. Mostly bargains from garage sales or estate sales, which I sometimes attend with her, but sometimes not because she goes pretty often. And too, I feel squidgy about wandering about those dead people's houses, touching the things they gathered over their lifetimes, the things not deemed worthy of keeping by the heirs and so offered for good deals to us shoppers with our grabby hands. I imagine the old couples ethereal, meandering around us as we explore their houses. They're always a little dismayed. They whisper, "Oh no, not that brush with the carved handle from my mother, not my Niagara Falls commemorative plate, not the good pots and pans. We saved for those."

Mom tells me Bubby enjoyed a good estate sale, but she complained they were too expensive. She adored rummage sales, though.

"Anything for a bargain," says Mom. "When we were little, Ellie and I would run down alleys looking through people's garbage to see if they put out anything good, and Mama was always interested in what we'd find. 'Any treasures?' she'd say to us. 'Any treasures for me today?' And later, when churches started having rummage sales, then yard sales popped up in the neighborhood, your Bubby was crazy about those. Was even willing to leave the house to let me take her." Mom goes quiet, thinking of Bubby, who entombed herself in her blocky white house in the crumbling neighborhood.

Mom loves old books, old compacts, pretty old buttons. She sells some, but mostly she likes to take them out and touch them, "My collections," she calls them, stroking them with her voice. For a while it was Depression glass, that cheaply made tableware that anyone could afford, even during hard times.

"It was so thin, so fragile, that lots of it broke. That makes what's left wonderfully collectable," says Mom. Right now, two dozen plastic bins of the stuff live in a crawl space in our basement, Mom having filled her own house to its dotted outlines. If Steven and I and Celia eventually move, we'll take it along, pay someone to carry it to the truck and into the new basement, because even though Mom hasn't touched this collection in years, it matters to her that that we have it.

When Celia was a little girl, she said to me, "I want to have collections, too, just like Gammy." She proceeded to gather flower petals that dried and dissolved to dust, the dust crushed into the cracks of her floorboards where it resides still. Over the years she's collected rocks, acorns, shells, burst balloons in interesting shapes, sticks, worms that I begged her to store outside. All these collections are fine—they're small. But like her father and me, like my mom and Bubby and Zaidy, she's loathe to let much of anything go.

Some of this is inertia, which explains the princess stickers on her wall. But more, Celia mourns the loss—even potential loss—of anything, anything at all. Celia, who entered this world with secret knowledge of what came before. Who had her first existential crisis at age three, while we were driving. Past the Jewish cemeteries on Woodward, one two three little graveyards all in a row. Celia in her booster seat in the back, looking out the window at the world rolling by.

"What are those?" she asked of the fields of gray stones. And I explained, because experts on NPR said I should, how our human bodies are our houses, how we live in them for long years, and then, when it's time, we leave the houses and go elsewhere.

Celia was silent for five minutes, long after we'd left the cemeteries behind. Then she began crying, sobbing, really, like stars exploding.

"Time goes forever," she said between hiccups. "How can anything be true when time is forever? Is anything I hold in my hands real?" And I could do nothing, bound as I was behind the wheel. I reached for clichés, for faith I never learned as a child. How she'd live in heaven—that tempting, non-Jewish notion—how Steven and I would live with her. How she'd eat candy all day, all the candy she could stuff into the biggest garbage bags in the world, that she'd never get a stomachache. It took a little while, but worked well enough, I guess. She stopped crying before we got home.

And a week later I came out of the shower to find her waiting for me, grabbing at my hand. Celia tugged me downstairs to the kitchen and pointed toward the recycling bin that had detonated into an installation art piece. There were ramps of milk cartons and pathways of newspaper and some old essay scraps and bottles and tinfoil become spaceships and black holes, all of it held together by Scotch tape and dental floss. And I cringed a little, knowing how she'd mourn when we eventually had to return the sculpture to its component parts, let it go.

"I call it *Time*," said Celia.

Now, a dozen years later, I'll sometimes find her beside my bed in the middle of the night, when she's having trouble sleeping. Once

Celia falls, she sleeps long and hard, but it's that first feathery slip into unconsciousness that seems to thwart her—like she doesn't trust herself to let go and tumble into blackness. And so she'll come to our room, stand there next to my head on the pillow—she knows her father will sleep through apocalypse—and I'll feel her through my thinnest, most jumbled veil of dreams, jerk fully awake.

"What is it, honey? Is everything OK?" I ask every time.

"It's fine," says Celia. "I couldn't sleep is all. And I wanted to see you."

"I'm here," I say. "I'm always here. I'll always be here."

But that's a lie and Celia knows it, so she comes to me. She comes for the same sense of rootedness that comes with stuff, with collections of all sorts, the things we keep to bind us to Earth, to honor the moments of our lives, to honor the dead who collected that stuff before us.

And because my scratchy words are sufficient for the moment, Celia turns around, trudges back to her room. And every morning I find her there, sprawled like a starfish across her blankets or curled around some old toys she can't bear to part with, the dog and cat curled around her, all of them profoundly, softly asleep.

Laura Hendrix Ezell

FUGUE

Because her dreams are terrible, relentless as dogs, Paulette thinks up games to keep her awake. In one of them, she walks around her apartment blindfolded and tries to memorize the exact texture and location of everything she has—end tables and footstools, picture frames, potted plants, ashtrays. She knows the size and weight of all of her books, the texture of their covers, the thickness of their pages. Other times she will make phone calls, to college friends who've settled at all ends of the country; to startled aunts or cousins; to people she knew in high school and who don't remember her; or to people who don't know her, who have the same names as the people she knew in high school, and usually hang up before she can explain her mistake. Another game she has is to bring a man home from a bar and keep him up all night. She will make him talk for hours, and when she senses he is about to leave, she moves on to music and dancing. She saves the sex until the end, until morning, if possible; she has learned to spot the very last moment before a man decides irrevocably to leave.

To keep herself awake, Paulette takes a job serving drinks and making grilled cheese sandwiches at Maidy's, the only bar in Sayree that stays open past midnight. The people who frequent this bar go there to drink. They sit alone, or occasionally in pairs and threes, and they drink as if drinking were an occupation, a solemn responsibility. As if there were an end in sight, a point at which they could say, *I'm done now*, and nod, and put on a hat, and walk out the door. Usually the patrons here do not make very much noise. Their drinks are simple: beer, gin, beer and a shot of bourbon. Because she does not have to bother much with juices or fancy liquors, Paulette catches on quickly to what each of the men, for they are mostly men, likes to drink. They warm to her for this, and she makes good tips, as good as can be made here. She likes her job. On slow nights, Marty, who owns the bar, tells her to help herself to a drink. No one asks questions about her life or tries to make her laugh. No one insists that Paulette pretend she is happy.

At home she has laid out a sleeping bag below the window in her den, the window that glows the brightest in the heat of midday, and this is where she rests, with the shades raised, in the afternoons, when there is enough sun to keep her from falling truly asleep.

She does not use a pillow. She wears her shoes. She keeps the television on and concentrates on the dialogue, on the plots. She wraps her mind tight around the plots, following them through her drowsy fog, never letting go, as if these words, these voices, were a tiny thread that she could follow to the other side. She knows that if she lets go there is falling, and dark.

This resting helps a little. Paulette looks forward to the hour that she will spend on the floor—the feel of the sun on her face, the coarse, hard fabric of muscle that lines her eye sockets going slack, like a tent collapsing onto soft, wet ground. All of this is so wonderful. When she stands up afterwards, Paulette feels a gratitude that borders on euphoria. The world takes on a faint pink buzz, a warmth. Paulette thinks she has found a way; these rests are enough to keep her going.

But her life is thinning out, turning to lace. She has trouble piecing together sequences of events and cannot always decide what is real and what never happened. Sometimes she finds herself making lists.

Pay the water bill.
Which holiday Tuesday.
Important: C, A, B12.
Find out where in Scotland.
Coal. Cole.

Sometimes, she finds herself sitting in the only chair in her kitchen, holding such a list in her lap, staring at it, and trying to remember what she could have meant when she wrote it.

They have noticed it at work. The hollows beneath Paulette's eyes look like gashes, spaded. Sometimes, she sees flashes of light that nearly knock her over, leave her stunned and silent. She forgets drinks and names and is prone to episodes of staring.

"Paulette." Marty has come in the front door. From across the bar, he claps twice in her face, his arms straightened before him like alligator jaws.

"Yes?" She looks up and remembers where she is.

"You OK?"

"Sure." But the answer is slow, followed by a thoughtful nod.

Marty assumes it is drugs. Paulette looks like it might be pills. *Bad news, pills*, thinks Marty. He knows. He's seen it.

"Listen." He lays a hand on her shoulder, and they lean their heads together, almost touching foreheads over the bar.

"Hmmm?" Sleepily.

"Why don't you go home, get some rest."

"Nahh, Marty, I'd rather stay here."

He hesitates. "Well, stay if you like—off the clock, though. This side of the bar. Pour yourself some coffee." Marty shakes his head as he walks behind the bar. *These girls*, he thinks.

Marty takes over for her, first serving her the cup of coffee he recommended, figuring she must not have heard him before. She slurps her way through half of it, and then pushes it back at him.

"Gin, please." Paulette giggles a little at her demand, at the way her head feels drunk already, though she's only had the coffee. It is strange, the things she finds funny these days. She is constantly being surprised by what makes her laugh and what sets her crying. The stimuli get all mixed up in her mind, and she fears that somehow, she has begun to feel things backwards.

Marty hesitates, but Paulette pushes the coffee mug farther away from her, and eventually, he takes it. He pours her a weak gin and tonic. Paulette nods her thanks and slurps for a while. Then she pushes the ice around with her straw. Looks up at Marty, slides her glass across the bar. Marty shakes his head and pours another drink, weaker this time. And each time after that.

The gin warms Paulette like a pair of arms. She forgets that she has no one to call. She forgets that she has parents and a sister, three states away, who do not even like her. She thinks about going home for Christmas. She smiles a little.

Across the room, a man flips through the leaves of the jukebox. When Paulette comes to her senses tomorrow, far from this bar, far from this town, this is the last thing she will remember, this image of an old man in a ball cap, bracing himself with one arm against the jukebox, head down, swaying slightly, almost like dancing, before the music has even started.

At some point, Marty looks up and realizes she is gone.

Hours later, somewhere else, Paulette opens her eyes. Above her, maple branches, heavy with leaves, catch dazzling chunks of light, like thousands of fish in a shivering net. For a moment, she believes she is on the living room floor, halfway to waking, still treading thickly through some dream of wind and light. In this moment, Paulette is achingly happy.

But slowly the mind shakes itself loose, casts off the downy fetters of dreaming, pecks through. Paulette wakes into the kind of confusion that does not know what questions to ask—a confusion like a foreign tongue, a language thick with tongue.

She stands and looks around her and does not panic. *This is a park*, she thinks, and the thought is comforting in the way that parks are always comforting—the familiar geography of flatness; the surety of grass, threaded through with gently bent concrete paths; the universality of lamppost, of bench, of garbage receptacle. Paulette knows she has never been here before.

This knowledge does not scare her. Something takes over. Something like the adrenaline wind that encircles the head just after a trauma, after a car wreck, when a woman looks down at her forearm and thinks, *That is not where it's supposed to bend*, and laughs, because it is all so very funny then, in those moments when the brain pads the body with a soft suit of chemicals, to protect it from all the different kinds of sharpness.

Paulette wanders through the park, and out of the park, and into the city. It is not much of a city. Three-and-a-half-story-tall buildings in the distance. Entire blocks deserted—lunch counters closed, or posting odd hours; miles of warehouse space, windows blacked out with spray paint. A long-closed train depot. She stops at a newspaper machine. Brighton. She's traveled twenty miles. This is somehow easy for her to accept. She believes it quickly and with great resolve, in the way that a person believes a thing when she doesn't want to know any more, when she doesn't want it to get worse. She nods and turns around, walks back to the park, where she's left her car. Paulette drives the twenty miles home. She goes back to work that night. She does not tell anyone what has happened to her.

☾

A few days pass. Paulette works, rests, drinks a little, cries at inappropriate moments (watching herds of some long-legged plains animal on the television, reading a magazine advertisement for disposable diapers). And then one night she leaves the bar and wakes up in a hotel bed in a room she's never seen. *Fuck*, she thinks. *FUCK*, as she slams the heel of her hand against the wall, gets up, and kicks the dresser by the bed. She cries then, curls herself into a ball at the edge of the bed, and cries like she hasn't cried since she was a child—until her face is numb and her diaphragm begins to seize up and the breaths come like jerks on a fishing line: sudden, unpredictable, very hard. She cries until she has cried everything out, worn herself out, and then she waits half an hour for the purple splotches to fade from around her eyes and mouth, and then she gets up to leave the hotel.

There is a woman behind the front desk. She is roundish, with short hair of some bland color and a ruddy complexion. She's wearing a turtleneck. She smiles at Paulette, a kind smile. A smile like the smell of bread. Paulette hesitates, then walks up to the desk. She wants to ask the woman the name of the city. She needs to know where she is. But she needs to know other things, too—where she is and how she got there and how she will get home, and what she will do when she gets home, and if she will ever be able to sleep again, to go to sleep in a bed and wake up there, and if there will ever be anyone for her to lie beside, someone to hold her down if she tries to get out of the bed and drive away. But Paulette cannot find the words. She opens her mouth, spits forth some air and some vowels, false starts, but she cannot make the woman understand. All she can do is to touch her arm. It is the only way Paulette knows to ask the questions. And when she does, she finds that she cannot let go. That this, the touching of the stranger's arm, is not only the question, but the answer; and Paulette cannot help herself when she gently closes her hand around the woman's elbow, and when she takes the woman's hand in her hand. *Please, please do not make me leave. Please do not make me let go.* This is what she says with her hands, her hands kneading and trembling, although there are still no words. The woman does not understand. She shakes Paulette loose and looks afraid, and picks up the phone. Paulette leaves then, as fast as she can go without running.

Outside, she wanders around for a while, looking down. After a while she comes to feel that it does not really matter where she is, after all. Paulette has two dollars and twenty-seven cents in her pocket. She walks into a gas station and buys a bag of chips. She locks the bathroom door, cups her hands, and drinks some water from the sink. Leaning over the sink, she cries again—quietly this time—splashes her face, and leaves the place.

In Abel there is a man who has lost his wife. Paulette sees him as she sits on the curb outside of the gas station. She is eating her chips very slowly and trying to decide what to do. Across the street, he is busy, taping flyers to telephone poles and windows. He has a stooped, caved-in look about him. His walk is a slow shuffle. It is the walk of a lonely child. There is something about him, something in his gait, or the low, side-slung angle of his head, or the way he is dressed—his shabby green cardigan, buttoned up despite the afternoon sun—that reminds Paulette of an uncle she had, who died before she could know him well—an uncle she has come to know through photographs, and whose loss she has always felt in her stomach like a homesickness, as though, somehow, she had loved him. This similarity seizes her by the heart. Her whole body swells with the idea of this man. She wants to help him. She thinks that he can help her.

But there is no way to explain this, and so she hangs back. She waits there at the gas station, holding the bag of chips in her lap, watching as he makes his slow progress down the street, taping his flyers to every pole, every window.

But she follows him at safe distances, camouflaging herself with plausible activities. She stoops to pick up some change. She deposits her empty potato chip bag in a garbage can. She stops and looks casually at the flier. The face in the photo resembles her own, she thinks—a little, through the eyes. Bettye Roby, the flier says, is the name of the woman in the photo.

For almost an hour she follows the man, and finally, into a diner where he takes a booth for himself. Paulette sits at the counter and tells the waitress she doesn't want anything. She is waiting for someone, she says, looking into the woman's eyes, which have narrowed.

In the booth, the man spreads his fliers out to cover the table and stares down at them. When the waitress approaches him, he doesn't look up.

Paulette picks at her nails while the man sips his way through two glasses of soda. He has ordered a bowl of oatmeal, but it sits cooling beside him. He looks at it and stirs it occasionally. Finally he walks up to the counter to pay.

Paulette does not know what to say to the man, but she stares in his direction. She tries to bend her eyes and mouth into good shapes, kind shapes. She has a sharp face, one full of angles, and she has been told before that this face of hers does not lend itself to approachability.

When the man turns to go, he sees her sitting there—wanting, with all the parts of herself, to help, and not knowing how. For a moment he stands completely still, looking puzzled, as if she were a letter held at arms length, an enchanting script that he cannot quite read. But then something changes. His face blooms. He softens. There is something of gratitude in his expression, and something also of apprehension. As if a gift has been given, but may yet be taken away. The man begins to glow.

"Bettye."

The word hits Paulette in the gut, makes her feel dizzy.

"What? No. I'm not. I'm not Bettye. My name is Paulette." She shakes her head and stands up. She backs away from the man.

He is walking towards her. He begins to cry.

"No, no, I'm sorry. No."

"Bettye."

The waitress looks on, her mouth slack, her forehead a loose swirl of skin. She looks at Paulette, looks at the flyer the man has taped to the counter. She looks again, shakes her head. She leans over the counter and tugs at the man's sleeve, gently, saying, "Come on, now, Mr. Roby, now, don't do this again. You know that ain't her ...."

The man takes hold of Paulette's wrists, softly, his long fingers encircling them like bracelets. He is barely touching her. She has never been touched so lightly, with so much love. The weight of his gaze is sinking her. Her head drops to her chest.

He lifts her chin and kisses her mouth, her temples, her eyelids, her jawline. And then there is no more resisting. Paulette's face melts into these strange kisses. She nips at his mouth with her lips: hungry, a baby bird. She will be Bettye for this; she would be anybody.

Bettye. The word slides over the man's trembling lower lip. He lays his head in the space between Paulette's ear and shoulder.

She closes her eyes. *Yes*, she whispers. *All right. Yes.*

Lee Ann Roripaugh

META / COUCH

When you go to the artist's retreat you bring along books written by each of your three lovers, all writers. You want to feel close to them, to hold their words next to you in the solitude. You imagine yourself laying down your own words alongside theirs, braiding your language into the currents of their language. For you, this feels like writerly intimacy, a kind of aesthetic sex.

It's lonely at the writer's residency. You don't call or text anyone because you can't afford international roaming. No one talks to you. You thought Canadians were supposed to be nice, but it occurs to you that maybe they don't like Americans. And why should they?

Some of it, though, is probably your own fault. After you spend all day alone in your room, writing, your focus becomes pulled so far back into your own head that by the time you wander down to the dining room you feel blinky and overlit—as if you're a pale grub who's just crawled out from under a fallen log. You feel floaty, strange, jetlagged. The altitude makes you a little dizzy.

But still. Days pass and you feel increasingly estranged and awkward. This seems to be in direct correlation to the degree in which the surrounding scenery becomes increasingly beautiful. The rain stops and blue-green mountains surface from behind their veils of mist like gigantic, dewy-faced brides. Clouds wobble and teeter above like excessively frosted wedding cakes. You, on the other hand, become more and more transparent—like Saran Wrap, or the Invisible Woman (pre-Malice era)—fading/melting into the scenery.

Sometimes, at mealtimes, when you get up from your table to re-fill your water glass, waitstaff clears your place setting and takes away your food before you're finished. One night, when you're relaxing on the roof deck after dinner, someone deadbolts the sliding patio door from the inside, leaving you locked outside on the deck. You call and call the switchboard, but no one answers. When you finally reach the switchboard, it takes security nearly an hour to come and let you back inside.

You become invisible to your lovers as well, even though their words are strong and vibrant in your head. One by one, they start to look straight through you, until they're meeting the gaze of someone else entirely.

The Ecuadoran Poet gets back together with her ex-girlfriend. They semaphore their happiness on FB. The Ecuadoran Poet posts that the Ex-Girlfriend Who is Now Her Girlfriend Again memorizes entire poems by the Ecuadoran Poet, recites them back to her in multiple languages in the evenings. That's the mark of true love, fans of the Ecuadoran Poet sigh ickily into the comments section. The Ecuadoran Poet posts a picture of herself in bed with the Ex-Girlfriend Who is Now Her Girlfriend Again in which their long perfect naked legs are intertwined. You feel chagrined on behalf of your not-long and not-perfect legs.

The Meta-Fictional Novelist Who May or May Not Be in the Midst of a Midlife Crisis seems to have broken things off with you as well, although he doesn't actually tell you this. Instead, he quits texting. One by one, he withdraws <3s at the end of his messages. Four <3s goes to three <3s goes to two <3s goes to no <3s. He only e-mails if you email first. His replies are blandly neutral. Harried, distant. He promises to send longer e-mails soon, then doesn't. It reminds you of the time you rode a horse that tried to scrub you off on a fence.

Minimal creeping reveals The Meta-Fictional Novelist Who May or May Not Be in the Midst of a Midlife Crisis is likewise semaphoring newfound conjugal happiness on FB. He's saying Yes! To the Universe! He posts a picture of himself captioned: Saying Yes to the Universe! He wears a tie! With a big Yes! on it. The woman he's apparently saying Yes to the Universe with simultaneously posts a corresponding picture of a red glass heart nestled on her pillow. It says Yes! A week later they get matching tattoos. The tattoos say Yes!

Now your only remaining lover is the Poet Who's Married to Someone Else. It's because he's married to someone else that you took the other two lovers in the first place. Because you want to move forward. Because you don't want to be perpetually hostaged in the poet's bad marriage to someone else. The Poet Who's Married to Someone Else is weird and brilliant and funny and sexy and kind, but being with him is like trying to untie an infinite series of Gordian Knots. The Poet Who's Married to Someone Else makes promises like bright extravagant runaway kites spiraling away in the wind. Of course you should know better, but you're a poet and you like kites, too!

Maybe, in your own fashion, you've been trying to find ways to Say Yes to the Universe. Although? For the record? You think Saying Yes to the Universe is a dipshit phrase. You'd rather gouge your own eye out with a rusted spork than ever say anything that dipshitty.

Everything comes unbraided. You hide your lovers' books in the closet and now there's only the sound of your own voice—disconsolate, but loud and true. You think maybe it's all sort of OK, but wish it weren't happening while you were alone on retreat in another country. It's the first time you've gone on an artist's retreat. You can't help but wonder if maybe you're doing it all wrong.

Now the Poet Who's Married to Someone Else keeps LIKE-ing saucy pictures of third-wave twenty-something poets *en dishabille* on FB. You can't tell if he's just being friendly or if he's articulating a newfound preference. But since he's the only one left it makes you anxious. All the saucy-pictured third-wave twenty-something poets *en dishabille* have Tumblrs. You wonder if you should start a Tumblr. You don't feel as if you can say anything to the Poet Who's Married to Someone Else about LIKE-ing the saucy pictures of third-wave twenty-something poets because you don't want to sound creepy and insecure, and because it seems hypocritical since, strictly speaking, the Poet Who's Married to Someone Else doesn't know about the Ecuadoran Poet or the Meta-Fictional Novelist Who May or May Not Be in the Midst of a Midlife Crisis.

And *fuck* FB anyways. What used to seem like a little harmless pointing and clicking's been visually blown all out of proportion. Now each time the Poet Who's Married to Someone Else clicks LIKE, a ginormous photo of a saucy third-wave twenty-something poet *en dishabille* shows up in your feed, below a blaring notification that the

Poet Who's Married to Someone Else LIKEs her saucy picture. It kind of makes it hard to get perspective.

One night over Skype you tell the Poet Who's Married to Someone Else about the secretary—the one no one liked because she was mean and incompetent. The one who was fired following a small-town local scandal in which it was revealed she'd been embezzling money from her bowling league. You tell the Poet Who's Married to Someone Else about how Embezzling Secretary was a hoarder—the kind with several broken-down cars in her front yard and drawers full of grubby rubber bands. At work, it was very difficult to thread one's way to Embezzling Secretary's desk to make Xeroxing or travel reimbursement requests (tasks Embezzling Secretary would grudgingly perform with a bewildering level of incompetence and at a date so late as to be no longer useful) because her work area was walled off with old file folders, magazines, newspapers, used toner cartridges, Styrofoam, dusty Christmas ornaments, and plastic fruit. Maybe these two things—embezzling and hoarding—were all really part of the same impulse for Embezzling Secretary, you tell the Poet Who's Married to Someone Else. It was hard to say for sure.

After the Embezzling Secretary had breast-reduction surgery, a different secretary, Gossiping Secretary, came over to the Embezzling Secretary's house with obligatory post-surgery hotdish. Gossiping Secretary reported that there were two couches in Embezzling Secretary's house—one planted right in front of the other. Apparently, when the springs in the old couch were shot and Embezzling Secretary's husband started to complain that his ass hurt, Embezzling Secretary bought a new couch and they just stuck it right in front of the old couch. After that, Embezzling Secretary and her ass-hurting husband sat on the new couch, pretending like the old couch directly behind the new couch wasn't even there.

And so here's the thing, you tell the Poet Who's Married to Someone Else over Skype: I don't want to be that couch.

Angel Egg, you're the furthest thing from a couch, the Poet Who's Married to Someone Else says. I love you so much.

I'm serious, you say. There are way too many couches here.

Wait, says the Poet Who's Married to Someone Else. Is this a metaphor? (The Poet Who's Married to Someone Else isn't *that* kind of poet.) Which couch *don't* you want to be?

Neither one, you say, and now you're trying to hide on Skype that you've started to cry. Please, you say.

I mean it, you say.

Don't make me be that couch.

Caridad Moro-Gronlier

FOURTH QUARTER

The Dolphins were winning—for a change
parties paved a path toward a perfect season
every Sunday measured by Marino's confetti-
cannon release, the assortment of aqua and orange
flung around a rotation of rooms united
in their hatred of the other side. Each week

I came and joined the wives, learned the couch-
to-kitchen shuffle, but never wore a jersey
or the right colors, keys in hand
at halftime, the only beer-run volunteer
with no pennant affixed to the antenna.

I was there, for you, but I never cheered
or submitted to the show of heart you held
toward me before every huddle, the hope
you dispelled after every hike. I didn't care
about the score, the offense, the defensive line,

but you did. I tried but couldn't
get past what I thought true—
game after game you did nothing
and called it a win, tallied
your success in sacks and yards
you did not run, the clock
on us winding down.

Sandra Marchetti

EXTRAS

It was late when I walked by the sushi place. Through the picture window, I saw a man and his son, the owners perhaps, sitting under an anticipatory glow. They were watching the ballgame in the dark dining room. So unlike you and me, these foreign men resting after restaurant work, faithful through extra innings. I had flipped off the car radio, but I remember now we won. It was their reward for not going home, for waiting on the pitcher to throw.

Joe Giordano

WILLIE MAYS WAS
MY FAVORITE PLAYER

Willie Mays lost his cap chasing fly balls, so I did, too. I dropped a truckload of Spaldeens practicing his basket catch. His baseball card was the highlight of my shoebox collection, and was handled with the care of Dead Sea Scroll parchment. When I lost my Giants to San Francisco, I followed Willie religiously through the radio broadcasts of Les Keiter not realizing that the games were re-creations. I saw that Willie was black, but I didn't notice.

My father was born in Naples, and Joe DiMaggio was baseball for him. After the "Yankee Clipper" retired, my father lost interest, but would take note if Sal Maglie pitched or Yogi Berra homered. He thought I should root for Roy Campanella because he was half Italian. The other time I heard my father say something about a black person was when he put on a 78 record of "Sophisticated Lady" by Billy Eckstein and laughed to my mother that he first thought Eckstein was Jewish.

I could slice a horsefly in two with a tossed baseball card. Don't snicker. OK, it's an exaggeration. Winning flipping competitions, tossing cards closest to the wall, was an alternative to spending a nickel for a pack. Lenny Spazzolatto and Gene Kaplan, my best friend, vied with me to expand our collections. I called Lenny "Cousin Weak Eyes" because his peepers protruded like a crab. The two of us tussled to see who was toughest, and we tied for the honor. Gene was a Jewish redhead from down the block. His grating-voice younger brother, Carl, would insist that Gene give him cards so he could compete. Carl tossed like a flounder with a broken fin and was soon cleaned out. So, he hung around like a poltergeist, doing his best to disrupt my concentration. I wanted to stuff Carl into a sewer drain, but my friendship with Gene kept me at bay. Carl would cry to his mother if he tripped on a sidewalk crack. If I retaliated for his pepper-in-my-butt behavior, Gene would be punished for not sticking up for his brother.

My technique for tossing was to fade the card's flight, which gave it a better chance to crawl up the wall and become a "leaner," a card inclined against the wall. The best leaners had two corners of the card gripping the wall, but if even a single corner was raised, the next player was required to make three tries to knock it down. Failing, the leaner owner profited the three attempts.

I'd sent my Al Kaline into a sliced arc and been rewarded with a one-corner leaner. Lenny's mouth clamped down. He looked like a walleyed pike.

Carl shouted, "Lenny, knock it down."

Gene gave his brother's shoulder a push, but Carl became adamant. "Lenny, you can do it."

Lenny crouched. He wiped his hands on jeans and gripped an Ernie Banks by the corner, thumb on top. With a sharp flick of the wrist, the card flew like a Nike Ajax missile. It bounced off the brick wall a millimeter away from Kaline, who was pictured with bat shouldered as if ready to swat "Mr. Cub" away.

As his second attempt, Lenny readied Lew Burdette, pictured with arms raised in pitching motion, face as grim as Lenny's. I gulped. This was trouble.

Lenny let fly. Burdette grazed Kaline. The Tiger star tottered but held.

I puffed out a breath.

Lenny had only one card left, Mickey Mantle. "The Mick" card was a prize of great worth. The baseball card producer knew that most New York kids regarded Mickey as their hero and printed fewer Mantle cards to keep them buying. Lenny wouldn't ordinarily flip his Mickey, but the rule mandated three attempts.

Carl crouched near Lenny like a fight trainer. "Lenny, take your time."

The tension in the air was palpable. Lenny took a deep breath and readied Mantle for the attempted take-down.

Just then, a shadow covered Kaline. The four of us turned toward a black kid, about our age. He said, "What are you doing?"

Mrs. Jackson had recently moved into the corner apartment building. I'd seen her rolling groceries back from the A&P in her trolley.

She had a dignified demeanor, but it was the sway of rounded hips that held my eye. She wore red lipstick and dangling purple earrings against dark skin. I still thought my mother was more beautiful. The Jacksons were the only black family on the block. I'd seen this kid bouncing a ball on the corner when I returned from school.

Lenny looked at the black kid like he was gum on his shoe. "You broke my concentration."

The Mickey Mantle was clutched in Lenny's fingers. I said, "Cousin Weak Eyes, you need to make another toss."

Lenny stood. "He broke my rhythm. I want a do-over."

"No way."

The black kid repeated. "What are you doing?"

Gene said, "Flipping cards. Who are you?"

"Samuel."

"Lenny," I said, "you need to flip that Mantle."

Lenny said, "No way. Sambo disrupted play."

Samuel said, "My name's not Sambo."

Lenny frowned. "I'm not tossing Mickey."

Carl said, "You tell him. Anthony, Lenny doesn't have to do anything."

As usual, Carl was the voice most unwelcome.

I said to Samuel, "You screwed up our game. What do you want?"

He said, "I'll play. Gimme some cards."

Lenny turned his back.

I said, "You need to buy them."

He moved close to me. "You have plenty. Gimme some."

"No way."

Samuel shot his right fist into my gut. The air went out of me. I doubled over and dropped my handful of cards. Samuel scooped them up and ran. Gene gave chase. To my surprise, Lenny and Carl followed. The corner apartment building door was heavy and Samuel was slow to get it open. The guys surrounded him.

Lenny's fists were balled. "Sambo, give back the cards."

Samuel was confronted by three angry faces. He threw the cards to the street like a folded poker hand. Gene picked them up.

Lenny said, "Don't come back." Smirking, he, Carl, and Gene backed away from Samuel and came over to me. Samuel ducked into the apartment building. I'd recovered by the time the three reached me. Even Carl looked solicitous.

"I'm all right. Thanks."

Gene said, "Why did he punch you? You didn't insult him."

Lenny said, "What do you expect?"

The incident put a pall on the game and we all went home.

Dinner that evening was my Mom's steak pizzaiola. My father had me bring in the jug of homemade wine from the backdoor step where it was kept during cool weather. My father poured me one finger in a tumbler. He cut his with Hoffman Cream Soda in a water glass. My mother took only a taste of red.

I told them about the incident with Samuel.

Their forks stopped in midair, and I assured them that I was all right.

I said, "The kid's name is Samuel, but Lenny called him Sambo."

My mother said, "Don't repeat that. It's impolite." She shook her head. "I've not met Mrs. Jackson, but maybe I should talk to her."

My father said, "And say what? Three kids ganged up on Samuel. We don't talk to the Spazzolattos every time Anthony and Lenny fight."

"Molly Spazzolatto said that the neighborhood was changing. It could affect home prices."

My father huffed. He left for the living room and returned with a book, *How the Other Half Lives*, by Jacob Riis. He read, "Cleanliness is the characteristic of the negro. In this respect he is immensely the superior of the lowest of the whites, the Italians." His eyes rose to meet my mother's. "Italians used to be bad for the neighborhood."

She nodded. "We won't say any more about it."

I said, "Why did Samuel try to steal my cards?"

My father said, "Maybe he didn't have money to buy some."

The next day, I saw Samuel bouncing a ball against the wall of the corner apartment building. I neared him. He gave me a brief glance, then continued to throw his ball. I took a handful of doubles from my card collection and placed them on the apartment step. The sound of the ball smacking sidewalk and brick continued. I sighed, turned, and walked back up the street. Willie Mays was my favorite player. Now I noticed he was black.

B.J. Best

TEMPORARY COUGH

The doctors at the local clinic hired me to be a cough, something to drum up business. Dirty work. I'd float in the air of the supermarket until some cabbage-buyer would suck me in. To be a cough is to be a leopard leaping from the lungs, claws catching the back of the throat.

Three weeks later, my wife and I awoke to the sound of a diseased trumpet. Our daughter was choking. We got dressed, checked her breathing, tried to ask logical questions—*Is she allergic? Did she swallow something?*—then careened to the ER. There, the doctor terrified her with a mask of steroids, the buzzing X-ray machine. It turned out to be croup. The photographs showed her airways like the top of a steeple. They gave her some syrup in a cup, a Popsicle, and sent us home, air flooding her lungs like a spring thunderstorm.

Coughing is different than choking, I told the clinic the next day as I resigned. But not different enough.

B.J. Best

NO GOOD MOVIES

Sophomore year of high school. First job. I rewind video tapes. A woman walks into the store. Says there was no video inside the case she rented. I open it up. Inside is a colony of bees. *Bee kind, rewind,* she says. The honey glistens like jewels. *Lady, this isn't an apiary,* I say, and slam the box shut, but get stung anyway. My arm swells up like a muscleman's. I take out my epinephrine injector and hand it to her. *Sign here,* I say, my tongue thick in my mouth. *There are no good movies anymore,* she says. *I'd like to see one about a hospital,* I say. *It's all special effects these days,* she says. *No one remembers how to tell a real story.*

John Picard

"THE ACCORDION POLKA"

"If you stop playing the accordion now," my mother said, shaking a finger at me, "you'll regret it for the rest of your life."

I was only ten and for all I knew she was right. From my child's perspective the only thing adults seemed to do besides work was sit around and talk. If I bothered to listen maybe I'd discover that this one would never forgive himself for quitting the trombone and that one wept whenever he thought about throwing away five years of banjo lessons.

Alarmed by such possibilities, I would haul my six-hundred-dollar accordion (big money in 1960, especially for a working-class family) out of its velvet-lined case and practice for thirty minutes. But that didn't keep me from hating it. I hated everything about the accordion, its whiny organ-grinder sound, its unwieldy bulk, its limited repertoire. Years and years of practice were preparation for playing nothing but "Lady of Spain" and a bunch of polkas.

My mother was not a motivator, except in a negative sense. If I didn't do my homework, I would fail sixth grade and be left behind by all my friends and never make new ones. If I didn't obey God and read my Bible, I would go to hell and burn forever in a fire seven times hotter than any fire on Earth. In addition to future regrets, if I gave up the accordion, she promised me I'd never be allowed to learn another musical instrument. I was fascinated by the drums and loved the sound and elegant shape of the saxophone, but any chance of playing them hinged on my devotion to an overpriced squeezebox.

The Music Man, a Broadway hit in the late 1950s and later a movie, was about a con man who would skip town after selling musical instruments prepaid to small-town rubes who'd been convinced by him of their children's genius for the trumpet, the snare drum, etc. My Music Man brought with him a portable keyboard to test my musical aptitude. I don't recall how he gained access to our home, but I do remember expressing an interest around that time in playing a musical instrument, as children will do without any idea of what that entails. However he got in the door, the deal was that if I demonstrated sufficient ability I would qualify for free accordion lessons for an entire year at the music school he represented, with the condition that my parents purchase an accordion from the same institution, which doubled as an instrument supplier. I was unaware of all this. I just knew I was being tested and I wanted to do well. I wanted to play the accordion.

The Music Man arranged the keyboard on the dining room table. My parents stood to one side, awaiting the verdict. He played a chord, then asked me to play it. He played another. I played that, too. He nodded, impressed. He played some scales in different octaves and asked if I could tell the difference.

Some were higher, I said, others lower.

Good, he said. Very good. Well, he told my parents, he would have no problem recommending me to the music school. My parents looked relieved, perhaps a tiny bit proud. Of course, he said, natural ability was one thing, dedication and hard work another. But, he assured my parents, I had a great future as an accordionist, provided I was willing to apply myself.

Was I? my mother asked me. Was I willing to apply myself?

Yes. Oh yes.

My parents grew up in the 1920s and '30s, when jobs were extremely scarce in Depression-era Louisiana. They hadn't been married long when they moved to Washington, D.C., where my father found work as a street car conductor and later a bus driver. He didn't make good money, though, until he became a route manager for *The Washington Post*, working seven days a week, 365 days a year. By the fifties, he could afford a thirteen-thousand-dollar house, a Dodge station wagon, and, for his musically gifted son, an accordion.

My father was a silent and insular man. As if to make up for his emotional distance, he would surprise me with presents: comic books, a toy truck, a baseball. But no matter how many gifts he gave me, it never got less awkward. He would give them in such an offhand manner, dropping them beside me on the sofa or the floor, then leaving me with the briefest of explanations ("Saw this at Woolworth's"), that before I could thank him, he'd walked away. Once he gave my little sister and me some coin albums, one each for pennies, nickels, and quarters, plus all the change in his pockets to get us started. I don't know what my sister did with hers, but as hard as I tried I couldn't get into coin collecting and after a week I took out all the money and stuck the albums in the bottom of a drawer.

The music school was a two-story brick building in downtown Washington. Entering the foyer, you heard the muffled sounds of a dozen accordion lessons in progress. The place had a distinctive odor, the bellows the accordion player continually pumps emitting a stale, plastic-y smell, like an old comb. The music school reeked of stale accordion breath.

I went there the first time to pick out my new accordion, walking with my parents and a saleslady (a woman my mother's age) into a wood-paneled, high-ceilinged room on the second floor. Apart from a piano in one corner, the only objects in the room were accordions in their suitcase-like cases, arranged in a large circle in the middle of the floor. Urged on by the saleslady, I stepped into the circle and started around, examining each one. They were all different sizes and combinations of colors with the elegant curves, the aerodynamic sleekness, of a sports car. When I paused at certain ones, the woman would suggest I try it. I'd put my arms through the leather straps, lift it out of its case and stand, fingering the keyboard and opening and closing the bellows, as if I knew what I was doing. My parents, neither of whom had played a note on any musical instrument in their lives, looked on impassively.

Naturally I chose the showiest, flashiest one. It was gold and black with lots of levers and buttons I never did learn to use, and white piano-style keys with pin-stripes running through them, and a piece of textured chrome with the manufacturer's name, ROYAL, buffed to a high sheen and attached to the front like a hood ornament. Caught up in the moment, I didn't notice how much heavier it was than the other accordions. It wasn't long after my father began making payments on it that I discovered I couldn't play my new accordion while standing up without getting a back ache.

I couldn't have been more gung-ho at first, practicing an hour or more every day except Sunday, the Biblically mandated day of rest. I didn't mind that I couldn't play my instrument standing up. I didn't mind that I couldn't play more than a few scales and the simplest of songs. I was infatuated with the look and feel of my accordion. I was just happy to hold it in my arms and admire its gaudy beauty.

On Saturday afternoons, when my father drove into Washington to pick up newspapers (the Sunday inserts: mostly comics and advertisements), he would drop me off at the music school for my lesson and return an hour or so later, his long, blue panel truck heaped with bundles of newspapers. He never asked me how my lesson went, any more than he urged me to practice or inquired about my progress. In the division of labor that characterized my parents' generation, these were elements of child-rearing, and child-rearing was women's work. My father had done his part by providing me with the best musical instrument money could buy.

Saturday nights *The Lawrence Welk Show* came on at eight o'clock. My mother and I would watch it together. (My father was in bed by then, his normal work day starting at 11:30 p.m. and ending around dawn.) The highlight for both of us was Myron Floren's performance on the accordion. A testament to his popularity, only the handsome, wavy-haired Myron Floren, with his insouciant dead-on gaze, debonair smile, and brilliant technique had a regular weekly solo. I sat on the floor in front of the TV, the better to observe his long bony fingers crawling up and down the keyboard. My favorite moment came when he would jiggle the accordion, making the notes vibrate. His smile would expand ever so slightly, partly in acknowledgement of the audience's applause, partly from the pleasure of making such a wondrous sound.

"He was really good tonight," I would say to my mother.

"Practice makes perfect."

The only thing marring this honeymoon period was my music teacher. He was a bald, stout, older gentleman with a foreign accent who wore wire-rimmed glasses and a white shirt and dark tie. In memory he looked just like Andrés Segovia. His flinty personality was also like the maestro of the classical guitar whose master class I would see years later on public television.

I dreaded this man's disapproval, expressed in sly ironies at my expense. I once asked him how long he thought it would be before I could play "The Accordion Polka," an accordion classic Myron Floren relied on to showcase his keyboard wizardry.

"Oh," he said, "any day now. Any day."

I complained to my mother about my teacher but she never seemed to take me seriously. In retrospect, I see that he was not a happy man, that underneath his sardonic wit was real bitterness, as though as a child Segovia had taken up the accordion instead of the guitar, leaving him with the permanent, niggling suspicion that he'd missed his true calling, that he'd wasted his life on an instrument unworthy of his genius.

It was not his fault, however, that by the seventh or eighth month the enemies of romance, familiarity and habit, had greatly diminished my accordion's allure. Slowly, ineluctably, my practice time began to fall off, dropping from an hour to fifty minutes, then forty-five, thirty-five, thirty—the recommended minimum suggested by Segovia—and then, when I thought I could get away with it, twenty-nine minutes, twenty-eight, twenty-seven, and so on. It was more and more the case that I didn't practice unless my mother made me.

When I was much older my mother would sometimes start a sentence with, "Your father's a good man, he's been a good provider ...." After the implied "but" would come her complaint that he'd never done anything to help her raise "you children." My father never disciplined us, never saw that we did our homework, never made us brush our teeth or take a bath. My mother performed such housewifely tasks as cooking and housekeeping without protest. But when it came to the unending, thankless labor that is raising a child she felt the burden too keenly not to be resentful. And if that weren't enough, my father had given me something that cost a small fortune, something for which he took no responsibility other than paying for it, and then left her to do the dirty work.

The music school sponsored an annual recital, and having completed a year of study I was urged to participate. Of course I wouldn't be able to use my own accordion. I had to borrow a lighter model from the music school. I applied myself to the accordion with some of the old vigor, practicing up to an hour a day, driven mainly by the fear of making a fool of myself in front of an auditorium full of people. I would stand before my mother's full-length mirror, feet together, eyes straight ahead (no looking at the keys), and play over and over the four-minute piece I'd chosen for what my teacher insisted on calling my "debut."

I almost enjoyed this run-up to my recital, playing music for its own sake, feeling somewhat competent at it. Segovia was unimpressed by my renewed dedication—nothing I did seemed to impress him— but at least my determination to learn "Little Brown Jug" gave him fewer reasons to scold me for not practicing enough. Leaning forward in the chair next to mine, his hands splayed on his knees, his black knit tie tucked into his white shirt, he would say, "That was better, but try it with more feeling this time. Technical virtuosity has its place, but for music to soar there must be a commitment of the heart as well as the mind."

Often I didn't understand a word he said.

The recital went well enough. I made some mistakes, but they weren't so blatant that anyone noticed. It so happened my aunt and uncle from Louisiana—and their many children, my cousins—were visiting us at the time. I had my own little claque that night. My father took a photograph of me in mid-performance. It shows a jug-eared boy holding an accordion high up on his chest and looking very fifties with his flattop and his pair of white bucks.

"How was your debut?" Segovia asked at my next lesson. He did not attend the recitals of any of his students.

"Okay, I guess."

"I'm so glad to hear it. I would hate to think all of our hard work had been in vain."

It turned out that my last bit of enthusiasm for the accordion was used up at my recital. I didn't even like the sound it made anymore, even when made by Myron Floren, who'd lost the ability to inspire me. I'd begun to catch on that he wasn't the coolest guy in the world (Myron?), and the accordion far from the hippest instrument. There were no accordion-playing rock-and-rollers on *American Bandstand,* no accordion-playing folk singers on *Hootenanny*. There was just no payoff with the accordion. I was old enough to start having crushes. I had a major one on Karen Rantovich, the most popular girl in my class. I daydreamed that this dark-eyed, dark-haired cutie in white socks and a Peter Pan collar, this sixth-grade vision who wouldn't give me the time of day normally, would somehow happen upon me playing the guitar, say, or the piano, playing with such dazzling skill that she would fall instantly in love with me. Try as I might, I could not imagine getting that reaction with the accordion, no matter how well I played "The Accordion Polka."

And so I would arrive home from school around four o'clock, grab some snacks, and, planting myself in front of the TV, watch reruns of *The Lone Ranger* and *The Cisco Kid*.

My mother would step out of the kitchen. "If you practice now you won't have to do it later."

"OK. After this show."

After "this show" was another show.

"We'll be eating in half an hour," she'd try again later. "That gives you just enough time to practice."

"In a minute."

"Not in a minute. Right now."

"*OK.*"

I would turn off the TV and go upstairs, but I wouldn't practice; I wouldn't go near the accordion case beside my bed, knowing that my mother was starting dinner and was too busy to bother with me.

But the glances she directed at me across the dinner table told me she hadn't given up the fight. After dinner I returned to my bedroom. Given the choice between opening my math book and opening the accordion case, I would invariable choose the former. And I loathed math!

"I'm not hearing anything up there," my mother would shout from the living room.

"I'm doing my homework."

She would appear in my doorway soon after, her hands on her hips, her brow creased. "You know perfectly well you can't practice after seven-thirty because your father will be in bed. You can always do your homework later."

"I could practice in the basement."

"No, you can't. No, you can't practice in the basement." She meant I couldn't practice in the basement—actually the subbasement—because she couldn't easily monitor my playing from two flights up.

I was no longer susceptible to my mother's vision of an accordionless future racked with remorse, and she knew it. More immediate and tactile measures were called for. Her eyes squinted into slits, her face red with fury and frustration, she would say, "If I don't hear that accordion as soon as I leave this room you're going to regret it. You hear me?"

"Yes."

"'Yes' what?"

"Yes, ma'am."

"Another thing. Look at me at when I'm talking to you. If you don't practice the whole thirty minutes—not twenty minutes, not twenty-five minutes—if you don't practice the whole thirty minutes I'm coming back here with a belt and you'll wish you'd never been born."

"I already wish that!"

The accordion brought out the worst in both of us.

So I would sit for thirty minutes with the accordion getting heavier and heavier on my lap, tapping out this and that scale to keep my mother at bay. She must have realized by then that they'd been duped, that the music school was essentially a front for selling expensive merchandise to unsuspecting parents and overindulged children.

I never told my mother outright that I wanted to quit the accordion, though clearly I did. She never asked me point blank if I wanted to quit, though she had to know the answer. We were locked in a kind of stalemate, my father the mute kibitzer who refused to intervene, a stalemate that only outside circumstances could resolve.

Every third or fourth Saturday my mother would get a babysitter for my sister and ride with me and my father downtown. While I was having my lesson she would shop at one of the big department stores in the area, Woodward and Lothrop's or Hecht's. After my father dropped us off one Saturday, my mother left for G Street and I headed down the corridor to my practice room, walking past the doors of my fellow sufferers as I thought of them, listening to the wheezing, hurdy-gurdy cacophony, breathing in the accordion stink. Segovia was waiting for me with the door open. I strapped on the accordion and arranged myself before the music stand. I played the exercises I'd been assigned that week, then some short pieces from memory. I knew this was a warm-up to my first attempt at a piece I was supposed to have been practicing that week, but with just a few minutes left in the lesson I thought I might get out of it. Then my teacher said,

"Let's hear it, shall we? The new one."

I put the sheet music on the stand, arched my back and began.

Segovia stopped me after three bars. "Again," he said.

I'd gotten to the fifth bar when he put up his hand.

"Once more, please."

After two bars he stopped me yet again.

"It may not be your fault," he said. "It could be I've brought you along too quickly. Do you feel you're not ready for "Pop! Goes the Weasel?" Or is there some other reason for your lack of preparation?"

I could feel tears welling up.

"Whatever the case," he continued, "I can't help questioning your devotion to the accordion—and not for the first time, either. If you lack the will to master its daunting technique, if you're unable to appreciate its complex harmonies, perhaps you should consider switching to a less demanding instrument. The harmonica, say. Or the bongos. Once again, please."

By the time I reached the sixth bar, massacring note after note along the way, I was crying.

"Did your mother come with you today?" Segovia asked.

I nodded.

He left the room and, moments later, returned with my mother. I noticed it particularly at church, where my mother taught Sunday school and sang in the choir, but it was true in general that out in public my mother was miraculously transformed into a lady of gentle manner and ready sweetness. Occasionally I benefited from this. Bending toward me with a shy smile, she took a tissue from her purse and dabbed at my face.

"He's been sick," she explained to my teacher. "He wasn't able to practice as much as he should have." This was true, sort of. I'd had a slight cold that week I used to get out of two days of practice.

"I do wish he'd told me that," Segovia said without a trace of irony, his face alight with Old World charm.

"I'll see that he practices harder this week," my mother said. "I'm sure."

"Are you feeling better?" she asked me.

"Yes."

"Yes, what?" she said with a tight smile.

"Yes, ma'am."

As I was leaving, I glanced back at my teacher in time to see his face assume its customary scowl.

Outside, my father's truck was parked at the curb. Climbing up and in, my mother and I situated ourselves on the bundles of newspapers behind my father. I was still sniffling.

"What's wrong with him?" my father said.

"He cried at his lesson."

"I don't like my teacher. He's mean."

"What did he do to him?" my father asked, turning around in his seat to address my mother.

"Nothing," she said. "He didn't do anything." She took a tissue from her purse, dropped it in my lap, then snapped the purse shut. "Well, I've had all I can take." She aimed a finger at me. "That was your last accordion lesson."

"It was?"

"There'll be no saxophone. I warned you. No drums, either. No more musical instruments of any kind—*ever*. Is that clear?"

It was. I didn't know how or why exactly, but it was over. Not until I was older did I understand that what had looked like my mother's diffidence in front of my teacher was actually acute embarrassment, that what had seemed like extraordinary patience was a cover for her mortification.

"The worst part of it is," she went on, "I knew this would happen. I knew it from the beginning. I told your father, I said, 'Give him a year—two at the most—and he won't want anything more to do with the accordion. It's a waste of money,' I said. 'You'll see.' Well, I was right. Here it is a year later and—."

My father revved the engine.

"Here it is a year later and that's—."

He revved the engine again, louder this time, then shifted gears, revved it a third time, and pulled into traffic. My mother stared at his back for a moment, then looked away. It wasn't long before we

214

crossed the district line into Maryland, my mother and I shifting uncomfortably on the piles of newspapers, my father riding high up in the driver's seat, taking us home.

My parents tried to sell my accordion, but there were no takers for a secondhand accordion no child could play standing up. Shut away in its plush case, it ended up in the subbasement, shoved into a corner with the other junk.

After I graduated from a local college and left home, I moved to another part of the country, but I still visited my parents at the old address twice a year, usually at Christmas and the Fourth of July. The years became decades. During one of my summer visits, when my mother and father were well into their sixties, I descended to the subbasement for a reason I don't remember, leaving my parents to their TV-watching in the living room. While I was rummaging around in that cool, damp place, I noticed that my accordion case was nowhere in sight. I sorted through the discarded household items, but I couldn't find it. It occurred to me to check the closet, and there it was, partially buried under a pile of old magazines. Pushing them aside, I dragged the case out into the room, flipped its rusty latches and opened the lid. The top of the R in ROYAL, the metal nameplate, had broken off, but the accordion itself appeared to be in good condition. Even though no one had been stopping me, as a grown-up with plenty of leisure and disposable income, I hadn't taken up the drums or the saxophone or anything else, which meant I was standing over the only musical instrument I'd ever played, and likely ever would play. I lifted it out of its case, put my arms through the straps and brought it to my chest. I passed the middle finger of my left hand over the rows of buttons until it found the one with the depression, what I remembered was the "C" note; my ring finger rested on the button diagonal to it. I guided the middle finger of my right hand a third of the way down the keyboard and settled it there, assuming the standard starting position for accordion playing. I opened the bellows. They breathed for the first time in thirty-plus years. I pressed down on the buttons, once with my middle finger, twice with my ring finger—*ohm pa pa, ohm pa pa, ohm pa pa*. I closed and opened the bellows again, this time running the fingers of my right hand up and down the keyboard, a la Myron Floren. Then I did both hands together. I thought I was actually playing something, perhaps a piece taught to me by my lordly music teacher. I was so engrossed it was a moment or two before I bothered to listen to what I was playing, and what I was playing it turned out was ... nothing. Nothing but a mishmash of wrong notes. Heat spread over my face and neck. I'd embarrassed myself. Then I was seized by the fear that my parents might have heard me, might come looking for the source of that strangely familiar sound. I slipped quickly out of the straps and dropped the accordion back in its case. I lowered the lid and snapped the latches shut. Hauling it back inside the closet, I grabbed up the magazines and spread them over the case. I closed the door and hurried away.

William Trowbridge

SERENDIPITY

Said to be among the ten words
hardest to translate, it's what happened

when Fleming, forgetting to clean
his pertri dish, discovered penicillin,

and Roentgen, fiddling with tubes
and gasses, hit on X-rays. Ditto

the stumbling onto cornflakes, matches,
superglue, vulcanized rubber, plastic.

Velcro, potato chips, stainless steel, Popsicles,
microwave ovens, and Viagra. All serendipity.

It means the opposite of "Edsel," "winged tanks,"
"sea-shoes," the "vacuum beauty helmet";

of Midas' magic fingers, or the mantis male's
after-sex come-hug-me; or when, as a toddler,

I tried to feed the neighbor's Doberman,
a mild rehearsal for teen romance,

when, coaxed by hormones and the boogaloo,
I held my heart out to Melody Capone.

Serendipity

Walpole coined the term after reading a fairy tail
about three princes of "Serendip," now Sri Lanka.

So genteel and foreign-sounding, the word can
make us ransack memory, grab the Webster's,

which we'd never need to do for "perfect storm,"
"Murphy's Law," or "clusterfuck."

William Trowbridge

DEATH RECOUNTS HIS FAMILY HISTORY

Grandpa Death acquired foreclosed properties
under the name of Meek & Co. (his little joke).
An avid churchgoer, he helped start the Inquisition
and was always there for last-minute conversions.

He could have been an ad man: "Call it 'The Black Plague,'"
he advised, "nice and simple. Round it off: 'The Hundred
Years' War,' 'The Thousand Cuts,' 'the Last Mile.' Go with
something upbeat, motivational: '*Arbeit Macht Frei.*'"

Things got so good he could almost let the business
run itself. He'd lounge in some seaside disaster area, taking in
the sights. Finally, he retired to Palm Desert, where he still
plays a mean handicap and dabbles in futures.

Walking in such a big shadow, so to speak, irked Dad, who tried
photography part-time—hand-tinted portraits of children
propped in their coffins. Your artsy type, he finally dropped out
and moved to Stockholm, where he got a part in a Bergman film.

So now it's just me, the family dark horse, you could say. "Quit
following me around, you little creep!" Dad used to holler,
sounding like the kids at school. Of course, it wasn't long
before I got the balance sheet back in order. Cigarette?

Michelle Ross

RATTLESNAKE ROUNDUP

Ray was irritable during the drive up to Sweetwater, kept removing his baseball cap from his head and shaking it as though to dislodge a stick-a-bur.

"State your grievance," Tess said from the passenger seat of the motor home as they left Houston. She watched her husband carefully.

The kids were in back, both insulated by earbuds.

Ray said, "This weekend is about Dad. Why the hell would Mom do something like this?"

"Bring a date?" Tess said.

She was savoring Ray's misery, and there was nothing he could say about it.

They were caravanning to Sweetwater, Texas, for the largest rattlesnake roundup in the country to release Tess' father-in-law's ash remains. For three years, Ray and his sisters, Joyce and Trudy, had asked their mother what she planned to do with Cash's ashes, and Lynette had said she didn't want to talk about it. She hadn't approved of Cash's wish to get cremated. For that and other grievances, her kids had worried she'd kept him in that recycled peanut jar tucked behind spare toilet paper rolls as punishment. Then, finally, she'd said it was time.

The roundup had been Cash's affair. While he'd never collected thousands of pounds the way the top contributors did (that's how the Jaycees, who hosted the event, paid for the snakes: by the pound), every year he'd brought in about a hundred pounds or so.

Nobody questioned Lynette's decision about *where*. Considering they'd been asking her *when* for three years, they couldn't very well object to the timing either, except insofar as her unexpected traveling companion was concerned.

He was almost stilt-walker tall, and he wore black leather pants and a T-shirt featuring a fanged human skull. Add to that his devilish black goatee, thin mustache, and shiny black hair, and he resembled one of the shadowy figures from the covers of the trashy romance novels Lynette sometimes read.

Twenty-six to Lynette's seventy. He was a dark cabaret musician—stage name: Enigma. He'd produced two albums: *Wet-Feathered Feeling* and *Miss Muffit Under the Tuffet*. Vampires, cannibals, and ghost lovers who sucked the brains out of your head while you were sleeping were his subject matter. All this Tess learned from the Internet on the drive up after Lynette introduced them all to him in the parking lot of a Walmart where they'd met to caravan to Sweetwater together, three trailers and a motor home. It was a bold move.

Before Walmart, Tess had been the gruff traveling companion. Ray had been out of work five months, no unemployment checks on account of his resigning from his position as radiation safety technician at the hospital's request out of fear that the situation could become a lot worse if he didn't. The story Ray told his family was that another employee had framed him for something he didn't do. His eldest sister Joyce's response to that had been to say, "Well, if they all die of radiation poisoning over there, serves 'em right." What his family didn't know was that the employee in question had been a summer intern and that what she accused Ray of was making her uncomfortable by talking about his "marital dissatisfaction," this while offering her shoulder rubs. Withholding these details had been Ray's idea. He'd begged Tess not to tell them, this despite swearing up and down that it had all been a misunderstanding and that he'd most certainly not been hitting on the young woman. "You know me!" he'd said.

He wouldn't have told Tess either, probably, if he hadn't been certain she would find out from her friend Nevia, who worked in HR.

Ray made a wrong turn upon entering Sweetwater. He drove the motor home past ramshackle houses that Tess initially presumed were abandoned, so many of them had boarded-up windows, but then she saw a pair of cats feeding from a dish set along a door stoop. Farther down the street, a dog dragged what looked like a T-bone, the meat long gone.

Recently, a sixteen-year-old girl had gone missing from the town Tess and Ray and all his family lived in. The girl's car was found abandoned alongside the highway just before the exit for the main road through town, the girl's purse and car keys on the passenger seat. Everyone believed this was proof she'd been abducted and probably they were right, but Tess wondered what details, like the cat dish and the T-bone, may have been overlooked. She wondered if the girl might have staged the whole thing. Once life got going on a certain course, it was difficult to change that course without taking drastic measures.

Tess said nothing about the unintended detour now, and she observed this as if from a distance. They were just two people traveling together along a road neither of them had seen coming. They were on an adventure. That was one way to look at it. Dr. Olive would see it another way. "When you avoid your feelings, the feelings don't go away. They're there under the surface, still doing their damage. Like a boil. You need to get the crud to come to the surface."

Despite having never met him, Dr. Olive seemed to think Tess should leave Ray. She'd never said this directly, but every week at their appointment she pressed Tess to focus on what she needed and wanted, and to forget everybody else. There were questions she urged Tess to answer, questions such as if her relationship with Ray were a story she could write any way she desired, how would she write it? What did she dare not hope for? These questions had bored into Tess like the larvae of botflies. She could feel them wriggling around beneath her skin.

Tess's head spun for hours, sometimes days, after her appointments with Dr. Olive. Like being a member of a cult was the analogy that came to mind, only she wasn't sure whether her counselor was deprogramming her or initiating her.

Tess's friend Nevia had been in and out of counseling for a couple of decades. She said, "That's because that doctor is taking a jackhammer to your snow globe. It feels scary, but trust me, it's a good thing."

Then again, Tess had long suspected Nevia didn't think Ray was good enough for her. After all, not even Coach bags or Godiva chocolates, things regular people would consider indulgences, were good enough for Nevia.

☾

A fat rattlesnake in the demonstration pit curled up like a house cat within inches of Tess's feet, only a transparent thermoplastic barrier between them. Its meek pose was betrayed by the sharp, black slits in its eyes, its lean snout, and its taut body. Its glistening tongue, which poked out here and there to smell her, looked like the tail of some pitiful amphibious creature the snake was teasing, letting loose its throat's grip only to suck the creature back in again.

The man in the demonstration pit stirred the snakes that had collected together like helpings of spaghetti, the reverse of the Halloween prank Tess had pulled when the kids were little, shoving their small hands inside a cardboard box that concealed a heap of cold ricotta-stuffed manicotti. The man explained to the crowd that he had to move the snakes around from time to time so they didn't suffocate each other.

Ray, the kids, and Tess' in-laws were outside the coliseum, eating sausages on sticks. They'd seen enough, or at least Ray had.

Within the couple of minutes he'd spent in the coliseum, his sullenness had morphed into anger the way it had the previous summer when she'd lured him into an art gallery to watch a performance artist cut a Texas flag into her chest with a razor blade as she stood naked before her audience and sang "The Yellow Rose of Texas." Ray hadn't cared what statement the artist was making. He'd said the whole thing was perverse. To make a statement of his own, he'd slept that night curled up in the back seat of his car, which resulted in a couple hundred dollars' worth of chiropractic adjustments.

The man in the demonstration pit had gentle blue-gray eyes, a color one might liken to a crystalline body of water, though the bodies of water Tess had known her whole life, the Gulf of Mexico and countless alligator-infested bayous and swamps, were brown or murky green. He wore a crisp white shirt and white Stetson hat and spoke softly about the importance of understanding the snakes. He said things like "When the sun has set the air on fire, I don't need my Kevlar boots. The snakes don't like that harsh sun. But when the temperature gets to around fifty at night and seventy or eighty during the day, that's when they're out looking for food, water, and companionship. They won't go out of their way to strike, but if I startle them, they will. They do it out of fear. They do it to protect themselves. I know this from living with them."

The majority of the Jaycees weren't so charming. "We stretch 'em and sex 'em, stretch 'em and sex 'em," a Jaycee in the weighing pit said in answer to Tess's question about what he learned by poking the snakes' tails with a metal probe. A Jaycee in the milking pit taunted her with a snake's pried-open mouth, like a school boy with a shiny new pocketknife. "Ah, come on. Give him some love." A Jaycee in the skinning pit spat out chewing tobacco as he slit a snake open along the length of its body, which hung from a hook above him. His bare arms were ribboned with tattoos of blue-skinned women, their hair fanning out as though they were under water, as though they had drowned, every last one.

The man in the demonstration pit pulled a yellow balloon from his shirt pocket and blew air into it. He rubbed the balloon up and down his body. To give it his scent, he said, though he'd told his audience that pit vipers sense their prey via infrared radiation.

The snakes hardly seemed to notice him. They lay placid as sunbathers. The only hint otherwise was the steady rattle that permeated the coliseum. The rattling hum seemed to come from everywhere and nowhere all at once as though Tess were situated inside the belly of it. When the man in the demonstration pit managed to gather a snake he'd been fishing for with a hooked metal rod and lift it onto the table at the pit's center, the animal's tail shot up like an antenna, but she perceived no audible change.

The first time he prodded the snake with the balloon, Tess shuddered. This was how some religious fanatics got themselves killed. It was the sort of thing she could imagine her father-in-law, Cash, doing, only the man in the demonstration pit didn't seem the least bit smug or cruel about it. He was nothing like Cash, who'd taken pleasure in riling people, as well as snakes. Sometimes Tess had gotten a kick out of watching him, especially when it was Ray's sister Joyce he was after. But he'd worn on her too. He'd made the kids cry, sent Ray into depressions that lasted weeks.

The man in the demonstration pit circled the snake, and the animal rotated to keep tabs on him. They were partners in a strange dance. While he intentionally aggravated the snake, it was true, there was nothing cruel about the performance. There was softness in his movements.

Finally, after what seemed like several minutes of taunting, the snake had had enough, and it struck and popped the balloon.

The man didn't flinch. He left the snake on top of the table. He stirred the snakes in the spaghetti heaps. He said, "What I'm trying to teach you is that rattlesnakes are not aggressive creatures. The only time they're generally dangerous is in September when the females are caring for their young. Then they'll kill you. Outside of that, they're passive. They just want to be left alone. Leave them alone, and they won't go out of their way to strike."

Lynette's boyfriend circled round the demonstration pit then and stood next to Tess. He didn't say a word, but even so, she felt as though he were absorbing her with some kind of extrasensory perception, as though he were "seeing" through her skin and skull and into the folds of her brain, as if he could read her synapses. This is how she felt under Dr. Olive's gaze, too. Like they were playing Blind Man's Bluff, except Dr. Olive's card was tucked away in her palm; Dr. Olive could see Tess's card and her own, but Tess could see nothing.

The previous year Tess had visited the world's quietest room, the anechoic chamber at Orfield Laboratories in Minneapolis, for a magazine article she'd written about the science of sound. She'd heard her blood moving through her brain and heart, the tiny firings of her auditory nerves, and squeaks along the joints connecting the bones in her skull. She hadn't lasted five minutes. After, she'd staggered to the toilet and hung her head between her legs for fifteen minutes before she felt her body was in sync enough to manage the task of maneuvering down a hallway without bumping into something.

Lately she'd suffered similarly disorienting bouts. She was tuning in to background noises she hadn't known were there.

Once when she awoke in the middle of the night to use the toilet, she was so startled by her own reflection that a curdling scream issued from her larynx. It seemed to ricochet through her, leaving a long hollow in its wake. She hadn't recognized her own voice. This, more than the unanticipated movement in the mirror, was what haunted her. It had not been the scream of someone young and vibrant. She'd pictured a stiff white nightgown that buttoned up to the neck, a lonely old woman afraid of her own shadow. When had she become the sort of a person who could produce such a sound?

Being the incredibly deep sleeper he is, Ray hadn't heard, thank goodness. In the morning when she'd told him about it, he'd said, "Everybody sounds like an idiot when they scream."

He was wrong, though. Ray hadn't known her when she was a teenager. Then she'd been a beautiful screamer. Tess and her friends, Cath and Kiki, used to take turns. The idea had been to imagine they were running from a psycho killer. The girl whose turn it was closed her eyes and imagined herself alone with the killer, and when she was ready, she opened her mouth and let sound rip from her throat like a hurricane.

Sometimes a psycho killer wasn't enough. Sometimes they had to taunt each other to get there, like when it was Cath's turn, they would pinch the fat along her bra strap and say she was as plump as a biscuit and that the killer was going to slice her open and butter her up. When it was Kiki's turn, they chastised her for having been so desperate for a boyfriend that she let Skip Nolan plant hickeys all over her neck during lunch break at the Burger Basket. When it was Tess's turn, Cath and Kiki went off on her crazy bitch of a mother and how she better hope she didn't end up like her, alone and angry and pathetic.

Always, always, when the screamer got there, when the fear penetrated the lacquered kernel of her core and shattered her from the inside as it burst forth through her throat, they all three knew it at once. They all three felt it. After, they collapsed, exhausted, a pile of sweaty limbs and smeared mascara. Except for the sounds of their breathing and their thumping hearts, they were silent. As the heat gradually left their bodies, they gathered themselves up and moved onto other things—talk of how bored they were, how depressed they were, of the boys they'd fooled around with and the boys they hoped to fool around with. This talk was like the hurried motions of pulling on clothes after the spell of intoxication had worn off.

Tess had been thinking about Cath and Kiki a lot since that sixteen-year-old girl went missing.

In the auditorium, Enigma produced a small black drawstring bag filled with black licorice jelly beans and offered it to Tess. She took a single jelly bean and slid it into her jean pocket.

She, Cath, and Kiki used to slip bags of the stuff into their purses before asking a sales clerk at the front of the store to sell them a pack of cigs, which they couldn't very easily steal. Tess stopped eating licorice at the same time she stopped smoking. That was years ago.

She was a little afraid to taste licorice now, afraid its pungent taste might make her want something she didn't want to want.

"I'm Tess, Ray's wife," she said, the words sounding dumb and inconsequential.

"Enig," he said.

For lack of something better to talk about, she told him she thought the man in the demonstration pit was a gem.

He said, "The guy speaks softly and uses words like 'companionship,' and you're won over to his side? All your judgments about what these men are doing vanished just like that?"

"What makes you think I had any judgments?"

He stared at her.

"I'm just saying I don't think this guy is like the rest. He's fond of them."

"So what if he is? They're prisoners. They've been yanked up out of their homes. Now they're going to be skinned and fried and made into dashboard ornaments. No pretty talk can justify that."

Then he said, "I'm going to free these poor bastards."

"And do what? Send the snakes out into the arena, the fair tents, the parking lot, the campground, and the carnival?" Even as she said it, she felt a thrill at the idea of the crowds being terrorized by the very animals they came to ogle. There was a lovely justice in it, one that Ray would be unable to appreciate. He disapproved of the event as well, but the difference, she thought, was that Ray's anger arose from a sense of his own suffering at having to bear witness, whereas Enig's anger was for the snakes, for their suffering.

"You heard him—people don't get bitten unless they present themselves as threats." Then, "Lynette tell you what we're going to do with the old man's ashes?"

"Lynette and I aren't close."

"We're going to feed him to the snakes. It's beautiful. That man was a gasser. You know that? He chased them out of their burrows with gasoline. And now he'll disappear into the black holes of the snakes' throats. It's like ouroboros, the snake eating its own tail. It's so damn perfect you can feel it in your gut."

What Tess felt in her gut was something else. She didn't feel bad for Cash. She didn't care what happened to his ashes. They were just carbon and other elements anyhow—elements that would get recycled again and again no matter where they were deposited.

It was Lynette she was thinking about. She'd been married to the man for forty-eight years. How was it that a person could spend her entire adult life with a person she despised so much she'd want to feed his remains to rattlesnakes?

Lynette stepped out of her trailer in a rockabilly-style black shirt dress like nothing Tess had ever seen her in before. Her long gray hair was pulled back into two French braids.

Enig stepped out of the trailer behind her. He was gargantuan next to Lynette. Together they looked like characters out of a freak show or a fairy tale. He leaned over and kissed her on the mouth, and Tess half expected the kiss to transform Lynette somehow, revealing some hidden identity cast away by a spell.

Ray bristled where he stood with his brothers-in-law, Fred and Buck, beside Buck's smoker. They drank beer as Buck piled on twenty pounds of pork for the barbeque cook-off because if they were going to come up all this way, might as well take home a trophy.

When Enig broke away from Lynette, he took off walking. He sang as he wove between other people's trailers. He had a voice like caramel—thick and rich and sticky.

Joyce and Trudy hauled the ice chest full of shrimp to a weathered picnic table several dozen yards away, and Lynette and Tess followed with bowls, knives, and newspaper. Ray's sisters didn't know about Lynette's plans for the ashes yet, for if they did, they wouldn't have sat down with their mother to remove the exoskeletons and intestinal tracts from twelve pounds of shrimp, Cash's favorite crustaceans, for dinner.

Joyce said, "I worry about you, Momma."

"What in hell for?" Lynette said.

They had to swat flies with their elbows as they worked, but none of them wanted to smell raw shrimp where they slept, so they battled the flies without complaint.

"The world is one heck of a crazy place right now," Joyce said. She gestured in the direction of the crooning with her eyes.

"You think he's going to bludgeon her in her sleep?" Tess said.

Joyce ignored her. "The two of you don't make any sense."

It was true that Lynette and Enig weren't logical. He was barely one-third her age and had penetrating brown eyes that had probably prompted whole crowds of female fans to offer themselves like trays of skewered fruit. But one thing Tess knew for certain was that lust wasn't logical.

And anyway, Joyce's constant negativity grated her. She was the type of person who would knock senseless fools out of the way to do CPR on you if you were unconscious, but as soon as you were resuscitated, she'd proceed to complain about your halitosis and critique the state of the bra she'd had to pull up around your neck. *How often do you wash that thing? That's not a good color on you, just so you know.*

For this and other faults, Tess wished a meteor would burn through Earth's atmosphere and shoot right through Joyce's skull, a hot little bullet by the time it reached her.

Then she immediately felt guilty for thinking it. There seemed to be an important distinction to be made between recognizing Joyce's despicableness and deriving pleasure from the notion of her suffering for it. The latter had been Cash's territory. If he hadn't been so convinced he could punish people with his actions and words, he would have kept a drawer of voodoo dolls.

"The world has been a crazy place for as long as I've been living in it," Lynette said. She wiped sweat from her forehead with the back of her hand. "Ain't nothing new about crazy."

In no time at all, they were talking about the girl who'd gone missing. The general consensus among Tess' in-laws was that the girl was lying at the bottom of the bayou running through their town, but who did it and how was still up for discussion.

Trudy blew a few strands of her bottle-red hair out of her face and said, "My money's on some shifty-eyed creep like that bagger at Kroger. Every time he asks me if I want help carrying my groceries out, I can see just what he has in mind. He'd scoop me into the trunk of my own car and drive me off to some secret hideout in the woods and do God knows what with me. Then he'd probably dump me and take my groceries and my money to boot."

"Goodness sakes," Joyce said. "What do you think that man could possibly want to do with you?"

"He'd rape her in the rear," Lynette said. "Remember that guy in Alvin who broke into widows' homes and raped them in the rears? Three women in all before he was caught. Same crazy look in his eyes."

Just then, Joyce's second-youngest child, Ruth Lily, ran all the way from the carnival to complain that her younger sister, Fern, had bitten her. Ruth Lily held up her arm to reveal human teeth marks. "Take it to your daddy," Joyce said.

None of the women said anything for several minutes. The clouds in the sky were stretched thin like plastic wrap. Tess became painfully aware of how sticky her hands were with the shrimps' inky innards.

"I read that that girl was giving her Momma grief all the time, staying out all hours of the night," Joyce said.

Tess slammed the table with her fist, surprising herself as much as her in-laws, who all froze.

People had said terrible things about Kiki when she stole five hundred dollars from her grandmother and ran off to Los Angeles. They hadn't known what Tess and Cath had known, that her scurvy stepfather had been molesting her since she was a kid.

They were supposed to have run away together, the three of them, but Kiki had gotten impatient waiting for them to commit. "You're scared," she'd said.

Tess and Cath had been so ashamed of abandoning her that they hadn't even said goodbye. They'd received one letter each from Kiki, in which she'd pardoned them, and then they'd never heard from her again. Their letters to her had come back unopened.

"Let's not blame the victim," Tess said now. She wiped shrimp guts onto newspaper. "Assuming she was abducted, assuming she didn't run away, we all know it was a man who did it."

The other women nodded their heads in agreement.

The talk turned to the violence that lurked beneath the surface of *their* men. Trudy told a story about how Fred punched a man in the stomach simply because he talked to her a little too long about the firmness of cantaloupes as Fred watched from across barrels of apples. "We lit the sheets *that* night," she said with a crooked smile.

Joyce recalled the time Buck repeatedly bashed the earth next to a bush in their backyard with the back of a shovel because she commented that it looked like a rabbit den and the last thing she needed was a whole litter of bunnies getting into her vegetable garden. "He ran out there quick as a snake," she said. "I didn't mean for him to hurt them. I was just saying was all. The whole time I was screaming for him to stop, and after he said he did it for me, so what was I making a fuss about?"

Lynette told a story they all knew—how she'd jumped between Cash and Ray after an eleven-year-old Ray freed the crate of rattlesnakes Cash had caught for the roundup.

Like Enig was scheming to do with the entire arena of rattlesnakes, Tess thought, and she wondered for the first time about Ray's motivation in freeing those snakes. He'd only ever talked about it as an act of kindness, to the snakes, but had it been? Or had it simply been a way to get under his father's skin?

"I thought he was going to kill Ray," Lynette said gravely.

Then she told them something they didn't know, that after that incident, she had no love left for Cash. "If trading him in would have been as easy as returning an expired carton of milk, I would have done it in a heartbeat."

There was a long silence.

Then Lynette said, "I feel like I can tell you this because I know now just what I was missing."

Joyce said, "With all due respect, I don't want to hear about it."

It was supposed to be Tess' turn, but they'd forgotten all about her. No one looked to her. No one said, *So what about Ray? In what ways is he violent?*

Lynette said, "Well, you're going to have to get over it because we're moving in together. We're getting a dog."

"A dog!" Trudy said. "I thought you hated dogs!"

Of course, the story occupying Tess was the one she'd promised Ray she wouldn't tell, and it would humiliate her as much as it would him. She didn't need to give her in-laws another reason to pity them.

"Christ's sake, Momma. Can you slow down for a minute and think about this? He's a kid. Quite frankly, he's a freak, too. And you could be that freak's grandmother," Joyce said.

"I've never been happier in my life," Lynette said.

And would it be a stretch to call what Ray had done violent? He was adamant that it had been innocent, that the young woman had misunderstood his intentions. Of course, his actions had indeed conveyed interest. That he wouldn't admit that felt like a kind of violence, the way he'd rather try to convince Tess she was mistaken than own up to the truth. What Tess could never be sure about was whether Ray really was so out of touch with himself that he didn't see this or whether he wanted so badly to believe he had done nothing wrong that he'd convinced himself he hadn't. Or: was he an exceptional liar?

"Momma!" Trudy said.

"Now that's simply a cruel thing to say," Joyce said.

"It's not meant to be cruel. It has nothing to do with you," Lynette said.

Lynette's boyfriend's singing seeped in like a fog: "All you little children, you better lock your doors and clean your mouths." Tess caught a momentary glimpse of his black-clad body in a sliver of empty space between trailers and trees. He was a phantom. He was not of this world. The same could be said of his and Lynette's relationship. Tess would have said that such a love was impossible, impractical, and absurd.

It was as though a fat yellow balloon were being waved in Tess's face. Her in-laws were trying to incite her to strike. They'd been trying all along.

She cleared her throat then and said, "So Lynette, why don't you tell Joyce and Trudy about your plan for their daddy's ashes?"

Lynette cocked her head at Tess. She looked out into the trees where Enig had momentarily passed through.

She said, "Might as well tell you, I guess." She paused. Then, "We're going to feed 'em to the snakes."

All motion stopped at once, but Tess' sisters-in-law's bodies seemed to buzz with the potential for movement like mousetraps that could spring at a feather's touch. Tess wondered if inside an anechoic chamber, she'd be able to hear the twitching of the women's muscles, if together they'd sound like an arena full of rattlesnakes.

Joyce and Trudy stared at Lynette.

"You can't do this, Momma," Joyce said.

"I most certainly can."

Joyce said, "If you want to be rid of them, give the ashes to me. Let me deal with this."

"I want to feed him to the snakes," Lynette said.

"Did that freak put this into your head?" Joyce again.

Trudy looked dazed.

"It's not an idea that really belongs to either one of them," Tess said. "Isn't that right? It blew into you like a divine wind? You listened to your gut and you just knew?" The words were hardly out of her mouth when her hands began to shake just as they had done before her last two appointments with Dr. Olive. She heard the words of the man in the demonstration pit: *They attack out of fear.*

Lynette said, "I lived with that man longer than y'all ever did. Those ashes are mine."

"He's our daddy," Joyce said. "I didn't drive all the way up here for this."

"He gave you both a tough time too. It wasn't just Ray."

Trudy stood then and took off running toward Lynette's trailer. She let herself inside and came out with the peanut jar.

"Things are going to get ugly if she doesn't hand him back over," Lynette said.

"They're already ugly." Joyce's eyes were on Tess.

As Trudy headed toward the coliseum, Ray grabbed her arm. Tess couldn't hear what was said, but he soon let go and Trudy was off, running clumsily, but faster than Tess would have imagined she was capable of.

"What in hell, Mom?" Ray said as he marched toward the table, but Lynette ignored him. She wiped her hands on the shirt dress and hobbled after Trudy.

Trudy stopped amid the last patch of yellowed grass just before she reached the pavement leading to the fair tents and the food venders and the crowds of tourists shopping for rattlesnake souvenirs. She twirled around like a sprinkler, spraying Cash's ashes in all directions.

When Lynette caught up with her, she got down on her hands and knees and scooped up what she could of the remains while Trudy kicked the ashes around with her feet to save some of her father from her mother.

Tess spit on the newspaper and tried to wipe her hands clean, but they were shaking so bad now that after dropping the paper three times, she gave up.

Joyce yelled to Buck that she was going to clean up, fetch the kids from the carnival, and then they were leaving pronto. She filled the empty plastic bags with the peeled shrimp and piled them back into the ice chest. She wadded up newspaper. She worked fast.

Ray said, "Will someone tell me what the hell is going on around here?"

"Why don't you ask Tess?" Joyce said. She slammed the lid down on the ice chest. She took off for the carnival, which was in the opposite direction of the fair tents and food venders.

The Ferris wheel, which loomed above the other rides, was motionless except for a slight jiggling, like a cog trying to come unstuck.

Ray turned to Tess. They were on opposite sides of the picnic table, watching each other closely like animals startled in the wild.

Tess stuffed her trembling hands into her pockets and found the jelly bean, sticky now. She imagined a beanstalk so huge it grasped the sky and cast a shadow over the whole damn town of Sweetwater. Would climbing it be an act of bravery or cowardliness? Strength or weakness? This was the sort of questioning that drove Tess crazy. To climb it or not to climb it, the decision could be interpreted so many ways. Like her not accompanying Kiki.

One day not long after that girl went missing, Tess pulled into a random hardware store parking lot, sat in her parked car, and tried to imagine Kiki hitchhiking halfway across the country alone, nothing but a suitcase and a few hundred dollars to her name. How terrified she must have been. Tess's chest ached to think of it.

When she'd considered running away with Kiki, she'd felt as though she were fawning over an unaffordable piece of clothing, like the spangled, gray leather jacket she'd fantasized about for years after she saw it at an upscale boutique she'd had no business browsing. Just do it, one part of her brain had said, while another part calculated interest and all that would have to be sacrificed in exchange.

Practical and cautious, she always placed such preposterous longings back onto their racks and got the hell out of there.

That was one way to look at it.

But what she thought of now was Miss Snake Charmer, the glittery teenage pageant winner who'd donned snake-proof chaps earlier that day and paraded around the inner perimeter of the demonstration pit with a live rattlesnake draped over her outstretched palms like a ceremonial object. Tess recalled the question a reporter called out to the newly crowned Miss Snake Charmer, "Aren't you afraid of all these snakes?" and the girl's answer, "There are a lot scarier things in this world than snakes. Like not fulfilling your dreams. That's the scariest thing I can think of."

Marc Tretin

THE WIRELESS PHONE THAT WAS DROPPED DOWN THE STAIRS

still has digits, three, eight, nine and sometimes
five able to call, but only Idaho,
and with crackles, buzzes, hisses, and chimes.
It wants to connect without saying "hello."
With nothing to communicate except the pain
of having nothing to communicate,
it dials four numbers again and again
in variations of five, nine, three, and eight.

Someone is breathing hard on the other end.
With no voice to muffle, silence can listen.
Unable to connect, but needing a friend,
it calls, not person to person, but phone to person.
Its content-less conversation says, "I'm here"
to someone saying, "Hello? Who's there? Who's there?!"

Reese Conner

THANK YOU

His name was Lewis
and my father loved him

        the way men
        of his generation,

        men who are not women,
        men who need to make
        that distinction

        love,

which is to say my father
met our neighbor,
received the bag
full of Lewis,

        who,
        like all dead cats
        that are carried,
        became broken rubber bands
        heavy as ball bearings,

and said *thank you*

        as if it were a kindness
        to yank a dog
        from the cat it killed,

as if the trespass of a cat
ought to end like this,

while that dog,
a chained-up shepherd,
still choked itself
over and over,
trying to admire
what it had done.

Contributors' Notes

Glen Armstrong edits the poetry journal *Cruel Garters*. He has a new chapbook, *Set List* (*The Bitchin' Kitsch*, 2015).

Tricia Asklar's poems have appeared in *Cold Mountain Review*, *juked*, *Neon*, *Poet Lore*, and other publications. Recently, her work was selected for the anthologies *ARTlines2: Art Becomes Poetry* and *My Cruel Invention* (Meerkat Press, 2015). She lives near Boston and teaches at Stonehill College.

Laura Bernstein-Machlay teaches literature and creative writing at the College for Creative Studies in Detroit, where she also lives. Her poems and creative nonfiction have appeared in numerous journals, including *The Michigan Quarterly Review*, *Oyez*, and *Redivider*, and are forthcoming in *The American Scholar*.

B.J. Best is the author of three books, most recently *But Our Princess Is in Another Castle* (Rose Metal Press, 2013), a collection of prose poems inspired by classic video games. *I Got Off the Train at Ash Lake*, a verse novella, is forthcoming from sunnyoutside. He lives in Wisconsin.

Melissa Boston's poetry appears in *Bird's Thumb*, *I-70 Review*, *The Fourth River*, *Blue Mesa Review*, and other journals. She currently lives in Fayetteville, Arkansas.

Sarah Browning is co-founder and the executive director of Split This Rock Poetry Festival: Poems of Provocation & Witness and an associate fellow of the Institute for Policy Studies. She is the author of *Whiskey in the Garden of Eden* (The Word Works, 2007), co-editor of *D.C. Poets Against the War: An Anthology* (Argonne House Press, 2004), and the recipient of artist fellowships from the D.C. Commission on the Arts & Humanities.

Susan Taylor Chehak is a graduate of the University of Iowa Writers' Workshop. Her most recent publications include a collection of short stories, *It's Not About the Dog* (Foreverland Press, 2015), and a novel, *The Minor Apocalypse of Meena Krejci* (Foreverland Press, 2015).

Andrew Collard lives in Madison Heights, Michigan, and attends Oakland University. Recent poems can be found online at *A-Minor Magazine*, *Juked*, and *Posit*. He co-edits *SiDEKiCK LIT*, a poetry journal.

Reese Conner's work appears or is forthcoming in *Spillway*, *Punchnel's*, *Fifth Wednesday Journal*, *Third Wednesday*, and elsewhere. He received the Katherine C. Turner Prize from the Academy of American Poets and the Mabelle A. Lyon Poetry Award.

Jeff Coomer lives in Charlottesville, Virginia, where he devotes his time to poetry.

Andrew Cox is the author of *The Equation That Explains Everything* (BlazeVOX, 2011), the chapbook *Fortune Cookies* (2River, 2009), and the hypertext chapbook *Company X* (Word Virtual). He edits *UCity Review*.

Jim Daniels' most recent books include *Apology to the Moon* (BatCat Press, 2015), *Eight Mile High* (Michigan State University Press, 2014), and *Birth Marks* (BOA Editions Ltd., 2013). He lives in Pittsburgh, where he teaches at Carnegie Mellon University.

John Davis is the author of two poetry collections, *Gigs* (Sol Books, 2011) and *The Reservist* (Pudding House Publications, 2005). His work has recently appeared in *One*, *Iron Horse Literary Review*, and *Kentucky Review*. He currently teaches high school.

Nandini Dhar is the author of the chapbook *Lullabies Are Barbed Wire Nations* (Two of Cups Press, 2014). Her poems have recently appeared or are forthcoming in *Potomac Review*, *PANK*, *The Los Angeles Review*, *Quiddity*, and elsewhere. She is the co-editor of the journal *Elsewhere* and works as an assistant professor of English at Florida International University.

Michael Don teaches in the English Department at the University of Illinois at Urbana-Champaign and is an editor and co-founder of *Kikwetu:*

A Journal of East African Literature. His recent work has appeared in *Washington Square Review, Fiction International, Per Contra, SmokeLong Quarterly*, and elsewhere. He grew up in St. Louis.

Sean Thomas Dougherty is the author or editor of fifteen books, including the forthcoming *The Second O of Sorrow* (BOA Editions, 2018), and *All You Ask for Is Longing: Poems 1994-2014* (BOA Editions, 2014). His website is seanthomasdoughertypoet.com. He works in a pool hall in Erie, Pennsylvania.

Shawna Ervin is a member of the Lighthouse Writers Workshop in Denver, where she recently graduated from the Book Project, a two-year intensive mentoring program. Recent publications include poetry in *Forge* and prose in *The Delmarva Review, Existere*, and *Sliver of Stone*.

Laura Hendrix Ezell is the author of *A Record of Our Debts*, winner of the 2015 Moon City Short Fiction Award. Her work has appeared in *McSweeney's, Kenyon Review, Mid-American Review*, and other journals. She holds master's degrees in creative writing and library and information studies from the University of Alabama and currently lives and works in Tennessee.

Alex M. Frankel's first full-length poetry collection, *Birth Mother Mercy*, was published by Lummox Press in 2013. He also has a chapbook called *My Father's Lady, Wearing Black* (Conflux Press, 2013). His reviews appear in every issue of *The Antioch Review*, and his website is www.alexmfrankel. com.

Jeannine Hall Gailey served as Redmond, Washington's, second Poet Laureate. She's the author of five books of poetry: *Becoming the Villainess* (Steel Toe Books, 2006), *She Returns to the Floating World* (Two Sylvias Press, 2013), *Unexplained Fevers* (New Binary Press, 2013), *The Robot Scientist's Daughter* (Mayapple Press, 2015), and the upcoming *Field Guide to the End of the World*, winner of the 2015 Moon City Poetry Award, due this fall from Moon City Press. Her website is www.webbish6.com.

Gary Joshua Garrison is a prose editor for *Hayden's Ferry Review*. His work has appeared or is forthcoming in *Southwest Review, Gigantic Sequins, The McNeese Review, Word Riot*, and other journals.

Ali Geren is an undergraduate creative writing student at Missouri State University.

Joe Giordano was born in Brooklyn but now lives in Texas. His stories have appeared in more than seventy magazines, including *Bartleby Snopes*, *The Monarch Review, decomP*, and *The Summerset Review*. His novel, *Birds of Passage: An Italian Immigrant Coming of Age Story*, was published by Harvard Square Editions (2015).

Sara Graybeal was raised in North Carolina and now lives in Philadelphia. Her work has most recently appeared in *Sixfold, Floating Bridge Review*, and the Head and the Hand Press's *Breadbox Chapbook Series*. She is the founder of the Poeticians, a spoken-word and hip-hop collective based in Philadelphia.

Mark Irwin's eighth collection of poetry, *American Urn: New & Selected Poems (1987- 2014)*, was published in 2015. His ninth, *A Passion According to Green*, will appear from New Issues in 2017. He is an associate professor in the PhD in Creative Writing & Literature Program at the University of Southern California and lives in Los Angeles and Colorado.

Stephen Jarrett is a fiction writer and musician from Pittsburgh. He writes and teaches in Tuscaloosa, Alabama, where he is an MFA in Creative Writing candidate at the University of Alabama. His work has appeared in *New Ohio Review, Quarterly West*, and *The Alembic*. He maintains a writing blog at stephenmjarrett.com.

Savannah Johnston is an enrolled member of the Choctaw Nation of Oklahoma. She received her BA from Columbia University and is currently pursuing an MFA in fiction at New Mexico State University, where she is the managing editor of *Puerto del Sol*. Her work has appeared in *Portland Review*.

Andrew Koch is a resident of Spokane, Washington, where he is an MFA candidate at Eastern Washington University and serves as managing editor of *Stirring: A Literary Collection*. He is the author of the forthcoming chapbook *Brick-Woman* (Hermeneutic Chaos, 2016), and his poems have previously appeared in *Gargoyle, Sugar House Review, Tusculum Review, Rogue Agent*, and other journals.

Dane Lale is a graduate teaching assistant at Missouri State University. He holds one master's degree in creative writing and is currently acquiring a second master's in rhetoric and composition. He is also an assistant editor at *Moon City Review*.

Marcia LeBeau has been published or has work forthcoming in *Burningword, Crack the Spine, Hiram Poetry Review, SLANT*, and other journals. LeBeau's poems have also appeared in *O Magazine*. She holds an MFA in poetry from the Vermont College of Fine Arts and lives in South Orange, New Jersey.

Sandra Marchetti is the author of *Confluence* (2015), a debut full-length collection of poetry from Sundress Publications. She is also the author of four chapbooks of poetry and lyric essays, including *The Canopy* (MWC Press, 2012), *A Detail in the Landscape* (Eating Dog Press, 2014), and the forthcoming *Sight Lines* (Speaking of Marvels Press, 2016) and *Heart Radicals* (ELJ Publications, 2016).

Katie McGinnis is from Kearney, Nebraska. She obtained her MFA in fiction from Washington University in St. Louis and is a current PhD candidate in fiction at the University of Missouri-Columbia. Her fiction may be found in *Portland Review, Potomac Review*, and *Gigantic Sequins*, among other journals.

Jennifer Met holds an undergraduate degree in molecular biology and a graduate degree in creative writing from the University of Colorado Boulder. Winner of the Jovanovich Award, her work has appeared in *Gulf Stream, Zone 3, Sleet Magazine*, and elsewhere. She lives in north Idaho and serves as assistant poetry editor for *The Indianola Review*.

Sarah Fawn Montgomery holds an MFA in creative nonfiction from California State University, Fresno, and a PhD in creative writing from the University of Nebraska-Lincoln, where she teaches and works as *Prairie Schooner*'s assistant nonfiction editor. She is the author of *The Astronaut Checks His Watch* (Finishing Line Press, 2014). Her poetry and prose have appeared in various magazines, including *Crab Orchard Review, Fugue, The Los Angeles Review*, and *Puerto del Sol*.

Nancy Carol Moody is the author of *Photograph with Girls* (Traprock Books, 2009). Her poems have appeared in *The Southern Review, The*

Los Angeles Review, *The Journal*, *Nimrod*, and other journals. She lives in Eugene, Oregon, and can be found online at www.nancycarolmoody.com.

Caridad Moro-Gronlier is the author of *Visionware* (2009), published by Finishing Line Press as part of their New Women's Voices Series, and the recipient of both the Elizabeth George Foundation Grant and Florida's Individual Artist Fellowship for poetry. She is Editor-in-Chief of *Orange Island Review* as well as an English professor at Miami Dade College.

Mike Nagel's essays have been published by *Salt Hill*, *The Crab Creek Review*, *The Awl*, and elsewhere. He and his wife live in Dallas.

Meganne Rosen O'Neal obtained her undergraduate and graduate degrees in art history and studio art from Drury University. She is a self-described intuitive formalist and paints large-scale, abstract works. She teaches at Missouri State and Drury Universities and is an active member of the local arts community.

John Picard earned his MFA from the University of North Carolina at Greensboro. He has published fiction and nonfiction in *The Iowa Review*, *Gettysburg Review*, *New England Review*, *Ascent*, and elsewhere. A recent essay was chosen as a "notable essay" by *The Best American Essays* for 2015.

Michael Ramberg has published two novels, *Jack's Boys* (Amazon, 2012) and *HempAmerika.com* (2013), as well as the zombie novella *The MZD* (2012). A native Minnesotan, he currently lives in Poland. More information is available at his website, www.grebmar.net.

Ron Riekki's books include *U.P.* (Ghost Road Press, 2008), *The Way North: Collected Upper Peninsula New Works* (Wayne State University Press, 2013), and *Here: Women Writing on Michigan's Upper Peninsula* (Michigan State University Press, 2015).

Lee Ann Roripaugh is the author of four volumes of poetry, the most recent of which is *Dandarians* (Milkweed Editions, 2014). She is a professor of English at the University of South Dakota, the editor-in-chief of *South Dakota Review*, and the Poet Laureate of South Dakota.

Michelle Ross' fiction has appeared or is forthcoming in *The Adroit Journal*, *Cream City Review*, *Hobart*, *Word Riot*, and other journals. Her work has won prizes from *Gulf Coast, The Main Street Rag,* and *Sixfold.* She serves as the fiction editor of *Atticus Review.*

Marvin Shackelford is the author of the poetry collection *Endless Building* (Urban Farmhouse Press, 2015). His stories and poems have appeared or are forthcoming in *Confrontation, Beloit Fiction Journal, FiveChapters, Southern Humanities Review,* and elsewhere. He resides in the Texas Panhandle.

David Sloan is the author of two books on Waldorf education. His debut poetry collection, *The Irresistible In-Between,* was published by Deerbrook Editions in 2013. His poetry has appeared in *The Café Review, Chiron Review, Naugatuck River Review,* and *New Millennium Writings,* among other journals.

Marc Tretin has published poems in *The New York Quarterly, Willow Review, Cloudbank, The Massachusetts Review,* and other journals.

William Trowbridge's latest collection is *Put This On, Please: New & Selected Poems* (Red Hen Press, 2013). His other collections are *Ship of Fool* (Red Hen Press, 2011), *The Complete Book of Kong* (Southeast Missouri State University Press, 2003), *Flickers* (University of Arkansas Press, 2000), *O Paradise* (University of Arkansas Press, 1990), and *Enter Dark Stranger* (University of Arkansas Press, 1989). His new chapbook, *Oldguy: Superhero,* is forthcoming from Red Hen Press this spring.

A. A. Weiss is the author of *Lenin's Asylum,* a memoir, forthcoming from Bleeding Heart Publications. Other work has appeared in *BOAAT Journal, Crack the Spine, Hippocampus,* and elsewhere. He is a recipient of the BRIO Award in Nonfiction from the Bronx Council on the Arts. He also serves as the nonfiction editor for *The Indianola Review.* Visit his website at www.aaweiss.com and follow him on Twitter @ronikenn.

The 2016

MOON CITY

Poetry Award

• The Moon City Poetry Award is for an original collection of poetry written in English by a single or collaborative author; no anthologies will be considered.

• Individual pieces in the collection may be published in periodicals or chapbooks, but not yet collected and published in full-length manuscript form.

• Open to all writers not associated with Moon City Press or its judges, past or present. Students, alumni, and employees of Missouri State University are ineligible.

• Manuscripts should be at least 48 pages long.

• Manuscripts should be submitted via Submittable, https://mooncitypress.submittable.com

• A $25 entry fee is due via Submittable at the time of submission; entry fees are nonrefundable.

• Simultaneous submissions are permitted, though manuscripts should be withdrawn immediately if accepted elsewhere.

• Deadline: May 1, 2016. Contest will be decided in late 2015 and the winner will be published in the fall of 2017.

• First prize: $1000, publication by Moon City Press (including international distribution through the University of Chicago Press), and a standard royalty contract. Ten additional finalists will be named and considered for publication.

• For questions, please visit mooncitypress.com or contact Moon City Poetry Editor Sara Burge at saraburge@missouristate.edu.

gingko tree review

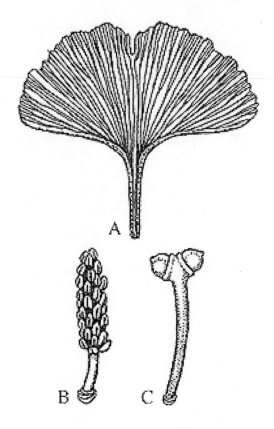

poetry, fiction, and nonfiction

www.gingkotree.org

2016 Fineline Competition

for prose poems, short shorts, and anything in between

$1000 First Prize • Deadline: June 1, 2016

2016 Final Judge: **Matt Bell**, author of *Scrapper* (Soho 2015), *In the House Upon the Dirt Between the Lake the Woods* (Soho, 2013), and *How They Were Found* (Keyhole, 2010)

500-word limit for each poem or short. $10 entry fee (payable online or by check/money order) for each set of three works. Contest is for previously unpublished work only—if the work has appeared in print or online, in any form or part, or under any title, or has been contracted for such, it is ineligible and will be disqualified. Entry fees are non-refundable. All participants will receive *Mid-American Review* v. XXXVII, no. 1, where the winner will be published. Submissions will not be returned. Manuscripts need not be left anonymous. Contest is open to all writers, except those associated with the judge or *Mid-American Review*, past or present. Judge's decision is final.

submit: marsubmissions.bgsu.edu

Mid-American Review
Department of English
Bowling Green State University
Bowling Green OH 43403
419-372-2725 • mar@bgsu.edu

SLIPPERY
ELM

Literary Journal

Annual contest: $1000
prizes in poetry and prose

$15 entry fee. All entrants will receive a copy of the
winning issue and be considered for publication.
For details, e-mail slipperyelm@findlay.edu
or visit http://slipperyelm.findlay.edu.

Deadline: Sept. 1st, 2016

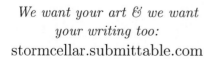

The 2017

MOON CITY

Short Fiction Award

- The Moon City Short Fiction Award is for an original collection of short fiction, written originally in English by a single or collaborative author.
- Individual pieces in the collection may be published in periodicals, but not yet collected and published in full-length manuscript form.
- Entries may include short shorts, short fiction, and/or up to one novella. Please include a table of contents and acknowledgements page (of previous publications).
- Open to all writers not associated with Moon City Press or its judges, past or present. Students, employees, and alumni of Missouri State University are ineligible.
- Manuscripts should fall between 30,000 and 65,000 words.
- Manuscripts should be submitted via Submittable, https://mooncitypress.submittable.com
- A $25 entry fee is due via Submittable at the time of submission; entry fees are nonrefundable.
- Simultaneous submissions are permitted, though manuscripts should be withdrawn immediately if accepted elsewhere.
- Deadline: October 1, 2016. Winners will be notified by spring 2017 and the winner will be published in spring 2018.
- First prize: $1000, publication by Moon City Press (including international distribution through the University of Arkansas Press), and a standard royalty contract. Ten additional finalists will be named and considered for publication.
- For questions, please visit mooncitypress.com
or contact Moon City Editor Michael Czyzniejewski at
  mczyzniejewski@missouristate.edu.

Moon City Review

SEEKING SUBMISSIONS

Fiction
Nonfiction
Poetry
Reviews
Translations

https://mooncitypress.submittable.com/submit